The Adventures of
Lew and Charlie Vol. VII

By Maurice Decker

Danger Isle

First published September 1942

Alaska Trail

First published September 1943

Pacific Outpost

First published September 1944

ISBN 978-0-936622-45-3

Table of Contents:

INTRODUCTION:

Lew and Charlie—the ultimate outdoorsmen—hunted, trapped and fished their way from Arctic Alaska to the jungles of Central America and back again. Along the way they also solved mysteries, caught crooks, and rescued the occasional damsel in distress.

The stories ran for 35 years as a serial in *FUR-FISH-GAME* magazine, beginning in 1926. Each novella-length adventure was broken into monthly chapters with cliff-hanger endings. The final chapter of the final story appeared in December 1961.

To mark the magazine's 60th anniversary in 1985, one of the stories was republished in its 12-month entirety. As the story was coming to a close, a new generation of readers who had become hooked on Lew and Charlie flooded the office with letters asking for more. Another of the original serials was republished in its entirety the following year. Then another and another. The magazine's readers are still hanging on every word.

None of the stories had been available in book format before 2012, when the first three were collected in *The Adventures of Lew and Charlie*. Volume II took up where the first volume left off, and then came III, IV, V, VI, and now Volume VII.

The magazine stories had to be edited for a book, but all of the adventure remains. This volume collects three adventures from WWII, when Lew and Charlie helped the Allied cause by fighting in the Pacific and also thwarting spies and saboteurs here in the homeland.

Danger Isle
Chapter 1 – War in the Pacific

The navigator on the Canadian navy plane flying Lew and Charlie back from White Goose Bay to their trapping cabin on Shadow Lake took the radio earphones from his head. "Give her the gun," he ordered the pilot. "Word just came through to deliver these men and return to headquarters with all possible speed!"

He turned, facing Charlie and Lew. "You're in the war," he said. "The Japanese just bombed Pearl Harbor."

"The nerve of them!" Lew exploded. "And on a Sunday, too. We shot them all down, didn't we?"

The navigator shook his head. "They sank several of your big ships and destroyed a lot of bombers on the ground. Guam and Wake Island were also attacked, and San Francisco is planning a blackout tonight."

"I'll be ..." Lew's voice faded out in utter amazement.

Charlie said quietly, "Turn the plane around. We're not going to Shadow Lake. We're going home to enlist."

"You bet we are," Lew agreed.

"You can catch a regular passenger plane from our base," the navigator said, "and get back to the States in a few hours. Your country needs men who can think fast and act right in danger."

They settled down in their seats, silently mulling over the unexpected turn of events. The long-predicted showdown in the Pacific had come. The United States was at war. They couldn't return to their trapline in the northern wilderness, not now.

*   *   *

Washington, D.C. was a place of ceaseless action. Traffic jammed the streets; men and women choked the sidewalks. Stores, restaurants, hotels all were filled. "There isn't any fresh air," Lew scowled, "not even outside. I can hardly breathe."

"The atmosphere doesn't compare to the North woods," Charlie agreed. "But we'll be getting out soon. Maybe in the morning."

"What I don't understand," Lew complained, "is why we had to come here at all. We passed right through a dozen towns where we could have signed up to fight."

"Listen," Charlie replied. "In an emergency like this, every man has got to take on the most responsible job he can handle. I figure our place is in Army Intelligence."

"Great!" Lew exclaimed. "But do you think we can get in?"

"I think we can," Charlie replied. "I have letters from Mrs. Malverson, from Captain Hardcourt of the Canadian destroyer, and from the Commander of his base. And I can get a recommendation from Colonel Bern, Sally's father. Chances are he is here in Washington right now, and he'll vouch for us, all right. No, I don't anticipate any difficulty. But if we don't get in, we can enlist as pilots."

When they reached their destination, they were a little surprised to see a modest office building. After a short wait in the vestibule, they were shown into a room quietly yet richly furnished.

No single thing seemed to stand out before the rest—not even the man behind the dully polished desk. His face seemed devoid of expression. His clothes were neutral, too. A dark gray, they decided later. Only his voice relieved the monotony of the place. That was crisp, yet low and pleasantly modulated.

"It may be we can use you," he said. "Provided, of course, that your references check out. I know Colonel Bern. He is here in Washington, and I will get in touch with him this evening. Give me your hotel address so I can call you before tomorrow morning."

"We couldn't get a hotel room anywhere," Lew said.

"I forgot how crowded we are," the man said. "I can give you a note that will provide reservations."

"Do we have to wait until tomorrow?" Lew continued. "I thought we might begin work right now."

The man behind the desk finally smiled.

"Of course, the present emergency has reduced the preliminaries. But it still takes a few hours to induct a man into this branch of governmental service. Confidentially, only one in 300 is accepted. But I don't think you will be refused. Your record of actual achievement is excellent. In fact, I think you will fit splendidly into a very special job that turned up this morning.

"Your work will be very dangerous," the man continued. "Two operatives who were on this assignment disappeared. It is almost conclusive both were killed." He searched their faces.

"We expect danger," Charlie replied matter-of-factly.

Lew nodded his agreement.

Two minutes later, they were back out on the sidewalk. "Gosh," Lew said, looking at his watch. "That took just 16 minutes. It must be my honest face that made him think we're OK."

"Maybe," Charlie said. "But I suspect the personal references didn't hurt. I hope he gets in touch with Colonel Bern tonight."

* * *

The train followed a crooked, twisting roadbed through the Cascade Mountains. Lew glanced out the window, saw nothing but sheer walls of bare rock, and looked inside again. "I wish we had stayed on the plane until we got to Tacoma," he grumbled.

"Stop griping," Charlie grinned. "You know why we took the plane only partway. It is much easier to check on people traveling by plane than by train. Chances are nobody is interested in our movements yet. But in case they are, breaking up the trip will confuse them."

"I want to get started working," Lew insisted. "There was a streamliner. Why pick this ghost of a slow train through Arkansas?"

"Same reason," Charlie said patiently. He knew Lew was just making conversation, that he was fully aware of the situation. He leaned back, closed his eyes and reviewed the instructions they had received from the man in the dark gray suit back in Washington.

"I believe," he had begun, "that this is a job exactly suited to you men. As you probably know, there are a large number of small islands off the coast of Washington State and British Columbia. They are rugged and rocky, covered with timber and mostly uninhabited. We suspect the Japanese may be cooking up a surprise for us on one of those places.

"As I said yesterday, two men we sent there to look around have fallen out of sight. I am sure both were murdered. When our enemies start killing, then we are sure their work is important."

He had paused to let his words print upon their minds. Then, "I know what you are thinking. We should send a naval force in to occupy the islands. We will do that, but not now. First, we need to know what is brewing there. If we let them go ahead and develop their scheme and then step in at the right time, we may grab off the lot. So, I will send you there to investigate. You can pose as fishermen, seal hunters, poachers, whatever role you believe is best."

He opened a desk drawer. "You will need expense money. Here is $600." Charlie took the stack of notes and saw they were old, well-worn bills of small denomination. Just another sign of how thorough this department was.

"You should be armed, too," their new boss continued. "Discard any gun you now own. You can give them to me for safekeeping, if you like."

From another drawer he produced a pair of .38 Super auto pistols. "The factory numbers on these guns lead nowhere. If you get in trouble with any local authorities because you carry weapons, tell them to phone Washington at this number." He wrote on a pad of paper and pushed it across the desktop.

"Memorize that," he ordered. "Then destroy it."

Charlie immediately pulled out a match, lit it, and burned the paper in a heavy bronze ashtray. When the paper was consumed, he carefully pulverized the ashes with the end of a pencil.

"That number can open a great many doors for you," the man behind the desk continued. "But never use it unless you absolutely must. We back our men to the limit, but we do it anonymously. I'm sure you understand why you must not appeal for help unless it is vital. Once you do, your usefulness in that section is over.

"There is only one contact you must make in Tacoma," he continued. "We have an agent stationed at this address." He wrote again, pushed the paper forward for them to see, then pulled it back and burned it as Charlie had burned the phone number before. Charlie was surprised to see it was a woman's name.

"This agent will make arrangements for you to contact the mainland when you have reports to make. And now, good luck."

That ended their instructions. He shook hands with them over the top of the desk, and they walked soberly out into the street.

Although transcontinental flights were booked for days ahead, their reservations were honored without comment. Alighting from the plane, they slept five hours and then climbed aboard this train. Now they were approaching their destination, Tacoma, where they would contact the local agent and begin their task of exploring the many islands off the coast.

Later, while walking down a Tacoma street, they were impressed with the number of men wearing lumberman's mackinaw coats. They found a second-hand store and made a quick swap. Their black and red plaid jackets showed slight wear and, moreover, looked clean.

They ate fried chicken, hot biscuits and shoestring potatoes in a restaurant then started off to the address they had committed to memory. It led them to the edge of the business district. Lew read the sign: Molly Moore. Latest Fiction Five Cents a Day.

"Not bad," Charlie said. "To pass information, all you have to do is put a note in a book."

Charlie glanced up and down the street. It was practically deserted. Streetlights gleamed dully through a curtain of mist drifting in from the Pacific. Anyone familiar with West Coast weather would have predicted rain.

He opened the door, and they entered a big room lined with shelves of books. A desk, table and three chairs sat in the rear. A girl sat behind the desk. She wore a suit with standing collar blouse and a black ribbon tie. Her glasses were thick and curved, her hair combed back and fluffed up just a little.

When she looked up and smiled, Lew realized she was positively beautiful, despite the severe clothing and the lack of any make-up.

"Good evening," she said pleasantly. "Can I help you?"

Charlie nodded. "We've come to get a book. One reserved for us yesterday. My name's Charlie, this is Lew."

He thought maybe her eyes flickered quickly behind the glasses, but he wasn't sure.

She frowned. "I don't remember saving a book for you," she said. "What was the name?"

"It hasn't a name. Just a number." He leaned down, picked up a pencil and wrote figures on her desk pad. Then he tore the sheet off, wadded it up and popped it in his mouth.

"I believe I have that book," she said slowly then stood up behind the desk. The girl opened the top drawer with her right hand and reached inside.

Charlie turned and saw a face pressed against the window.

"Wait," he said sharply. "Somebody is looking in."

Then the lights went out, the door burst open, and four dim shapes came leaping through.

"Look out!" Charlie cried as he jumped forward to meet the intruders head on. He caught the first with a swing of his long arm just under the chin. The blow sent the man reeling back into a book-lined wall. The second sprang at him, hissing. The man held a knife, and Charlie backed off warily. Japanese assassins, all right, he thought grimly.

The man swung the knife up viciously. Charlie leaned back, yet the point of the blade found his shoulder and bit into the flesh. Then Charlie stepped in, seized the outstretched arm, bent it powerfully over his left wrist and heard a bone snap.

There was no cry of pain, but the hissing stopped. Charlie swung again and sent another body spinning into the bookshelves.

As he turned to meet the remaining assailants, he realized too late that one had stepped in behind him. Something crashed down on the back of his head, and he went out like a broken hurricane lamp in a wind storm.

Chapter 2 – Never a Dull Moment

Charlie had no idea how much time had elapsed from the moment he hit the second man until he became conscious of someone jerking at his arm and whispering terse commands in his ear. He raised his head from the floor.

"Get up," the voice insisted. "Get up and get out of here before the police come."

For a second, Charlie thought it might be nice to meet a few well-armed policemen. Then, as his thoughts cleared, he remembered his own peculiar position here on a job of secret army intelligence. Through the fog, he recalled the words from the man in the dark gray suit who had told them back in his office in Washington:

"When you have to contact the local authorities, your usefulness is over."

He struggled to his feet. His legs were a bit shaky, but they held. The lights in the little bookstore were still out. Lew grasped his arm and was peering anxiously through the dim light at his face.

"Hurt bad?" Lew asked.

"No. I got a scratch on the shoulder from the second man's knife, and my head aches like the devil. It always does when it gets a bump like this. Where's Miss Moore?

That was the name of the local agent they had been directed to contact once they arrived in Tacoma. It was in her bookstore they had been attacked.

"Miss Molly Moore," Charlie repeated to himself. It sounded more like the name of a movie actress than of an employee of Military Intelligence.

"I'm right here, getting my coat on," her voice answered. "I'm getting out, too."

"Where's the gang that rushed us?" Charlie asked.

Lew waved an explanatory arm. Charlie looked about. Four still forms were sprawled on the floor. "It turned into a real knockout session," Lew said. Charlie knew from his voice his companion was grinning.

"Including yourself," Lew added.

"Just the same, I got my share, two of them," Charlie defended himself.

"You bet," Molly Moore said. "Lew only slugged one."

"What happened to the fourth?"

Lew laughed softly. "She clopped him on the head with a hammer she keeps on her desk to open the boxes of books. He went down like stocks when the war broke out."

He was urging Charlie on to the door. When they reached it, they paused to wait for Molly. She came briskly across the room carrying gloves and a purse.

"Maybe you better stay here and explain this to the police," Charlie told her.

"Not me. It's just as important I get away."

"I don't agree," Charlie said. "The Japanese already spotted you. They waited until somebody who looked like they might be in the same business came inside. They've been watching you all along, which means your usefulness to the service has ended. You can stay and try to settle this mess."

He and Lew were already through the door, and she pushed firmly after them before closing the door and locking it with a long key pulled from her purse.

"My usefulness has not ended," she said. "On the contrary, it has just really begun."

"Come on, Charlie," Lew urged. "You and no other man ever got anyplace arguing with a woman. There's a cab over at the opposite curb. Let's get in it and get out of here as fast as we can."

Molly jerked him back. He halted, surprised at the strength of her slim fingers.

"Don't be a dope," she whispered. "What do you think that cab is doing over there? It's waiting to pick up saps like you, of course. We're not taking any taxi within a dozen blocks of this place. Follow me."

She walked swiftly past the next building before darting back into a narrow, poorly lit alley. They followed through ill-smelling gloom and came out on a wider, better illuminated street.

Molly led them across it, turned left and walked two blocks, turned right and covered three more. Stopping at an intersection, she finally held up a gloved hand to stop a city bus. The vehicle was almost empty, and she walked passed the driver to the empty center section before sitting down.

"Just where are you taking us?" Charlie asked.

"To my home, of course."

Charlie's eyes widened a little with surprise. "Aren't you sticking your neck out? If this gang knew about your lending library, they also know where you live."

"Sure, and I suspect some of them will be there waiting for me to arrive."

Charlie looked at her expectantly.

"There are things I must get," she explained. "And some I must destroy. You wouldn't understand. And I have no time to explain it to you."

Charlie grinned. "You win. I'll keep my mouth shut."

"I brought this," she said and then opened her coat a little. He saw the head of the hammer she had wielded so capably before.

"You got what it takes," Lew said, not trying to hide the frank admiration in his tone.

They rode about 3 miles through the dimly lighted, foggy streets. Then Molly jerked the signal bell. The bus pulled up close to the curb, stopped, and they got out. She walked swiftly along the sidewalk and then turned abruptly into a perfectly dark alley.

"Keep quiet and follow close behind," she whispered. "We're going in the back door."

She stopped suddenly. "Shove me up over this fence," she whispered.

Charlie caught her around the knees. He hoisted her straight up the side of the tight board barrier. She hooked her fingers over the top, swung her legs over and they heard her drop lightly down on the ground.

Charlie followed in a hurry. One of them, he thought, should have climbed over first.

Molly stood, listening, one hand inside the front of her coat. He wondered why she hadn't already pulled the hammer.

Lew dropped down beside them. Molly whispered, "If anyone is waiting for us, they will be just inside the door."

The building loomed up big and black, a three-story apartment house. The lower part of the first floor was absolutely dark.

Molly reached inside her purse and brought out a small flashlight. Then she walked boldly, making no attempt to muffle her noisy steps. She went to the door, seized the handle with one hand, shoved it open, and with the other hand, shot a beam of light inside.

A dark face, with cap pulled down close over cheeks and forehead, sprang out before them.

Charlie stepped in past the girl. His long arm shot out and seized the fellow by the collar. The other hand, starting at the same moment, came crashing into the face.

Charlie struck twice. Then he let the body slide down.

Charlie looked down at the unconscious man.

"What'll we do with him?"

"Kill him," Molly replied matter of factly.

"My gosh, woman," Lew protested. "You want me to kill a guy who is knocked out and helpless? I suppose you want me to use that hammer?"

She held it out silently. Lew waved it away.

"You got to remember, Molly, we're new in this business. I can't kill an unconscious man. He won't be very dangerous for the next quarter-hour."

"You can't be tender-hearted in this game," she declared. Her voice sounded a little bitter.

They entered the hallway and found the door at the other end closed. Molly pushed it open, and they went into a larger hall. One end terminated in a pair of closed doors. The other connected with the kitchen.

"They only put one man back here because they expected we would enter at the front. There must be at least two or three of them in there."

"And one or two more up in your room," Charlie whispered.

Molly pointed to the right at a plain flight of stairs that disappeared through the stained ceiling. They followed her up. The carpet was threadbare but it muffled their shoes, and the treads were too solidly built to squeak.

At the top of the third flight she paused. There was another door, of dark varnished wood. "If there is just one inside my room, we're OK, but if there is one back of this door ..." she shrugged.

The door swung open soundlessly. They saw a long, narrow hall covered with a strip of carpet down the center. Two ceiling lights burned at opposite ends. Charlie closed the door behind them and noticed dark streaks below the hinges and said, "Somebody has oiled them recently."

Molly nodded. "Me."

It was an old building with narrow glass transoms above each door. Molly halted at the third room on the left, beckoned them close. "Bring that chair over," she whispered.

Lew set it down silently beside her.

"Climb up and look through the glass," she ordered. "This switch looks like it controls one of the hall lights. But it doesn't. I installed it last week. It turns on the light inside my room, and I put a 150-watt bulb in the socket this morning. If there's a spy inside, he'll get the surprise of his life when it goes on. You watch through the glass, see where he hides."

Lew patted her on the shoulder in admiration. She frowned impatiently at the gesture and pointed to the chair.

When her hand went out to the switch, Lew was waiting, face against the transom.

Snap! The room flooded with brilliancy, and Lew had a perfect view of the other side where a man stood poised just to the right side of the door. When the light came on, he started in astonishment and then hurried over to the window where he slipped in silently behind heavy, dark red drapes.

Lew stepped down off the chair and whispered what he had seen. Molly nodded and pushed him away from the door.

She opened it, and then sighing wearily, stepped inside. Her shoulders were sagging, her head seemed to droop with fatigue.

"Come on in for a minute, Bill," she said, her fingers on Charlie's arm, pulling him in with her.

"It won't take long to fix you a cup of coffee. Then I won't keep you any longer."

Charlie walked across the room toward the window.

"I'll keep my coat on. I'm only going to be a minute." Then he carefully laid his hat on the old-fashioned hot water radiator that stood about 4 feet from the window, glanced casually at the drapes, and estimating where the man's head was, took a vicious swing.

The spy was shorter than he supposed. Instead of striking the man's face, Charlie's fist smashed against the forehead. The blow was effective, however. It banged the fellow's head against the solid wall behind, and he tumbled face forward out into the room.

"You pack a wallop," Molly said.

Lew came in, shut the door behind.

"Six in a row," he said. "I thought they were tough."

Molly frowned.

"Don't be such a dope," she said. "Trigger men are a dime a dozen. Wait until you bump into the men who hire this scum. And when you do, look out! They're as deadly as a truckload of TNT."

"Okay," Lew promised, "I'll watch out. But in the meantime, there must be a few more trigger men, as you call them, waiting at the front door."

"You needn't worry about going downstairs," Molly told him. "They'll come up in a few minutes." She went over to the closet and took out a leather dressing case.

"Good grief," Charlie said. "Did you come back here and face these killers just to get some clothes?"

"Partly," she replied. "And this." She stepped under the overhead light, unscrewed the ornamental cap at the bottom of the big brass stem, and a neat roll of currency slid out into her hand.

"And this," she continued, taking swift steps over to the radiator. The shut-off valve loosened under her fingers. She removed a long, thin packet covered with vulcanized rubber. She shook the water from it and shoved it in her purse.

"It's a darned good thing none of these Japanese are plumbers," Lew said.

"Lock the door," Molly ordered.

Charlie shot the bolt. Then the door creaked, as if someone pressed against it. They backed away, keeping out of range of bullets that might come through the door panels.

Molly pushed up the window sash and stepped outside.

Glancing over her shoulder, they saw an iron fire escape running past the window.

"Some of them may be waiting below," Lew warned.

She nodded.

"Sure. But we're not going down. We're going up."

They followed her, Charlie coming last. He shoved the sash shut behind him. As he did, he heard hard blows beating upon the locked door. "We just made it," he whispered.

They reached the roof and started across the gravel-covered surface. Molly went straight to a second fire escape and started down. Charlie wondered if she had rehearsed this escape. Then he tried to pass her on the second section of iron ladder.

"I ought to go first," he said.

"It isn't necessary," she protested and almost ran down in order to stay ahead. She walked out on the pivoted bottom until its weighted end raised and let the other touch ground. Molly turned around at the bottom of the narrow ladder to watch them.

A figure darted up behind her and jerked the bulging purse from her grasp. With a little cry, she whirled about and started to follow. But the figure disappeared into the shadows.

Charlie dropped down the last feet and ran after the man. But after he stumbled over several ash and garbage cans, he realized pursuit was hopeless. He walked back in time to hear Lew say, "What I like about this business, Molly, is there's never a dull moment. Where do we go next?"

Chapter 3 – Dead Man on the Floor

Molly Moore, the local agent for military intelligence in Tacoma, showed signs of alarm. Until now, her cool sureness had almost irritated them. But the theft of her purse had shaken her confidence. Her shoulders trembled, and Lew wondered if she would break down and cry.

"Is it very bad?" he asked.

"Yes," she replied. "It had written instructions I dared not carry back and forth to the book shop. Also, it had what evidence the two men who were on this job before you had collected. It wasn't much, but it would have saved you much guesswork."

"There's a chance," Charlie said, "the man who snatched your purse is only a petty thief. We don't know for sure he's part of this gang of Japanese gunmen who have followed our trail. If he is only a thief, he'll search the purse as soon as he can, take the money and throw the bag away. I think he would discard the purse just before he turned out of the alley into the street. Let's give him five minutes, and then search the other end."

The farther end of the alley was lighted, and they stopped before they reached the edge of the glare to begin searching the garbage cans.

Lew felt carefully down into each can. Some were empty, some partly full. And then his fingers encountered the smooth feel of leather.

"Okay," he said. "I've got it."

He handed the purse to Molly.

"Now, pal," Lew said firmly, "you open that thing and give us any instructions and also the evidence you have for us. Next time, we won't get the dope back nearly so easily."

Molly silently handed him a legal-size envelope.

Lew opened his coat, his vest and his shirt. Then he thrust the envelope in next to his skin and buttoned up.

"Now," he said, "take us some place where we can read without being disturbed."

"The safest place," Charlie interjected, "will be among a lot of other people. Let's go to the lobby of the biggest, busiest hotel in this town."

The hotel lobby was large, luxuriously furnished and filled with people. Charlie looked at the people nearest. In front of them was a big chair filled to overflowing by a very fat man. His head lay back on top of the chair, and gentle snores indicated his peace of mind. Traveling salesman, Charlie thought, judging by the sample case beside his feet.

To the left on another couch sat a young man and woman, so obviously aware of each other they could not possibly be aware of anyone else. They looked harmless enough, so he motioned for Lew to produce the envelope.

Charlie turned to Molly. "Before we open this, I want you to tell us how it came into your possession."

"The two agents who had this job first came into the bookstore twice," she said. "The first time was right after they arrived in town, the second time five days after they started their investigation. They told me it looked like something big. But that was all they said. Then, a day after that, this envelope came by messenger. I never saw or heard from the two again."

Lew asked, "You holding out?"

When she replied with a look of disdain, Charlie cut in.

"What do you think happened to the men?"

"Same as would have happened to us tonight, if we hadn't outfought them."

Lew slit the envelope and drew out a single folded piece of paper. He opened it and out fell a piece of seaweed curiously colored a brilliant yellow. Lew turned it thoughtfully in his fingers. Then he spread the paper out flat on one knee.

"This is a map." His fingers traced the course sketched in pencil over a section torn from a regular Coast and Geodetic Survey chart. The sketch included numerous bearings taken from lighthouses and buoys. Lew read the first leg of the course.

"Where's Seal Point?" he asked Molly.

"Down on the sound, west of town."

Lew started adding up mileage.

"This takes us out to what must be an island 128 miles offshore. There's just a pencil dot marked 'Danger Isle.' I'm sure that's the place we have to find."

Molly examined the yellow seaweed. She smelled it, shook her head and gave it to Charlie.

"This map puts it all right under our thumb," Charlie said with satisfaction. "I thought we would have to search half a hundred islands before we found the right one. But why would anybody dye seaweed yellow?"

Molly had no answer for that, and Lew looked puzzled.

Charlie got up, looked at his watch, and then he looked around the lobby. No one was paying any attention to them.

"We better start moving, Lew. If we can buy a boat tonight, maybe we can get to the island by morning."

"Okay," Lew replied and then looked at Molly.

"If you'll tell us where you want to go, we'll see that you get there safe. I think your best bet is to leave town now that the Japanese have you spotted as a secret agent."

She looked at him defiantly and said, "I'm going with you."

"Don't kid yourself," Lew said. "We can't be handicapped with a girl in this business. Besides, the Japanese will recognize you, and you'll be a dead giveaway."

"They know what you look like now, too," she retorted. "That's why I told you to finish off the guys you knocked cold."

Lew rubbed his chin thoughtfully. He had to admit she was right on that one.

"Don't be a dope," she said flatly. "I did my share of the fighting tonight, didn't I? And I kept you out of that planted taxi, where you would have had your throat cut like a Thanksgiving turkey."

Lew wriggled uncomfortably. He couldn't think of anything to say to that, either.

"Besides," Molly administered the knockout punch to his objections, "do either of you know where you can buy a boat at this time of night? Well, I do."

They stared at her in amazement.

"I got one all picked out and partly paid for," she continued. "Come on. Don't stand there like a couple of cigar store Indians. Let's get going."

"Don't you need to pack some clothes or something," Lew objected feebly.

"I have everything I need in this case."

Charlie grinned at his companion.

"It's all right, Lew," he said. "From now on we treat Miss Moore just as we would a man on the job."

"You better not try anything else," she replied.

Then, to both of their utter amazement, she dropped the dressing case and covered her face with both hands. Then her body shook with sobs.

"For goodness sake," Lew said. "What's the matter?"

"That—that man I hit with the hammer," she sobbed. "He just sort of collapsed like his bones had turned to rubber. I know I had to do it. But I wish I could forget."

Charlie grasped her arm. "Don't worry about it, kid. You did what you had to do. But if it helps, you didn't kill him. I checked his pulse just before we left the store. He'll wake up with an awful headache, but he'll wake up."

Molly's sobs ceased, and she asked in a soft, plaintive voice, "Are you sure?"

"Absolutely," Charlie declared and then added, "I think you're a brave and clever girl. But we're tackling a problem that is vital to America's defense. Suppose after we buy the boat, we talk everything over. If we decide you can help us without increasing the risk, we'll count you in then."

Molly nodded and then stepped out on the curb, held up a slim gloved hand and stopped another bus. Its twin headlights bored a tunnel through the gray fog that had descended over the city.

Molly stepped inside and glanced carefully around before again taking a seat near the empty middle.

"Where do we buy this boat?" Lew wanted to know.

"At Pop Meeker's fishing dock. I got to know Pop last summer. He used to take out books from the store, about the sea and stories about famous ships and naval battles."

She stopped talking and sat up a little straighter as one of the men behind them got up and walked to the exit.

"After a while," she continued after the man had passed, "I started going down to visit Pop when there wasn't much business at the store. He was always fun, and besides, I thought he might help me find a boat if I ever needed one on short notice.

"I told him I liked to fish, which I do, and said I'd buy a boat to cruise around the sound if I could find a good one reasonable. Last month he showed me a boat with an outboard motor for $110. I had plenty enough money to buy it on the spot but thought it would look more natural if I made monthly payments. I've paid two installments. We can finish the balance tonight and take the boat."

The next time the bus stopped, Molly stood up. They followed her to the door. The unmistakable smell of the ocean struck their nostrils as they stepped down.

"Shut your eyes for a few seconds, then when you open them you'll see better in the dark," Molly said. "If anybody followed us, they'll attack somewhere in the next four blocks."

The bus was already two dots of red light down the street. Charlie and Lew drew their pistols then Charlie walked slightly ahead, on the curb. Molly followed at his left side, and Lew kept a pace behind. The hoarse blast of a steamer sounded out on the water. They reached an intersection and Molly turned them down an alley. The dark outline of a building loomed ahead. Molly walked very close to Charlie, and he felt her tremble.

"I don't like it," she whispered. "Pop always keeps a light burning up over his door. There should be a light, too, in that left-hand lower window. That's where he sits to read at night."

They went slowly to the door. It stood open about 4 inches.

"Give me your flashlight," Charlie whispered. He shoved the door hard then shot the light through. It disclosed a short counter along one side of the room. Behind were shelves piled with fishing rods, reels and line. Coils of rope lay on the floor. Several long nets hung from the ceiling to the floor.

Molly pushed him on into the room, towards a closed door at the opposite end. "Quick! In there. I know something has happened to him."

But Charlie still moved cautiously. He walked to the door, turned the knob and pushed. The panel swung noiselessly in, and he shot the light in to reveal a combined living room and bedroom. Charlie played the light across an easy chair with a magazine rack beside it, a floor lamp and a studio couch made up as a bed. The room seemed empty, and yet something indefinable sent the nerves tingling at the back of his neck.

"Stay here," he whispered. Lew pulled Molly over so their backs were against the wall at one side of the door. Charlie walked in, directing the light over the floor and on the walls. He noticed a draft in the room. A window was open, the curtain of cheap muslin blowing out into the night.

Charlie walked past a studio couch that stood out from the wall, and when he turned the light down upon the narrow strip of faded carpet, he saw the body of a man partly hidden under a brown blanket that hung down from the bed.

The head was bald on top with a thin fringe of iron gray hair about the sides and back. That made him fairly sure it was Pop Meeker. The worn carpet all around was sopping with blood. That told him Meeker was dead.

Chapter 4 – Charlie Borrows a Boat

Charlie turned away from the murdered man on the floor. He held the flashlight in one hand, his .38 pistol in the other, and he spread them out now to herd Lew and Molly along before him. He said, "We need to get out of here as fast as we can."

"Is Pop dead?" Molly asked.

"Did Pop have a bald head with a little gray around the sides and back?"

"Yes."

"They got him, then. Not very long ago, either. Wipe off both doorknobs as you come out, Lew. Don't leave fingerprints or anything else in this house. We can't risk getting mixed up with the local police."

"Why did they kill Pop?" Molly cried out. "He wasn't working for Military Intelligence."

"Japanese agents knew every place you went, every person you visited. There's an island tied up with their dirty business, and when you made friends with a man who sells or rents boats, what do you suppose they thought? I think they were just making sure we couldn't get a boat tonight."

They went outside and Molly guided them down a rough gravel walk to the water. The sound ahead looked black and oily. The dock was built of heavy planks, and when they stepped out upon it, none of the boards creaked.

Molly ran ahead then pointed down to a boat tied to a big iron staple driven into the dock. "This is it," she said. "We can start right away. Hurry."

Charlie gripped her arm firmly.

"We'll have to get a compass and some supplies first," he said. Then he leaned closer and whispered, "Careful what you say. This looks like a worse trap than that parked taxi."

He continued aloud, "Do you know where we can get the things we need in a hurry? We got to get out of here in less than half an hour."

"I'll take you," Molly said.

Charlie grasped each of his companions by an arm and pulled them along. When they had left the dock, he whispered rapidly.

"They want us to get in that boat. Otherwise, they would have sunk it. My guess is gunmen are waiting nearby in a faster craft, so they can run us down and sink us in the sound. Both of you go back to the house and wait. Don't make a move and don't make a sound until I come for you. Understand?"

Something in his voice told them it would be futile to argue. But they left him reluctantly.

Charlie pulled off his shoes and went back out on the dock, walking close to the edge where the planks were solidly supported. His sock-covered feet made no sound and, when he reached the end of the platform, he knelt and looked down.

The end was open, and there was at least 4 feet of clearance between the dock and the water, which showed he was right in thinking it possible that an enemy craft might be hidden under the dock itself.

A thick pile was driven at each corner of the dock end, and Charlie crouched down beside one and waited.

If they were underneath the dock, as he believed, they had heard him say they must be back in less than 30 minutes. When that time lengthened out into an hour, they would become impatient and finally come out to investigate the delay.

The wind off the ocean was cold, and his muscles were beginning to chill. He drew the wool coat tight up about his neck. He wished now he had brought his shoes along.

Of course, Charlie realized there were a couple of possible flaws in his thinking. The enemy might not be under the dock. And, again, someone else might come to the house up on shore, discover the murdered man, summon the police, and get them caught up in a lot of trouble. He began to wonder if there wasn't some way he could hurry up the confrontation.

A long bamboo fishing rod lay along one edge of the dock. He picked it up and studied it thoughtfully.

The pole was just long enough to reach across the floor, and he held it out level, poised over the opposite edge of the planks. Then he began to tap in a regular rhythm.

Tap. Tap. Tap.

Once every three seconds he brought the tip of the rod down

with the same even force. The pole was light, and he knew he could keep this up for hours, if necessary.

He knew, also, that the sound would be plainly audible to anyone under the dock and would arouse suspicion. Then it would grow monotonous, and finally annoying.

Tap. Tap. Tap.

Every half-minute he looked up at the house of Pop Meeker, fearing he would see lights in the windows. But the black bulk of the place stayed dark.

Tap. Tap. Tap.

A faint splash sounded below, and Charlie grinned. He was sure now his scheme was working.

Tap. Tap. Tap.

Silence ensued. Charlie, however, wasn't worried. That single splash had been accidental, and it would not be followed by another careless slip.

Tap. Tap. Tap.

It seemed like a half-hour had passed before he heard the second splash. Then a series of light noises that moved closer, and he knew a boat was coming.

He continued tapping.

He didn't stop when he saw the black prow of a craft push out into view. But he did crouch closer to the post as he kept bringing the bamboo pole down upon the planks.

The boat cleared out from under the dock and swung sideways. There were three men, two plying short paddles. The boat was 24 feet long and powered by a heavy inboard motor.

Tap. Tap. Tap.

The men sat in the boat, looking up at the dock. Finally, one started to climb up onto the dock. Big spikes driven into one of the end posts provided a convenient ladder for this ascent, and the man's head came up level with the floor then turned both ways, glancing along the planks.

Charlie shrank back, thankful the spikes had been driven into the opposite side of the post that shielded him. He wondered if his muscles were too stiff for a fast move as the man pulled himself up and stood motionless, eyes turning toward the place from which the taps had come.

Charlie leaped forward without making a sound and wrapped

his strong fingers about the man's throat.

He poured all of his strength into that deadly squeeze. The fellow's arms flapped twice and then fell limp against his sides. The grip choked down any cry of alarm.

Charlie soundlessly laid him down on the dock. The man would stay unconscious several minutes, at the least. Charlie crouched down behind the post again, waiting.

The men in the boat moved restlessly. Then a cautious voice called, "Sado?"

Sado, of course, didn't answer.

Charlie peeked around the edge, face screened by remnants of old netting. A second man stood in the boat, preparing to climb.

Charlie knew this wouldn't be as easy. He shrank back until he was almost out over the edge of the dock. He gripped the wood with one hand, his pistol with the other.

This man came up more swiftly than the first. He leaped lightly on the dock and then stiffened when he saw the prostrate form of his companion. He held a pistol, but he made the mistake of bending over the unconscious man before glancing around.

Charlie was within striking distance in a split second and brought the heavy slide-covered barrel of his gun down on the man's skull, neatly caught the gun that dropped from the other's limp fingers, and then supported the body with the same hand. There was only the faint scraping sound of the man's shoes as Charlie laid him down beside the first.

Charlie knew he wouldn't have to act so silently when he took the third and final man. But this man would be more wary. Charlie watched him stand in the boat and look around for nearly a minute.

Then he took a hitch with the boat's rope about a spike in the post and started climbing.

They're gluttons for punishment, Charlie thought.

When the man had climbed enough so he could just see over the edge of the dock, he stopped. But that was good enough for Charlie. He brought down the barrel of the gun, and the impact jammed the man's chin against the edge of the dock so it absorbed the full force of the blow.

Charlie seized the unconscious man's coat collar and swung him up over the edge. Then he quickly searched all three. Each had a long knife thrust in a leather sheath inside the belt of his trousers. Charlie tossed them out in the water. The last man's gun had dropped off the dock. Charlie kicked two more overboard to join it. Then he ran back to the other end of the dock and called softly. Lew appeared, immediately followed by Molly.

"We have a boat," was all he said.

They walked rapidly, no one saying anything more even when they reached the end of the dock and stepped over the three prostrate forms.

Charlie jumped down in the captured boat and searched it. There were two lockers, one forward, the other aft. Charlie opened the hatch at the prow and discovered a big fuel tank, unscrewed the cap and saw it was full to the very top.

He crawled back to the stern, passing several coils of rope and a rolled up tarp. In the aft locker were three seaman's slickers, a five-gallon can of water, and a store of packaged food. He saw rice, tea, dried fish, cans of meat and fruit, boxes of crackers and cheese.

It looked like the three of them could, if necessary, eat for at least a week.

Charlie started back to the prow and stumbled over a compact leather case he hadn't noticed before. He laid it on one of the seats and snapped the cover up. The case held a submachine gun, or tommy gun, with two 50-shot magazines, both loaded. The barrel and breech were worn bright from use. Charlie put the gun back in its box and then took the pilot's seat. He found the starting switch, and the big engine kicked over immediately. Then a throbbing but smooth hum filled the still night air.

Lew looked down from the dock and said, "You going to wait for us, or are you starting off alone?"

"All aboard," Charlie said.

Lew helped Molly down into the boat then dropped beside her. Charlie let the motor warm a minute while he examined the map Molly had given them. There was a light on the instrument board especially for reading maps. There were thumbtacks there, too, and he fastened the paper down flat so it could be checked at any time during their cruise.

"Get those coats from the locker," he told Lew. "We'll need them to break the wind when I open this baby up."

Lew untied the mooring rope. Charlie put the boat in reverse and backed out clear of the dock, turned her about, and started off into the night.

"Didn't you forget something?" Molly asked. The big engine under the hatch was so soft and smooth she had only to raise her voice a little.

"What?" Charlie asked.

"Deciding whether you would take me along or not?"

Charlie laughed. "I figured it was easier to take you than try to talk you out of going."

Charlie picked up the first station on their mapped course, a flashing buoy, and after they passed it, he knew it was going to be easy to follow the chart. He ran easily along at about half-throttle. Too much speed would draw attention, and they could not afford an inspection by harbor patrol.

Charlie slipped into the rubber coat Lew handed over. It was a bit small and threatened to split from the pressure of his thick shoulders. He settled back in the padded seat, thoroughly relaxed.

Lew said, "If we're going to be up all night, we need to eat. Give me the flashlight and I'll see what they got."

"Sit down," Molly said. "That's an order." She crawled back to the aft locker then said, "Give me your knife."

"Not to open cans," Lew protested.

"I want to slice cheese, you dope," Molly retorted.

She gave them sandwiches made from cheese and crackers, the big, wide, flat sea biscuit sort. Charlie ate with one hand, keeping the other on the wheel. He figured they were making 25 knots.

"Want me to steer?" Lew asked.

His tone showed he wasn't anxious for the job, so Charlie said, "No. I got the course doped. I think I ought to finish."

"I'm going to sleep," Lew replied. "But call if I'm needed."

Lew did quite a bit of sleeping that night. In fact, he didn't open his eyes again until the boat stopped the next morning. Then he sat up quickly and looked to Charlie.

"There it is," Charlie said, pointing at a chunk of land some hundred yards away, rocky and timbered.

The surf broke easily on a narrow strip of white sand beach. Behind, the land rose steep to a height of at least 100 feet. They were too close to the island to judge its size, but Charlie decided it had to be at least a mile in diameter.

Suddenly, Lew cried, "Look!" Then he pointed to a man

standing on the high ground. The man waved a flag of white cloth, up and then down sharply three times. Then the man rolled the flag up and, holding it in one hand, plunged down the incline toward them. In the other hand he carried a rifle.

"It looks," Lew said, "like the reception committee."

Chapter 5 – Disappearing Men

The sight of an armed man running down the bank of that tiny bit of land somewhere off the Pacific Northwest Coast washed the sleep from Lew's eyes in a hurry.

"We'll have to do something about him," Lew said.

Charlie nodded. "I know. I figured on getting here before dawn. But I ran right on to the island before I realized. Must have been half-asleep."

Lew picked up the machine gun and snapped in a 50-shot drum. He laid the weapon across his knees and shook Molly.

"Wake up," he said.

Molly yawned, sat up and pushed the tumbled hair back from her face. One hand went into a pocket of her suit coat and came out with several bobby pins. "Where are we?" she asked, pinning back the unruly locks of hair.

"We've arrived," Lew said, "at Danger Isle. And there's a man with a rifle coming to meet us."

Charlie punched the motorboat's starter button.

"Going to turn about and run out to sea?" Lew asked.

"No. I'm going to land."

"You want to get closer so he can't miss?" Lew grumbled.

"There may not be any shooting," Charlie explained. "At least I'm hoping to avoid it. This fellow was expecting this boat. Didn't you see him signal with the flag? He won't shoot until he's sure something is wrong."

They cruised in until the prow hit sand and stopped the boat. They were about 30 feet from shore.

"I hope you know what you're doing," Lew said.

"I want you to lie down in the bow and train your gun on him," Charlie replied. "I'll go ashore. If he aims at me, shoot him."

"What should I do?" Molly asked.

"Stay on the rear seat. Lean over against the gunwale like you're asleep."

Charlie stepped out of the boat and began wading through knee-deep water. After he had taken several steps, he paused.

"There's seaweed," he said without turning. "But none of it is yellow like that piece Molly had."

That bit of curiously colored seaweed, and the map they had used to reach the island, was the only information passed on by their predecessors. But judging from their own experiences of the past 20 hours, Charlie hadn't the slightest doubt that the two agents had been killed by Japanese spies.

The rifleman came through the brush about the same time Charlie stepped up on the beach. The man halted abruptly. Both hands grasped the rifle. Charlie pulled an old letter out of an inside pocket and held it up. The man stood motionless, suspicion filling his darting eyes.

Charlie smiled, took a step forward. He hoped his expression was reassuring. It must have been a surprise to this sentry to see a total stranger wade ashore from the familiar boat.

Charlie waved the letter again and grinned a little wider. The man approached warily. Only 6 feet separated them when the fellow stopped. Charlie stopped also and tapped the letter with the fingers of his other hand.

That seemed to help, for the man lowered his rifle a few inches and extended his left hand for the envelope.

Charlie stepped forward, and in the same motion sent a short-arm jab straight into the man's chin.

He staggered back but recovered swiftly and swung the rifle up into Charlie's face. But Charlie's other fist swept in past the weapon and again landed on the other's chin. This time the man went down like a head-shot deer.

Charlie picked up the rifle and shook the loose sand from the breech. It was, he saw, an older Arisaka model, standard issue for Japanese infantry.

Lew jumped out of the boat and waded ashore. He stood over the unconscious man. "You get all the fun," he complained softly.

Charlie wiped the sweat from his face. "Get some rope out of the locker and tie him up. Put a gag in his mouth, too. Then we'll roll him in the brush where he won't be found so easily."

Lew turned around, facing the boat. "Come ashore," he told Molly. "And bring some rope."

She took off her oxfords and stockings and waded in. She looked down at the unconscious captive, then glanced at Charlie and said, "Did you ever consider boxing professionally?"

"That's what clean living does," Lew replied for his companion, already wrapping rope around the man's ankles and wrists.

Charlie turned a serious face toward Molly.

"Can you run the boat?" he asked.

She nodded.

"All right. Cruise out about a couple hundred yards. Stay there until you see us wave to you. Then come in and land. If you see anyone else on the beach, go farther out. And if we don't come back by noon, open that throttle and get back to the mainland as fast as you can. Phone Washington and have them send help. Got all that?"

"I thought I was going with you," she objected.

"Don't be a dope," Lew said. "If we leave the boat, some of this gang can take it and maroon us. Then they can hunt us down at their leisure. Get moving, and don't argue."

Her mouth fell half-open, but Lew had already turned.

He waded out to the boat and came back with one of the coats. Charlie set the captured man's rifle in the crook of his left arm, and they started into the thick growth of stunted trees and vines that crowded the narrow beach. Lew looked back once.

Molly was climbing back in over the side of the boat.

They couldn't find a path leading from the beach to higher ground. That meant if the craft they had taken from the Japanese made frequent trips to the island, it almost certainly used some other landing point. It was a nasty place to be ambushed, and they proceeded cautiously. Then, after they had pushed their way some 60 feet, larger trees replaced the twisted saplings and brush, and the going got a lot easier.

They headed for the spot where they had first observed the sentry. The ground there was stony, also without any sign of path or trail. They were only about halfway up the ridge and kept on climbing to the rim. Instead of a bird's eye view of the rest of the island, they saw another, higher ridge inland.

Looking back toward the sea, they could see the boat plainly. Molly was standing offshore, around 200 yards.

"She ought to go farther," Lew grumbled. "A good rifleman could pick her off easy as pie at that range. Suppose she could see me wave from here?"

"Don't do it," Charlie cautioned. "She might think you wanted her to land. She's only waiting for an excuse to do that, anyway."

Fifty yards farther on they found an old game trail that showed plain sign of recent human use. They kept walking, but with even greater caution than before.

A fallen tree blocked the trail. When Lew turned left to walk around, Charlie followed.

Later, Lew could give no reason why he had taken the longer way instead of swinging right, but when they were abreast of the obstacle he stopped, hesitated, and then pulled Charlie back in among the feathery branches of the big spruce.

They crouched and then flattened their bodies back among the boughs. A squad of five men appeared, walking briskly, alertly. Their soiled garments were the same as worn by fishermen along the coast but could not disguise their military identity.

They were soldiers, trained and disciplined—Japanese, of course. Each man had a small canvas pack slung over a shoulder. So far as they could see, none were armed.

The men came up to the fallen tree, turned to the right and detoured around the uprooted butt. When the sounds of their passing died out, Lew stood.

"My ears saved us that time," he said with a grin. "We got to follow them, of course, and see where they are going."

"Of course," Charlie replied, "but we're not going to get close enough for any brawl. Those men are veterans. Did you notice each was middle-age? They could put up a good fight."

They started back on the trail, keeping well to one side where they were partly hidden by the trees. The sun was above the horizon when Lew stopped and grumbled, "We forgot all about breakfast. We could have brought some of the grub out of the boat."

Then Lew raised a hand. "Ssshhh ... I think I hear them."

The ground broke away ahead and the path dipped sharply. They could hear waves breaking gently along the beach. The thud of the enemies' stiff shoes was still audible. Then it ceased.

They crept to the edge of the thick jungle that lay between them and the sea. There was a little cove in the shoreline about 100 yards wide, fringed with narrow reefs.

They exchanged silent but knowing glances. It was an ideal place to beach a small craft.

The Japanese soldiers had spread out and were walking slowly along the edge of the sea. Their heads were bent as if searching for something. Each man had taken the pack from his shoulder. Every few seconds one would reach down, pick up something too small to identify, and put it in his pack.

"I wish I knew what they were picking up," Lew said.

It took the Japanese nearly half an hour to search each side of the little cove. Then they assembled in military formation and marched back up the trail. Charlie and Lew crept well back into the brush until they passed.

Both were intensely curious about the beach, but they did not dare walk out upon it, fearing they would be too visible to men climbing in the high ground behind. They saw one place, however, that was effectively screened by trees, and Charlie said he believed he could crawl out to it without being seen. He wanted to examine the edge of the sea.

When he reached the water, he dipped his fingers in then smelled them. He repeated this twice, and then, after glancing up and down the strip of sand, crawled back to Lew.

"It's oil, a thin film on top of the water," he said.

Lew pursed his lips in a noiseless whistle. "Submarines?"

"Probably. My guess is this is a refueling stop."

"We better start following them or they'll escape," Lew said.

They walked fast now to overtake the enemy squad. But Lew stopped every half-minute to listen with his keen ears. The ground lifted again; they crossed two more ridges, dipped down through a couple of small valleys, and then started climbing a third rise before they heard the men ahead.

Charlie estimated they had walked some 2 miles, indicating the island was larger than they had first supposed.

Finally, they saw the squad march up a grade then poise momentarily on its crest. Charlie and Lew could again hear the sea breaking upon the shore, and the nearness told them the ground ahead was a rather steep cliff or bluff directly above the water.

The soldiers strode on until it seemed they must be at the brink and would plunge over unless they halted. The leader whirled about facing back down the path. Charlie and Lew quickly drew back into the trees. Then they crouched close to the ground waiting.

There was the sound of several feet scuffing over the ground, and then silence.

Finally, Charlie crawled out to the edge of the trail. His eyes widened. The brink of the bluff was empty. There was no sign of the five men. Lew walked up the path, machine gun at the ready.

On either side was rocky slope covered with dead grass and scantily scattered brush. Before him, the ground fell abruptly away into a sheer drop to the water. The men had simply disappeared as if an airship had picked them up.

Chapter 6 – Molly Has a Mishap

Lew looked over the almost sheer cliff to the sea 50 feet below. "I'm a son-of-a-gun," he said. "Five men walk up to the edge and disappear. We don't hear a splash, and there aren't any bubbles on the water. So where did they go?"

Charlie was walking slowly back and forth, searching every foot of the rocky surface.

"When we find out how they disappeared, we'll know a lot more about what is happening on this island," was his only reply.

"Look," Charlie said a minute later, pointing to a number of shallow gashes at the very edge of the drop. "Suppose these marks in the rock mean anything?"

Lew frowned. "Not to me."

Charlie studied them for more than a minute then said, "Well, let's go."

"Where?" Lew replied.

"To the beach," Charlie replied. "So we can get away. We're badly outnumbered. They have complete control of this island, or they wouldn't risk marching across it in broad daylight."

"We must get Molly away from here, too," Lew added. "It's no place for a girl."

It didn't take long to walk back. But when they came to the edge of the ridge overlooking the little strip of beach, they stopped in dismay. The sea before them was empty. They couldn't see the boat anywhere.

"She wouldn't run off and leave us, would she?" Lew said.

"Not Molly," Charlie said. "Something bad has happened."

They ran down the steep incline, slipping between the larger trees until they hit the thick belt of jungle at the bottom.

As they forced their way through this last barrier, they saw Molly standing on the beach. She was dripping wet from her black turban hat to her broad-heeled oxfords. Her hair had fallen down and lay plastered across her face. She shivered, but her eyes blazed with anger.

The girl looked so forlorn yet so belligerent Lew could hardly keep from laughing.

She saw his attempt to keep a sober face as they crashed through the last tangle of brush and snapped, "You two make more noise than a herd of elephants."

The turban hat started to unwind just then, and when one end fell over her eyes, she jerked it off and threw it down.

"What happened?" Charlie demanded. "Where's the boat?"

"I'm not sure," she said and then hesitated.

"I ran out 200 yards like you said. The sun was so warm and felt so good I got drowsy and must have dozed off. All at once the boat lifted up, turned over on one side, and spilled me out. I woke up pretty fast when I hit the water, and then I started to swim. The boat turned on over and missed me by only a few feet. I saw a rip in the bottom a couple of feet long. It went down in less than a minute. I swam back here as fast as I could."

Charlie studied her face with grave eyes.

She kicked the sand impatiently.

"I don't know what did it. I didn't see anything. The boat just lifted up out of the sea and flopped over."

"You squeeze the water from your clothes," Charlie finally said. "Then we'll go inland and build a fire to dry you off."

Molly spread her suit coat over a bush and, starting at the hem of her skirt, systematically squeezed her attire as dry as possible.

"Now tell me what you found on the island," she said.

Charlie briefly told her about the five soldiers and how they had disappeared at the edge of the cliff.

The anger in Molly's eyes was replaced by anxiety.

"Do you think a whale might have hit the boat and spilled me out?" she finally said.

"It's possible," Charlie agreed. "Did you notice any wake in the sea?"

"I'm not sure, but I think there was a tumbling sort of commotion under the water. I was concentrating on swimming back to shore as fast as I could. It wasn't any too easy, with my clothing soaked and heavy."

Lew picked her hat up and brushed off the sand.

"Better hang on to this. Clothes will get scarce if we have to play Robinson Crusoe a couple of months."

Charlie was walking around them in a little circle.

"We won't last here a couple of hours, if the Japanese find us," he said. "We have to get off this island."

"We could make a raft, start swimming, and push it along with us to rest on when we got tired," Lew offered.

Charlie shook his head. "No chance. It's too far."

"Don't forget we have a man tied up over there in the brush," Lew continued. "He's going to become more of a problem the longer we have to stay here."

"Better see if he's all right," Charlie suggested.

Lew went over to the thick brush, parted the branches and pushed in. Almost instantly he leaped back, his face distorted.

"What's the matter? Isn't he there?" Charlie demanded.

Lew swallowed hastily and replied, "He's there, all right. But he isn't a problem anymore. He's dead!"

Charlie strode swiftly into the brush. Molly came along behind, but Lew put out an arm and stopped her. The man lay half on his back, just as they had left him, but his hands and feet were untied and the gag had been taken from his mouth. The bloodstained fingers of his right hand clutched a straight-bladed dagger fully 12 inches long.

"Killed himself, didn't he?" Lew asked.

Charlie nodded. "Suicide. Or harakiri, as they call it. The Japanese penalty for failure of duty. Somebody with authority released the ropes then let him go through with the terrible death. And that someone can't be so very far away, either."

"You are right," a soft voice spoke behind them.

Whirling, they saw a little man squatting at the very edge of the jungle, scarcely 8 feet away. He wore a neat blue suit and a blue cap with a narrow strip of gold braid above the visor. His hands held a submachine gun similar to the one Lew carried, and the muzzle was pointed directly at them.

The face above the muzzle was cut with thin cruel lines. Although the mouth smiled, there was nothing pleasant about it.

Molly gasped. Charlie and Lew started to lift their hands.

The man spoke again.

"The gun. Place it on the sand. But don't drop it. We must not get sand in the breech of such an excellent weapon."

Lew deposited the gun gently on the beach. Then he straightened up and raised both hands over his head.

"Good," the stranger replied. "Now you will tell me, please, how you found this island and why you came."

The three of them stood silently watching the face above the gun muzzle. Some of the smile vanished.

"Of course you will die," he said, "but there are so many ways. If you tell me what I must know, you can have an easy way. Otherwise, it will be long and hard. A gentleman would not let a lady suffer so needlessly."

"Don't tell him anything," Molly spoke to her companions. "He won't keep any promises, anyway."

The smile came back to the cruel face.

"You are trying to taunt me so I will shoot," he said. "You have one minute to decide. Then I will blow this," one hand left the gun briefly and touched a small silver whistle hanging from his neck, "and call my men."

"All right," Lew said. "Promise to shoot us so we die immediately, and I'll answer your questions."

The dark face relaxed a little. "I knew one of you would be wise. Tell me why you ..."

He didn't finish because his mouth was suddenly filled with sand. Lew had carefully worked his right foot deep into the loose stuff, and his wide shoe had kicked quite a load straight into the fellow's face.

Wham! Wham! The machine gun fired twice and then the action froze, clogged by sand.

The first bullet burned along Lew's right hip, but the second missed. The man's fingers flew to the breech and frantically tried to free the bolt. Failing, he dropped the weapon, sprang to his feet and reached into a back pocket for a pistol.

But before he could draw, Lew swung up from somewhere down around the level of his knees and caught the man squarely under the chin. Then Lew caught him with his left hand and struck again. The second blow wasn't necessary, but Lew was boiling with rage over the insinuated threats against Molly.

He stood over the loose heap of blue clothing.

"You made a lot of mistakes, chum," he said. "A guy in your line of work should know better."

He turned to Molly. "So what about the wallop in my right arm?" he asked. "Can I hit as hard as Charlie?"

"You'll do," she said. "Only don't brag. Charlie doesn't."

"We got to do something fast," Charlie spoke up. "Get those pieces of rope we used on the first man and see if we got enough to tie up this guy."

Charlie picked up the jammed gun. It had a simple breech mechanism, only six moving parts, and it took him just a few seconds to dismount it.

He quickly wiped the sand from each piece with a handkerchief, put the breech back, and loaded and ejected three shells without a miss. He threw the Arisaka rifle captured from the sentry back in the brush.

Molly was searching through the pockets of her suit for pins to fix her straggling hair. She put her turban hat back on and got into the damp coat.

"I know I look terrible," she said defensively.

Lew grinned. "You look like the very devil. Are you cold?"

"No," she answered shortly. "I'm not cold."

"A brisk walk will help," Charlie said, "Come on. We're going back to the cliff where we saw the five men disappear. I know what you're thinking, that we're sticking out our necks asking for the axe. But nobody wins a war by staying on the defensive. We can't hide in the brush and wait for them to find us. There is a chance for us to throw a few wrenches into the machinery the enemy has assembled on this island. If we can do that before they get us, I'll feel better when I face the end."

"Okay," Lew agreed. "Carry on."

"I'm sorry you got mixed up in this," Charlie told Molly.

"Forget it," she said. "I'm an intelligence agent, too. I have a duty to perform, same as you."

"I apologize for what I said about the way you look," Lew said. "You're a swell gal, and I'd put my money on you any day."

"Which must mean you think I look like a horse," she replied. But there was a lightness in her tone that told Lew she was not nearly so annoyed.

"If you kids have finished, suppose we move on," Charlie said dryly. "And stop talking. "

By this time, so many people had forced their way through the dense brush separating high ground and beach, a sort of path had been formed. But Charlie led his companions down the strip of sand some 50 yards and then started through the barrier at a new point.

They got through the brush all right, and started towards the trail that wound along the top of the ridge. Then, without warning, two Japanese soldiers leaped out of the cover and confronted them.

Each held a pistol. But Charlie had wasted no time. Even as the men leaped out to block their way along the trail, he was raising his machine gun. Some time back he had removed the safety lock.

This was going to be a case of the survivor firing first. He pulled the trigger and hoped he had moved swiftly enough to save the lives of his companions and himself.

War is, indeed, an ugly affair.

Chapter 7 – The Secret of the Cliff

Charlie's machine gun ripped out two short bursts. The stock and forearm handle jammed back into his hands, but a crude gas compensator on the end of the barrel softened the recoil and kept the muzzle down. He didn't waste time lifting the weapon but fired from the hip.

The two Japanese wilted to the ground. One managed to get off a shot, but the bullet went wide. Charlie slipped the safety catch back on the gun and let out a deep breath. "In this business, there are but two kinds of men," he said softly. "The quick and the dead."

"Thank goodness you were quick," Molly said in a tight voice. Then she bent over and took a pistol from one of the dead men's fingers. "It's about time I had a gun to carry," she declared.

When they reached the trail on top of the ridge they did not walk along it but rather moved back among the trees to one side.

"We'll use infiltration tactics," Lew said. "It will take more time, but it's safer."

They did not gain the top of the cliff where the five men had disappeared until just before noon. Lew squinted one eye up at the sun. "Been a pretty busy morning," he mused. "In fact, it has been a pretty busy 24 hours." Barely a day had passed since they had contacted Molly and started in this fast-moving espionage.

Molly went up to the brink of the cliff and looked over. "Where do you think they went?" she asked, referring to the disappearing Japanese soldiers.

"Down, of course. All we need do now is wait until some more come along so we can watch how they do it."

"I just noticed you lost your glasses," Lew said to Molly. "That bother much?"

"Not really. I wore them so I would look like a librarian."

They searched each side of the path near the cliff and finally found a place where they could lie unseen yet watch what happened at the edge of the break.

Lew had to grumble a bit. "We may waste the whole day here. Suppose they don't come?"

"Have to chance it," Charlie said. "Unless you have a plan?"

Lew had to admit he didn't, but added that he would probably starve to death if they didn't find food by nightfall.

It was cool in the shade of the brush, and Molly started to shiver. Charlie wrapped his coat about her shoulders. After awhile her even breathing showed she had fallen asleep. Charlie was getting drowsy, too, and decided he might as well recover some of the sleep he missed last night when he drove the motorboat over from the mainland.

The minutes passed slowly for Lew. For one thing, inactivity always irked him. For another, they had lost their grubstake when the boat sank, and he was hungry.

Lew preferred his meals to be regular and plentiful.

He wondered if there was any kind of game on the island. He had seen a few gulls wheeling in from the sea and some small birds among the bushes. But that was all.

Thirst bothered him, too. He found a small pebble, rubbed it clean then put it in his mouth. That, he had read, would relieve thirst. After a couple of minutes he spat out the stone in disgust.

It actually seemed to absorb the little moisture that remained on his tongue and made him feel the need of water more.

It was 3 o'clock when he heard the faint sound of feet pounding along the trail. He woke Charlie with a silent grip on his arm. Charlie sat partway up, then remembering the situation, sank back to the ground. "Somebody's coming," Lew whispered.

Charlie reached over and touched Molly's shoulder. She sat up, too, and brushed the hair from her eyes. Charlie motioned for her to lie flat, and she did without any protest or making a sound.

Five men emerged from the forest, in formation same as before: two pairs with one man in the lead.

They tramped up to the edge of the cliff, and the leader flung up an arm. At another gesture, each man slipped off his pack and laid it down on the ground. The pack flaps were jerked open, and out of each pack came a coil of rope.

The men lined up along the edge of the cliff, uncoiled the ropes and dropped one end over. At the other end was a steel grappling hook. The men set the sharp points of the hooks on the edge of the rock. Then, holding the grapple straight up with one hand so the point couldn't slip, they expertly lowered themselves over by holding onto the rope with the other hand.

In half a minute, the entire party had disappeared.

"Pretty neat," Lew whispered. "They must be trained acrobats. It's no cinch going down a rope that way with one hand."

"Hold on," Charlie cautioned, for Lew had started to get to his feet. "Let's see what happens to the ropes."

A few seconds later the ropes went slack. That meant the men had reached the bottom of the cliff. The top-heavy hooks fell over, the sharp points disengaged, and the rigging plunged from sight.

Five minutes later, Charlie decided it would be safe to approach the edge and look down.

When they did, the face of the rock was bare and smooth as before. There was no sign of a boat or the five men.

"There has got to be a hidden shelf or ledge where they stand to disengage the ropes," Lew said.

"And a tunnel or cave that leads back into the island," Charlie added. "That cave or tunnel is headquarters for this gang. We've got to get to it. And, apparently, we need a coil of rope with a big hook on one end to do it."

"Sure," Molly said. "And if we had a couple of torpedo boats and a company of Marines, we wouldn't need the ropes."

"Say," Lew exclaimed. "I just remembered the two who jumped us back on the beach wore the same kind of canvas pack. I'll bet a square meal there are ropes in those packs."

He picked up his gun and started off, walking as swiftly as he could and still be cautious.

When he reached the dead men they were lying exactly as they had fallen. He stripped the packs, and walking up the incline, opened one and saw it contained a rope and steel hook as he had expected, and what pleased him almost as much—food.

There were four slices of bread with chunks of hard, dried fish. The bread was dark and had a musty smell, but he didn't mind. There was a canteen in the pack, also, and when Lew unscrewed the stopper, he found it filled with cold tea.

He eyed the edibles for a second and dropped them back in the pack. He walked so fast he finished the round trip from the cliff in less than an hour. He nodded when his companions asked if he had obtained the rigged ropes. "Sure," he replied, "and look at this."

He spread out the bread and fish and the canteens of tea.

Charlie got out his knife and divided the bread in three portions. The canteens held about a quart each.

"There's no use trying to ration food for tomorrow, but I think we should hold one canteen in reserve."

They each drank the contents of one cup-shaped cover.

No one spoke for the next few minutes. The bread was coarse and the smoked pieces of fish had a rather "high" flavor. But their keen appetites overcame that. Lew picked up a couple of bread crumbs from his knee and swallowed them.

"I'm ready to tackle that cliff anytime," he said.

"We're not going to climb down in daylight," Charlie said. "That would be plain suicide."

He picked up one of the ropes and uncoiled it. The cord was tight and strong. The hook had been forged by hand, and it had been browned after forging to prevent any gleam in sunlight.

In another two hours it would be dark enough for their attempt, and Lew cut strips of canvas from the cover of the pack to hold their machine guns while they descended.

Molly watched him clean the barrels of both guns with a rag tied to one end of a shoelace.

"What am I supposed to do while you go down there?" she finally said.

That stopped them, and they looked at her blankly.

"Can you climb down a rope?" Charlie finally asked.

"I don't think so," she replied.

"Then the only thing you can do is wait here until we return. And if we don't, well, you know what to do. Keep on shooting as long as there are loads in the pistol."

"I'm not sobbing about what will happen to me," she snapped. "I want to know what I can do to help."

Lew spoke quickly.

"We're going to be outnumbered, and heaven only knows what we'll find down there. Watch the trail, and if any more of these fellows starts to climb down, you wait until they are dangling and run out and slice as many ropes as you can. That will cut down the odds against us."

He handed her his sheath knife. The edge had been whetted keen enough to shave. They were all quiet after that.

Finally, as the sky filled with tiny stars, Lew got up, slung a pack over his back and then pushed out from the protecting brush. He ducked back in so precipitously and unexpectedly he almost fell over Charlie's legs.

"There's one of them sitting on top of the cliff," he whispered. "How the devil he got there without me hearing beats me."

Charlie thrust his head cautiously out and took a look. As he watched, a match burst into flame and he caught the sight of a dark profile. The stench of burning tobacco drifted to them.

They lay under the brush for almost an hour, and Lew began to get impatient.

"You don't suppose they keep a guard up here all night?" he whispered. "We can't wait much longer, you know."

Another hour passed. At intervals, the sentry got up and paced slowly back and forth along the edge of the cliff. The sky got a little brighter from the moon rising at the other side of the island.

That started Lew grumbling again.

The sentry stood up and peered steadily out across the sea about every 60 seconds.

Lew held his watch up so light from the sky fell upon it.

"Almost ten o'clock," he groaned. "I don't think that guy is ever going away."

"Look," Charlie said. "He's signaling."

The man had taken a small electric lantern from his coat and was holding it so the bright beam fell out onto the water. He cut the switch on and off three times. Looking off into the gray clouds, they saw three flashes in reply.

"A boat," Charlie whispered.

The sentry set his lantern facing the sea. He turned the switch on, got up and walked towards where they lay hidden. Charlie got to his knees, but 50 feet from the light the sentry stopped, produced another light, and set it down on the edge of the cliff.

"He's marked out a landing place for the boat," Lew decided.

The Japanese sentry went back to adjust the first lantern a little. The beams were yellow and dull, but the lenses were specially made to cut through fog for considerable distances at sea.

They strained their eyes, searching for the boat they knew was approaching. Then they heard the motors. There was a thin haze down close to the surface of the water, although the air up on top of the cliff was clear.

A long, dark hull finally slid out of this haze and passed under the rim of the cliff. "Dang," Lew whispered. "It got past before I could see what kind of a boat it was."

The sentry waved an arm. The motors cut suddenly and everything was still. Then they heard the rattle of chains and three splashes. The sentry picked up his lanterns and turned off the light. Then he picked up a coil of rope from the ground, threw the free end over and climbed down.

Lew set down his gun.

"I'm going over and see what's cooking below."

Lew was hardly gone a minute when he came back, eyes shining. "It's a submarine, alright, not very long but twice as wide as any I ever saw before. And there's a swarm of guys running back and forth across the deck. They must have their shoes off because they don't make a sound.

"Nobody talks, but they're busy as the devil doing something, and, whatever that is, you can bet it stinks."

Chapter 8 – Cargoes of Death

Charlie simply had to get a look at the submarine anchored at the base of the cliff. So he crawled out to the edge of the sheer drop and took a look. The craft was not so very long but of immense width. It lay low in the water, and some 20 men scurried over the wet deck. A big hatch up forward had been raised, and, as he watched, something like an inclined tower slid up through it.

Then the end of a huge boom emerged from the base of the cliff. Men grasped the boom with wrenches in their hands. Charlie could see a little better now through the thin moonlight, and he realized that the tower and the boom were conveyors with moving belts, and he knew the sub was ready to discharge its cargo.

A stream of cylindrical metal objects poured up from the hold. The objects were 5 feet long and 2 feet in diameter with streamlined ends. Charlie started to count the cylinders, but after he passed 200 he stopped.

"Suppose they're bombs?" Lew asked.

"I don't think so," Charlie replied. "Bombs have stabilizing fins. Both ends of these cylinders are smooth."

"Did you ever see so wide a sub?" Lew asked.

"It must have been built expressly to carry heavy cargo," Charlie replied. "I'd say the hull would hold at least a thousand of those cylinders."

Molly joined them peering down at the activity below. When the conveyors finally stopped, Charlie looked at his watch. It had taken 1 hour and 40 minutes to discharge the cargo.

"Look out there," Lew said. Standing off a hundred yards was a second sub. "Is there a fleet of the blamed things?" he demanded.

The long boom retracted back into the cliff. The elevated conveyor settled back out of sight in the hold of the sub, and the hatch cover was battened down. Men appeared, jumping out onto the sub's deck. They raised anchors and cast off mooring ropes. The motors hummed and the big boat moved out from the cliff.

Five minutes later, it disappeared into the fog. Almost instantly, the second sub warped in and took its place.

Lew glanced anxiously at his watch. Then he looked at the eastern sky. It was only a few hours before sunrise. Charlie knew what Lew was thinking, because his thoughts were similar. Tomorrow might be too late to climb down and investigate the interior of the cliff. They couldn't expect to survive another day undetected on the small island.

It was 3 o'clock in the morning when the second submarine finished unloading. Lew stood up and worked the stiffness from his muscles. "Don't move around too much," Charlie cautioned. "There may be yet another sub. We should wait half an hour."

"It's going to be daylight then," Lew argued.

"I never saw anybody so impatient to get killed," Molly said. "You know you haven't a chance in a hundred, don't you?"

"When my number's up," Lew said, "I figure there isn't anything I can do about it. So I'm going ahead with my job. I'll wait half an hour to see if there is a third submarine. But no longer."

As it happened, Lew didn't wait 30 minutes. A few minutes later, they heard a marine engine start. A small boat pushed out from the cliff, circled away and sped down along the coast.

Then Lew got busy.

"I'll go down first," he said, tying his submachine gun with the straps so it would ride on his shoulders. "If there's a guard below, he'll see me before I see him. There's no use in both of us getting picked off. When I'm ready for you, I'll signal with three jerks on the rope. If you hear a gunshot, you'll have to figure out what to do then yourself. Just take as many of them with you as you can."

Lew took off his shoes and put them in the canvas pack, snapped a cartridge in the chamber of his pistol and shoved it in a coat pocket. Charlie uncoiled one of the ropes, set the hook firmly in the edge of the cliff. Lew backed over the edge, got his knees astride the rope and dug them into the cliff to slow his descent. He went swiftly hand over hand down out of sight.

As he slid down, Lew began to understand why they could see so little of the bottom of the cliff from above. The face of the rock bulged out, effectively blocking their view of the point where cliff and sea met.

Lew descended to within 10 feet of the sea before he saw the entrance to the tunnel. It looked more like a crack or fault in the rock than like an entrance made by man. The opening seemed to be at least 7 feet wide and an average of 6 feet high.

The rope had been luckily placed. It fell along one side of the opening, so he was able to cling to it and look inside without exposing his body. Everything was dark, no sound of men or machinery. He lowered himself down until his feet touched the water.

Lew slid down deeper into the sea until his feet touched stone. Feeling about with his toes, he decided he was standing on a ledge about 15 inches wide. He released the rope and stepped forward towards the entrance. He went down into deeper water then found another shelf where he could stand. The rocks were slippery. The floor slanted up. When he was 6 feet inside, his outstretched hand touched a barrier.

He tested it with his fingers, decided it was canvas, heavy and stiff with paint. That would explain the absence of light from the cavern beyond.

Lew edged over to one side, fingers brushing along the cloth. He wanted to find out just how this curtain was stretched so evenly and smoothly across such an uneven space. The answer to this question was plain enough when he reached the side of the wall. A groove had been skillfully chiseled back into the rock so it left a shoulder on the outside of the curtain. In behind this shoulder were many small hooks embedded with cement in the rock. Lew had to admit now that he was up against a real problem. In order to pass the curtain, he must unhook one edge. If an armed sentry waited, his fate would be swift.

He noticed that the water crept up a little higher over his feet. The tide was coming in. I'm not getting anyplace standing here, he thought. So he slipped off the pack, untied the machine gun, put the pack back on his shoulders and carefully unhooked a row of the canvas grommets. He pulled the edge of the canvas back several inches. The space behind was even blacker than where he stood. He unhooked more of the curtain, waited several seconds for something to happen. When it didn't, he loosened enough to shove his head through. The tunnel was perfectly dark. He undid more hooks and stepped inside. Walking with his hand outstretched, he suddenly touched a second curtain. It was installed like the first, but around the edges were traces of light.

Lew went back to the first curtain and fastened it shut. The curtains formed a double seal across the mouth of the tunnel. The floor was dry here.

He stopped and his shoulder brushed against something on the wall that swung from the blow. Exploring with his fingers, he found five queer objects suspended in a row. He lifted one down and turned it over in his fingers for several seconds before he realized it was a gas mask. Things began to click in Lew's brain. The puzzling mystery of Danger Isle began to take shape, and it frightened him. He now had a pretty good idea what was inside those big drum-like cylinders. Lew wadded the gas mask up and stuffed it into his pack. He decided he wouldn't go back to the cliff and signal Charlie to join him. Better, he thought, to explore alone.

Face pressed close to the second curtain's junction with the rock, he searched all along the edge. The lower corner seemed to let fewer splashes of light escape. That indicated some sort of obstruction on the other side. This, he decided, was the most advantageous place to open. He carefully loosened a half dozen of the hooks, pulled the curtain back and thrust an arm through. His fingers brushed against something hard, smooth and cold. It was a gas cylinder. He loosened more of the curtain and felt a second cylinder stacked upon the first. It was going to be easier getting inside than he had dared to hope.

For Lew had decided upon a desperate act, if necessary. Lew was determined to break open as many of the cylinders as he could, to release their deadly contents and perish if he must.

He squeezed under the last curtain and entered in a narrow space between a long tier of drums and the wall of the cavern. Lew looked around the end down into the cave. The space opened up to a full 100 feet wide and almost 30 high. The tier of cylinders followed the lifting ceiling until they were stacked 10 and 12 high at the opposite end. Halfway along the tier was doubled. Farther down, tier after tier extended farther than he could see.

Lew saw three men sitting on a bench at one side of the room. Four others lay on the floor covered with blankets. Back of the men on the bench was a long row of gas masks hanging from a wire stretched across the space. Lew counted 16 of them. That probably meant there was around the same number of Japanese living in this underground chamber.

Then his keen ears caught the sound of a motorboat. It died with a sputter just beyond the outer curtain. Lew drew back into the narrow aisle and faced the sea. He heard fingers fumbling at the curtain. The inner curtain was ripped open, and three figures appeared in the mouth of the tunnel.

Two walked ahead and behind them a third. The first two were inches ahead of a short machine gun held by the third. Lew's heart came up in his mouth when he recognized Molly and Charlie.

Chapter 9 – Prisoners of War

It was a jolt for Lew to see Charlie and Molly driven into the cave ahead of a machine gun. It seemed as if he had left his companions up on top of the cliff only a few minutes ago.

The left side of Charlie's face was bloody, and he limped a little. Molly seemed unhurt, although her clothes and hair were disheveled, and she was obviously quite angry.

Two Japanese carrying a third brought up the rear. Seeing this made Lew feel a little better. Charlie had got in at least one good lick before they overpowered him.

Lew started to raise his gun, wondering if this might not be the time to begin the fight. But he didn't. The man behind Charlie walked very close, and he constantly poked the muzzle of the machine gun into Charlie's back. Besides, Molly was on the wrong side, almost in line with his fire. Lew decided to wait for a better opportunity before he opened fire.

No one spoke a word. Those who came inside said nothing about their captives. There were no words of greeting, no questions from the men who had stayed.

Why didn't somebody speak? Then Lew saw the man who carried the gun turn around to face those supporting the unconscious man. He lifted one hand shoulder high and moved the fingers swiftly. The fact flashed on him that these fellows were all mute. Lew recalled that the only one he had heard talk was the one he had overcome by kicking sand in his face down on the beach.

It was a devilish clever way to make absolutely sure their unholy work would be carried out in silence.

The pair of Japanese dumped their unconscious companion on the floor and then followed the prisoners into the room-like space up ahead. The men there jumped up from their seats and gathered around. One of them reached out and seized Molly's chin in his fingers. She spit in his face. The fellow slapped her across the mouth, so hard she staggered a little, and for the second time Lew brought up his gun, fighting an almost irresistible urge to shoot.

Then the men stepped back and snapped to attention.

Lew looked around to see what had brought this quick change. A man in a white uniform stood at the opposite side of the room. He was short, a little stout, and the abundance of gold braid on his jacket and cap indicated high rank. He advanced smartly with rolling step. He came up close to the prisoners.

It was too dark for Lew to plainly see his face, but he could easily imagine a smile of cold triumph. The officer spoke in flawless American English.

"You have made some trouble, but not too much," he began. "I knew your bungling would eventually make you my captives."

Charlie answered quietly. "I thought we were doing all right. That is, up until a few minutes back."

"That is what you were meant to think," the man replied.

Gosh, does that guy love himself, Lew thought, rubbing his fingers over the magazine of the submachine gun.

The officer spoke sharply to the man who still stood stiffly behind Charlie and Molly. "The other man?" he demanded. "I assume you killed him when you captured these two?"

The gunman looked like he was swallowing hard and then provided an exception to Lew's belief that all of them were mute, for he saluted and said, "No, Excellency. We searched the cliff and the woods but could not find him."

That, thought Lew, will wipe some of the smile off the big shot's face. The officer spoke sharply again, this time to Charlie. "Where is he?"

Charlie took his time answering. "I don't know. He left some time back. I'm wondering if he got scared and ran off."

Lew winced. The Japanese won't swallow that, he thought. They aren't dumb.

But to his amazement, the officer seemed to swell up a little as he said, "That is typical of your kind. But he can't escape. He is still on this island, and we will capture him, too."

He turned to his subordinate. "Send men to find him."

Charlie was looking around the cavern. "This is some layout," he said casually. "I suppose the cylinders are poison gas?"

The officer nodded. "A very special kind. One breath paralyzes all of the muscles for as long as six hours. Continued exposure brings death."

Then he looked proudly at the immense tiers of terrible stuff.

"Of course, the use of poison gas has been prohibited by international treaty," Charlie suggested.

The man sneered.

"That is for the democracies. Besides, your lying government is making its own poison in a dozen arsenals. But they will bungle their opportunity. They will wait until we strike first, just as at Pearl Harbor, and then it will be too late."

"I've heard you used gas in China," Charlie said.

"Of course. We had to test it," the officer bragged coldly.

"A plane can make one round trip from this island to the mainland," he continued, "including the time needed to load and refuel, in less than 90 minutes. They will shuttle back and forth until every large city within air reach is wiped out."

Then he smiled like a demented serpent. "We do not want to destroy the factories, the stores of equipment and food. We will simply liquidate the inhabitants and march into undamaged cities."

Charlie spoke again.

"You have a pretty big stock pile of cylinders in here. How many, a thousand?"

The officer sneered again.

"A thousand? We have almost two hundred thousand!"

Charlie isn't doing badly, Lew thought. The blowhard doesn't even realize Charlie is playing him into telling us their plans.

The officer continued.

"Our gas is so powerful, each cylinder will wipe out all life within an area of four city blocks."

Good Heavens, Lew thought. There's enough in here to kill millions of people.

"You've done a lot of work on this island," Charlie said.

The officer's arrogant pride started him boasting again.

"We began in 1937. This cave was nothing but a wide crack in the rock. Our fishing boats started coming then, two, three a night. We heated areas of rock and pumped cold sea water over them. The broken pieces were hauled away and dumped in the sea. The cave extends back almost a quarter-mile, now."

Lew almost whistled aloud with surprise. What a monstrous storehouse of death, and only a few miles from thickly populated areas of the West Coast.

The officer's ugly pride kept him talking.

"We worked two years enlarging the cave, and your military never suspected. For the last four months our submarines have been bringing in the gas and fuel for the planes. There are thousands of gallons of it back beyond us."

Of course they would need high-octane aviation fuel, Lew thought. The planes will come in from a great distance, and their tanks will be about empty when they land.

The officer stepped forward, laying a hand fondly on one of the big cylinders.

"Even the Germans have nothing this good. Every precaution is taken in the eight factories that manufacture it 24 hours a day. But in spite of that, more than 20 workers die daily because of small accidental spills and leaks. Most of them are women, so the loss is small. They are proud to give their lives."

"You must be just about ready to begin," Charlie suggested.

"The planes have been dispatched, are already on their way."

"I suppose you'll kill us?" Charlie asked indifferently.

"Yes. You will have the honor of testing our gas. We have a small, tight room in which some of every shipment is tested. We have used mostly dogs and goats. Occasionally, some of the men who have failed in the tasks set for them."

He's a cold-blooded devil, Lew thought. Somebody had to do something, and it looked like it was up to him and Charlie.

"I'm to be used to test the last shipment?" Charlie asked.

"Exactly. There is some pain. It also has a curious effect on flesh and vegetation. It turns all yellow."

The yellow seaweed, Lew thought, must have been exposed to the stuff, and the agents on the job before us brought it back as evidence of how it acts. Danger Isle was right. How many innocent people had this gang murdered already? How much longer was Charlie going to keep that devil talking?

He figures Charlie and Molly are already good as dead, Lew realized. But he doesn't know I'm here.

Charlie asked another question.

"This morning, our small boat was tipped over and sank. Was that one of your planned actions?"

The officer seemed puzzled.

"I must look into that. Somebody slipped. One of our submarines came too early and had to wait until night to discharge its cargo. Your boat must have been struck."

Now, for the first time since his appearance, the officer appeared to notice Molly.

"You will go into the chamber first," he said to Charlie. "Then later, the girl. We do not have women on the island. It is not permitted. But perhaps she can make our awkward life more pleasant before she dies."

Now he scrutinized Molly closely. "She is so dirty. But we have some soap and sea water, and I can give her a suit of white linen to wear."

Molly lifted her chin and spat directly in his face.

Chapter 10 – Poison Gas

To Lew's surprise, the Japanese officer did nothing when Molly spat in his face. Instead, he stepped back a little, pulled a white handkerchief from his pocket, and calmly wiped his cheek.

The guard, however, wasn't so composed. He stepped around to one side and struck Molly heavily in the face. She fell against Charlie, caught his arm, regained her balance, and straightened up.

No cry escaped her lips.

That girl's got what it takes! Lew exulted to himself. His own teeth were clenched, and this was the third time he leveled his gun, finger itching to spray the room with bullets. He would have probably done just that, too, if Charlie had not acted first.

Charlie struck out with his left hand, hitting the breech of the guard's gun and knocking it to the floor. Then Charlie's right hand came up, landing on the fellow's jaw. It hurled him back against a tier of gas cylinders.

How that boy can hit, Lew thought. We won't have to worry about that one for awhile. I wish there was some way I could let Charlie know I have them covered if he would just get himself and her out of my line of fire.

Then Charlie grabbed Molly's arm, dragged her along the tunnel a few yards, and hurled himself and her down behind a row of the gas cylinders. They were only partly concealed, and not very well protected from the men back in the room, but Charlie called out, "Okay, Lew. Let 'em have it!"

Lew thrilled at the words. He realized now that Charlie had known all along he was hidden somewhere inside the cavern.

The officer in white uniform had drawn a pistol and was running forward. A few steps more and he could lean over and pump bullets into Charlie and Molly. But before he took that last step, he ran squarely into a slug from Lew's gun.

Lew didn't worry about him after that. But right behind him came one of the men who had stood in the back of the room with a submachine gun in his hands, and the way he was holding the weapon showed he knew how to use it.

Lew shot twice. Every second was precious, but he figured he should finish that guy off. He called to Charlie, "You two get out of here, fast. All hell's going to break loose in a moment." He could hear feet pounding the rock floor. Reinforcements were coming.

Charlie scrambled up, pulling Molly with him. The pair dashed past, and Lew started pumping bullets into the row of gas masks that hung from the ceiling. He waited, wondering if any of the men he knew were back out of sight in the space beyond the room would fire. Then he realized they dared not fire for fear of breaking one of the brittle gas drums.

He heard Charlie ripping at the final canvas curtain. He shouted, "Give a yell when you're clear."

Charlie answered immediately, "Let her go, Lew!"

Lew reached back in the canvas pack he had been wearing all this time and took out the gas mask. The mask seemed a little small when he fitted it over his face. But he tried a few deep breaths, and a valve somewhere in the rubber clicked noisily. He had to trust that the thing was working; there wasn't anything else to do.

Lew waited 10 long seconds to give Charlie and Molly a little time to start up the face of the cliff or swim off in the sea, whichever plan his companion decided was best. Then he slipped the catch from his machine gun, turned it to full automatic, aimed as far down ahead as he could see, and smashed a hail of bullets into the tiers of poison gas cans. The plastic containers smashed like eggs. A thin, yellowish vapor arose from the broken containers and seeped out into the tunnel.

One cylinder held enough gas to kill all living things in four city blocks—at least, that's what the Japanese officer had told Charlie. Anyway, Lew figured he had smashed 20, so that should take care of this gang of murderers.

He eased out of his cramped space against the cavern wall. The air was getting so thick now he could scarcely see, and he started groping his way with one hand pressed against the rough wall.

But then he choked suddenly with a sharp pain that started at the roof of his mouth and shot down his throat into the very bottom of his lungs. Panic seized him, but he fought it off, expelled all the air from his lungs with a deep breath, and pressed the gas mask closer over his lips. Something had gone wrong with the device, or perhaps the concentration of gas inside the narrow space was so deadly no mask could filter that much yellow death. He had to stop and steady himself by leaning against the rock. His tortured lungs were demanding air. But the deep pain had left, and he knew he dared not breathe again. He knew, too, if he went down he might never regain his feet.

Step by step he fought his way toward the tunnel exit and life. He forced his feet to move, turned and took a step through the first open canvas curtain. The machine gun slipped from his hand, and then he felt his body settling slowly but surely down. His brain cleared momentarily, and he felt a short thrill of exultation. They were going to get him, but he had taken plenty along for company. Besides, Charlie was outside now, safe and able to put the final check on this hellish business.

That was all Lew remembered for a long time. He didn't feel the strong arm slip about his shoulders and drag him out through the last doorway. He didn't feel the splash of cold water in his face.

Charlie pulled Lew through the shallow water until they were a dozen yards from the cave mouth. Then he propped his insensible companion up against the cliff and reached up for the dangling rope end. He lashed it under Lew's arms, making the knot firm with no slack in the line. He had to work fast, for poison gas was surging out of the open cave and seeping towards them. The wind, fortunately, was holding the stuff back, but Charlie knew he had only a few seconds to work.

Assured that even if Lew lost his feet and fell he would not slide under water, Charlie jumped up, caught the rope above his companion's head, and went up it hand over hand. When he reached the top Molly was standing close to the brink still wearing her gas mask. Charlie could feel her eyes questioning him, but he didn't have time to speak. He leaned over and began hauling desperately on the rope. Molly pulled beside him.

When Lew's head came up level with the top, Charlie backed off a step and with a final heave dragged his companion over onto level ground. He motioned for Molly to untie the rope, picked Lew up in his arms, and started inland away from the sea. He didn't know how much of the deadly vapor would rise up the cliff and follow them in among the trees, so he had to keep going until there was no chance of it overtaking them. Charlie ran almost a mile before he finally stopped, gasping for air. He laid Lew down on the ground and jerked the mask from his face.

Lew's eyes opened, shut, opened again, and after some fluttering stayed open. One hand came up, and he muttered, "You look so darned funny."

And then Charlie remembered he still wore his mask. He pulled the thing off. Molly did the same, and when Charlie looked in her eyes, he saw tears.

"He's all right?" she pleaded.

"Of course he's all right. I'll bet a dollar the lazy son-of-a-gun has been playing 'possum all this time so I'd have to lug him here."

"You aren't fooling me, not any," Molly told him softly.

Lew sat up.

"How you feel?" Charlie asked.

Lew shook his head. "Rotten," he finally managed to answer. But his head was clearing, and there was nothing of the sharp pain that had seared his lungs.

They were on top of a high summit. The moonlight had faded, and the ground was shrouded in deep shadows. When the nausea left, Lew was able to walk fairly straight.

"All right now?" Charlie asked.

"I guess," Lew replied. He glanced over at Molly, saw the tears in her eyes. "What's wrong with you? Did you get some of that stuff, too?"

"My jaw hurts," Molly said briefly, "where that soldier hit me. He loosened three of my teeth."

Hot anger gripped Lew. "None of that gang will hit a woman again," he said grimly.

"That wasn't all of them," Charlie reminded him. "I expect to see more sometime during the day. We have to make sure they don't see us first."

"I lost my gun," Lew said.

"They got mine when they captured us," Charlie replied. "But we can get more down in the cavern."

Lew shivered. "I'm not keen about going back there. But I guess we must. Maybe the gas will thin out after awhile. That one breath almost got me."

"I don't think your mask fit right," Charlie replied. "I didn't have any trouble with mine when I went back to drag you out."

"A few seconds more and it would have been too late for me,"

Lew said, nodding gravely. "It was lucky you found the masks hanging in between the two doors."

They sat quietly for several minutes. None of them felt much like talking. Each sensed the deadly danger that still hovered over the tiny island.

"What do we do next?" Lew finally asked. His own head still ached too much to permit much clear thinking.

Charlie was silent for some time before he replied. "We can't do anything except hide in the brush. There are armed Japanese searching for us, and we can't make a slip. If we are captured or killed, the Japanese can go right on with their plans."

The silence was heavier than ever after those words.

"There's only one thing to do," Charlie continued. "We must capture the motorboat the Japanese are using and get off the island. To do that, we need guns, and to get guns, we have to go back down in the cavern."

Chapter 11 – Cave Full of Death

Even though he had almost succumbed to the poison gas he had deliberately released in the enemy's cave, Lew wanted to return immediately and get weapons. "If we have to return to the cave for guns," Lew asked, "why wait? I'm ready to go now."

Charlie disagreed. "Not the way your legs wobble. Your gas mask isn't very good, either. A few hours may give the gas a chance to thin. I figure about the middle of the morning will be good." He glanced at the sky. Everything was black—that brief spell of intense dark that precedes the dawn. "Morning isn't far away," he added.

They went back into the brush, walking carefully so as not to leave a trail that could be followed. The place they finally selected had a good view of the path for 100 feet each way.

Charlie sat down, leaning back against a small rock. "I'll watch for them. You two try for some sleep. You look washed out."

Molly rubbed her jaw then said, "First, I'm tipped out of the boat. Then two goons slug me on the jaw, jarring my teeth loose. I don't know how much skin was scraped off my legs when you dragged me up over the side of the cliff. I'm bruised and raw."

"I'm too hungry to sleep," Lew growled, suddenly remembering how long it had been since he last ate.

There was a trace of fog in the air, and Molly began to shiver. Charlie and Lew wrapped their coats about her, and she fell asleep almost immediately.

It was an hour before the sun's warming rays reached them. Then, despite his keen hunger, Lew fell asleep, too. A grasp on his arm woke him a short time later.

"The enemy is coming," Charlie whispered. "We must get out of here fast if they start searching the woods."

Lew watched two figures treading doggedly along. What I wouldn't give for my tommy gun now, he thought.

The pair passed by and continued straight to the cliff. Half an hour later, they returned. They kept looking to each side now, but at no time did they make a move off the path.

"They don't look very happy, do they?" Lew whispered. A

few minutes later they heard the sound of the motorboat. The shore, apparently, was closer than they had suspected.

When the sound faded away, Lew stood up. "Charlie, I'm going down into the cavern. We need those guns, and I just got to have grub. Why keep on dodging those fellows if I'm going to die of starvation in the end? I'll be so weak soon a baby could tie me up."

Charlie thought this over for a minute.

"All right," he said. "Go ahead. But you better take my gas mask. And just as soon as you get into the cave, look for a gun. When you find one, tie it on the end of the rope so I can haul it up. Then I can cover you while you search for more guns and grub."

Lew quickly agreed to these suggestions. But then they both had a job trying to convince Molly she should stay hidden in the brush while they returned to the cliff.

"I'm going," she insisted. "I'd be scared to death up here alone. I want Lew to send up a gun for me, too."

When they reached the top of the cliff, there was no taint of gas. A strong cross wind coming off the mainland was apparently siphoning the gas away from the cave and pushing it out to sea.

Charlie threw his rope over the side and held the iron hook firmly against the rock. Lew put on Charlie's mask and started down, still wearing the canvas pack. When he reached the bottom he saw the first canvas curtain was open. The water was only a few inches deep over the ledge, and he waded quickly through it inside.

He took an experimental breath, found the mask was working then passed through the second curtain. Enough light came over his shoulder to illuminate the passage some 30 feet. Beyond that was darkness. But he plainly saw his submachine gun lying on the floor a few steps ahead. The magazine was empty, but he picked it up anyway. There were more guns somewhere, and some would certainly contain filled cartridge drums.

His toe touched something. Bending down, he saw the body of a dead man who still clutched a rapid-fire gun. Lew unclenched the fingers, saw the gun was the same model as the one he carried. He tied the loaded gun to the end of Charlie's rope, tugged a signal, and then waited until his companion had drawn it up and out of sight. Feeling relieved, he started back into the cavern. Charlie was armed now, and he need fear no attack from behind.

The air in the first room was tainted yellow. Lew remembered seeing a pair of electric lanterns on a table at the rear, and he went straight to them, walking carefully so he wouldn't trip. When he turned on the lamp, he was pleased to see its powerful beam cut through the yellow haze and light the passage for almost a hundred feet beyond.

Lew found three more submachine guns. He took the cartridge drums from each, shoved one in his own gun and the others in his pack. Then, with gun in one hand and lamp in the other, he started into the passage that led deep into the bowels of Danger Isle.

The tunnel grew wider. On either side were the same high tiers of cylinders. Three times he passed breaks in the tiers where brown curtains covered passages branching off from the one he followed. Then a square pillar of rock split the tunnel in two, and curtains filled in the space at each side. Lew pulled the right one back.

When he shot the light beam through, he saw a seemingly endless room that lay off at an oblique angle from the main passage, a room filled to the ceiling with 50-gallon drums. This, he knew, must be the aviation fuel, thousands of gallons ready to refuel the Japanese bombers.

Lew lifted the other curtain. When he saw what was behind, he stood motionless for almost a minute. Then, with shaking hand, he dropped the canvas and backed away. This room was filled with double-deck bunks, and the bunks were mostly full.

"You kill or get killed in war," Lew told himself. But the wholesale death still unnerved him. He turned and went back.

There were three side passages to investigate. He struck it lucky at the second. Behind the curtain were piled wooden cases, some of which had been opened. One contained 5-pound bags of rice. Lew put two in his pack. He found bundles of dried fish, and he stocked up heavily on this. It could be eaten without cooking. He took tea, cheese and dried peaches.

The next thing was to locate the kitchen and drinking water.

Lew left the storeroom and opened the last curtain. It was filled with tables and benches and the walls were lined with cupboards. He jerked a cupboard door open and saw what he had been hoping to find—a stack of bread loaves securely wrapped in moisture-proof paper. He put three of these in his pack, which was beginning to bulge. He found a pound of butter and added that to his stock.

But one want remained unfilled—water. There had to be some

supply, and it proved to be an iron pipe coming out of the side of a huge cistern made by walling up a portion of the room. Lew filled two canteens. Then he found a battered saucepan with lid and started for the outside.

Once outside, Lew tied his pack and his gun to the dangling rope and called out to Charlie, who hauled up the stuff. Lew went up when the rope appeared again. He didn't waste any time grabbing the pack and starting for the brush.

No less hungry, his companions followed. Lew told them what he had seen. His companions didn't comment.

When they were hidden deep in the undergrowth, Lew started a small fire using dead sticks that made almost no smoke. He filled the saucepan with water and, when it boiled, he dumped in some tea. The fragrance almost brought tears of joy to his eyes. They cut slices of the heavy dark bread and of the cheese and broke the smoked fish into pieces. They drank from the cups that covered the tops of the canteens.

They rested for some time afterwards, and Lew grinned when he heard the sound of the motorboat approaching.

"We can handle them quite nicely now."

He picked up his gun, worked a half-dozen loads through the breech and out upon the ground. He picked up the ejected loads, wiped them clean on his shirt sleeve and put them back in the drum. Charlie tested his own weapon. Molly shoved what was left of the food back into the pack.

"They'll probably come along the path just like they did before," Lew said. "The top of that little hill will be just the place for an ambush. You can stand on one side behind a tree; I'll stand on the other side."

This time it didn't require any argument to keep Molly in the background until the shooting was over.

Below, about 100 feet away, the path swerved sharply towards the sea. When the enemy rounded this turn, Lew planned to take them. But when they heard the sound of feet trampling the ground, Lew, on impulse, stepped out from behind his tree and stood motionless beside the trail. He just couldn't bring himself to shoot a man from an ambush.

When the Japanese soldiers came around the turn, the one slightly ahead looked up and saw Lew, snapped up his gun and fired. Lew knew the man would move too fast to aim. He fired his own gun, and the man fell. Charlie got the other one before he could do any harm.

And then, while they stood there feeling the grim satisfaction that comes when one wards off death, they heard sounds that dashed their satisfaction and changed it to fear. Feet pounded heavily along the trail, the feet of many men escaping back to the beach.

"Oh no," Lew cried. "There were more of them. They must have picked up some of the posted guards."

"We can't let them get away," Charlie said. "We have to get that boat. Everything hinges on it."

Chapter 12 – A Voice from the Fog

Lew and Charlie put everything they had into running down the Japanese soldiers before they reached the sea and the boat on the beach. They needed that boat themselves to escape Danger Isle and warn mainland authorities of the plot they had discovered to drop hundreds of tons of poison gas on West Coast cities. Sweat ran down their faces despite the cold wind blowing in from the water.

When they crashed through the final jungle barrier, they saw the boat drawn prow first on the sand about 40 yards away. Two Japanese soldiers were inside, one bent over the motor, the other shoving on a paddle to get the craft afloat. Charlie and Lew brought up their guns and tried to steady them against their own breathing.

The man holding the paddle saw them, let the paddle drop and picked up his own gun. He rushed a shot that missed, and then Charlie squeezed his own trigger, right elbow pressed tight against his chest to control the sights. It was the best position when firing a short-stocked machine gun.

The Japanese soldier pitched headfirst over the side of the boat. The other then dove over the stern into the shallow water and swam away. Since he was unarmed, Charlie and Lew let him go.

When Charlie climbed in the boat, he saw it was a duplicate of the one they had used on their cruise to the island. Then, to their surprise, Molly came limping out of the jungle and across the sand beach. What had been left of her stockings had been ripped away by the brush. Her legs were bleeding, and a long red welt ran across her face. She climbed into the boat and sank down on a seat.

"I thought I told you to stay put?" Charlie tried to sound stern.

"Your hard knocks are over," Lew assured her in a softer tone. "And so are ours. We're going back to the mainland just as fast as this boat will travel. And what a story we'll have to tell."

"Take a look at our fuel tank," Charlie said.

Lew unscrewed the cap and thrust the muzzle of his gun down for a better check. When it came up, only two inches of the end were wet. "We must go back to the cave for gas," he told them.

That was bad news. It was vitally urgent that they proceed

with all speed, but they had no choice—they had to take on more fuel if they hoped to reach the mainland, more than 100 miles away.

As they approached the entrance of the big underground storehouse, they put on their gas masks. Molly had carried them down with her in one of the packs. Charlie ran the boat in as close as he could then stepped out into the trickle of water that covered the ledge of stone. Lew had left the electric lantern just inside. He picked it up and guided Charlie back to the big room filled with drums of gasoline. They filled a five-gallon can then made five more trips with it before the boat tank was full.

Night hovered over the ocean when they shoved off again. "Ease her off," Lew ordered. "I hear a plane."

Charlie cut the motor. A light fog was dropping, and they could hardly see 300 yards. Charlie's hand gripped the throttle, impatient to send the little craft plunging over the waves. But Lew raised his arm in warning.

They all heard the splash, followed by a succession of lighter splashes, and then something immense swung in towards them. A long-distance bomber loomed up in the fog, painted a deep blue gray that blended skillfully with the twilight. Four propellers idled so slowly they could almost count the blades.

"Maybe one of ours," Molly whispered hopefully. Then the huge craft swung, and they saw the rising sun painted on its wing.

"It's Japanese," Lew said shortly. "The first of the fleet coming to spread poison gas over our towns. This is the night they planned their attack."

"Well, this is it," Charlie said. He gave the motor a little more gas and started to turn it around.

"Where are you going?" Molly demanded.

"We've cancelled our trip home," Lew said.

"But you're going," Charlie added.

"What are you two going to do?" she demanded.

"Do what we can to delay the poison gas attack. That plane is pretty far out and we ought to be able to cut back to the cave without being seen. You must drop us off; then drive this boat like hell itself was behind you. You know what to do when you get home."

As they coasted quietly near the shore, Molly said softly, "I think you're awfully brave."

"We're scared to death," Lew replied. "At least I am."

He picked up the gas mask and put it over his face.

Their boat swung into the cave mouth and they stepped out. Lew patted Molly on the shoulder. Charlie squeezed her fingers in his big hand. "It's been fun," he said quietly. "Now get going."

She swung around even as he spoke, hit the throttle and powered away into the fog.

"Only one thing for us to do," Lew said, "blow this whole place up."

Charlie nodded. "There's enough aviation fuel stored inside to lift the island's top half a mile high. But I'm still trying to figure out a way so we don't go along with it."

"If you can't," Lew told him, "we still got to touch her off."

"Of course. Listen, did you hear another splash?"

"Yes. Another plane has set down. They'll come up to the cave soon to start loading fuel and poison gas."

Charlie said, "I'm going inside to handle that part. You keep them off my tail until I'm through."

It took Charlie a minute to run back into the room where the drums of gasoline were stacked roof high. He set the electric lantern on the floor so its beam played upon the tall tiers of barrels, and then he began shooting. He put one hole in the end of each of a score of drums. Unlike in the movies, he knew that he could shoot a full drum without causing it to explode, and if it did, well, the important thing was to destroy this storehouse of death.

Charlie had noticed that the floor of the room lay several inches lower than the passage outside. That meant several minutes should elapse before the gasoline would flow toward the entrance of the cave.

Somewhere along the passage was the door leading to the cooking room. He had not seen the place, but Lew had described it in detail. The first curtain he ripped aside exposed the storeroom filled with packages of food.

Charlie was getting edgy. If the fuel overflowed and ran into the passage before he set a fuse to ignite it, he would have no chance to escape. But behind the next curtain he found the place he sought. He ran to the cooking range, opened two burners, and lit a match.

The fuel was cold and would not ignite. A little panic crept up his back when he remembered it might require minutes to ignite one of these fuel oil burners. He had counted on the curtains that sealed the fuel room and this one to keep the fumes out long enough. But he thought he could smell gasoline fumes.

On his third try, one of the burners flared. A yellow flame flickered around the top. The other burner caught. Charlie watched as the flickering flames slowly turned a steady blue.

Then he ran for the door. There was a strong smell of gasoline in the passage. He had to get out of there in a hurry.

Lew stood out at the cave's mouth, staring into the fog bank. Funny, he thought, how slow the Japanese were to swing their big bombers in near the cave. Then he saw a light blinking through the mist, flashing out some signal. They're waiting on a reply, he thought. Pretty soon they're going to come in anyway, even if they don't get an answer.

Then he heard another loud splash, then another. Planes were dropping out of the sky like blackbirds into a cornfield. Next, he heard the muffled sound of Charlie shooting the drums of fuel.

His keen ears caught the sound of paddles, and he moved back farther into the cave entrance. Two men in a rubber raft headed straight to the cave mouth. When the boat was 40 feet out, the men stopped paddling and one hailed softly. Then Lew heard them talking rapidly, and they started paddling closer.

Lew waited until they were no more than 10 feet away. He couldn't afford to put a bullet in that rubber raft, but he had to take out the crew. That boat, he figured, might save a couple of lives — and his was one of the two.

War is about survival. He stepped forward and shot the Japanese soldiers. Then, swimming with one hand and holding his gun above the water with the other, he reached the raft. Lew tossed his gun in and, finding hand straps sewn on the edge, crawled aboard. He brought the prow up against the cave entrance and held it.

At that exact moment, Charlie ran outside, jumped in the raft, and yelled, "Paddle for all you're worth! She's gonna blow any second now!"

They paddled with every ounce of their strength. But the blunt-bowed craft was slow and clumsy, and the power they put in their strokes almost lifted it from the water.

"What did you use for a fuse?" Lew asked.

"Cook stove. Lit two burners." Then he added, "We'll make it all right." Only he didn't have much confidence that they would. He knew a gigantic stock of high test was due to explode any second.

A searchlight cut through the fog and, after wavering up and down the edge of land, finally fixed itself upon the dark mouth of the cave.

"I was afraid of that," Charlie said. "They'll pick us up now."

The shaft of light left the cave and searched along the cliff. Their rubber boat had covered at least 300 feet before the Japanese airman picked it up in his beam and began to follow them.

The little boat was illuminated in a brilliant glow that, despite the surrounding fog, revealed them in every detail. A hail of bullets splashed the water behind them. By simultaneous impulse, they changed course, Charlie pushing ahead, Lew backing water with his paddle. They swung the craft off its course, then dogged back again in time to escape a second blast of machine gun fire.

Just ahead the island jutted out into a narrow high point. If they could just get around behind that screen of rock, they might have a chance.

Two guns blazed at them, coming from different angles. A third gun started and, strangely enough, it seemed to come from behind because bullets screamed by to plumb in the water yards ahead. Japanese soldiers on the cliff must have joined the shooting.

They dodged the boat frantically, desperately. But it was only a matter of seconds before the gunners would get their range and cut them to bits.

Then it happened. A low roar surged against their eardrums, a roar that swelled into a thunderous blast that almost capsized their low-riding boat. A giant sheet of flame blazed into the sky. They steadied their boat as well as they could and kept on paddling.

The searchlights went off, and the machine gun fire ceased. Fragments of rock began to crash down into the sea all around them, and they had to use every bit of the skill developed when piloting canoes through bad water to keep afloat. Smaller bits of earth pelted their heads and shoulders, but by some miracle they escaped the big chunks.

They knew two grave dangers were on the way. One was the inevitable tidal wave that would result from the terrible shock of that explosion. And even more serious was the immense quantity of poison gas the blast would release.

Flames still erupted into the sky, but the air was so filled with a yellow, murky haze they could scarcely see as far as they could before the explosion. Then a huge chunk of rock dropped from the sky, missing Charlie by inches, and struck the front of the rubber boat, shearing it off. The back of the craft flipped up and flung them into the sea.

They came up swimming, but knew there wasn't much hope now. Their gas masks were gone. First the tidal wave, then the flow of poison gas.

Charlie looked back over his shoulder. A big part of the island had vanished, and grim satisfaction gripped him. They might not live, but they had done their job well.

Then a voice hailed from out of the fog, "Lew? Charlie?"

"My gosh," Lew yelled. "What are you doing here, Molly?"

The motorboat drove at them, swerved sharply but still plowed into Charlie, who thought he heard a couple of his ribs crack. At least it felt like two.

"Get in!" Molly cried.

They needed no urging and floundered over the gunwale head first. Lew's legs were still outside when she spun the wheel, jammed on the throttle, and powered away from the island.

"I told you to go home," Charlie reminded her.

"You know how long ago that was?" she demanded. "By the clock on the instrument board, it's been exactly 22 minutes."

Had so much actually taken place in that short span of time?

"What difference would 22 minutes make in my warning the mainland?" she continued. "Those Japanese planes are practically out of fuel. Our fighter squadrons will run them down in daylight tomorrow. I knew you were going to blow up the gas. And I knew this boat was your only hope of escape."

Molly smiled and said, "I must look like a real devil now."

"You look like an angel," Lew corrected her as he bent over and kissed her lightly on top of the head.

The end

Alaska Trail

Chapter 1 – Some Dead Men Do Talk

L ew had spent a lot of time in the North, but this Alaska rain was different. It just floated in the air, soaking trees, ground, their clothing. It felt good to come in out of such weather, even if the shelter was a morgue.

Lew wiped the water from his face, shook his hat a couple of times and followed Charlie and Chief of Police Howell across the cement floor to a closed door. Howell pushed it in. The air that emerged was heavy with the smell of formaldehyde, and a fly buzzed somewhere up over their heads.

It was the first fly Lew had noticed in this frontier town of Wild Horse. "Summer can't be far off," he thought.

Howell punched a switch, flooding the room with light. It looked like a big vault with concrete walls. This addition to the old frame police station was so new it hadn't been painted. Howell half-apologized, explaining that only since the completion of the highway had such an addition been needed.

The body lay on a sort of cement tray almost in the middle of the room. Grimly, Lew forced himself to step forward and study it.

The man had been about 30 years old, shorter than average and thick in the body. The hairy legs were slightly bowed. Marks of spectacles were impressed on the nose bridge and along each cheek back to the ear. The hair was coarse, straight and dark, and the skin below it curiously blotched. This gave a surprising contrast with the rest of the body, which was uniformly dark as if tanned by long exposure to wind and sun. Seven puncture wounds with blue edges were scattered over the chest.

Howell stabbed a forefinger at them. "Good shooting, I say. The guards on the trucks carry short 12 gauges with buckshot."

"Is the guard still here in town?" Charlie asked.

Howell shook his head. "He had to go on, but I can tell you all there is to know. I questioned him myself right after the shooting.

"The drivers stopped for supper and lined the trucks up alongside the service depot, like they always do. One guard stayed while the rest ate. When he heard a truck hood lid being lifted, he went to investigate and found this fellow leaning over the truck engine. Brown, the guard, asked what he was doing. The fellow didn't answer, just whirled around with one hand raised. Brown thought he was either going to shoot or throw something, so he fired."

Howell pointed at the chest wounds. "Buck doesn't usually kill so quick. The coroner said this guy was unlucky. One slid between two ribs into the heart."

"Who was he?" Lew asked.

"He was a waiter at the Wild Horse Tavern. But when we questioned Strumley, who runs the place, we learned he had worked just two days. The only name they knew him by was 'Pete.' Help's hard to get up here, so nobody asks many questions of a man who says he wants work. They figure they're lucky he stopped instead of going on to the road construction camp, where they pay real dough.

"He lived at 205 Tenth, an alley off the main street. We searched the room but didn't find anything. There wasn't a scrap of paper. Hardly any clothing — a sweater, two shirts and a raincoat."

"Maybe some of the other waiters knew him," Lew suggested.

Howell's eyes turned belligerent. "We know what we're doing. We questioned the whole lot. Nobody could tell us anything."

"They have cooks and cigarette girls?" Lew replied.

Some of Howell's belligerence faded. "Sure, they got hostesses, too, that dance with the boys for four bits a dance. We haven't got around to them, yet, but we will."

"I'd rather you didn't," Charlie said. "Let us have a try first."

Howell looked doubtful. "Well, I suppose I can let it go until tomorrow. I got my orders to show you all the cooperation I can."

"Thanks," Charlie replied, closely studying the dead face.

Howell started talking again. "The guard was worried maybe he shot too quick. This fellow hadn't damaged the truck any. I don't know what he was trying to do, but he didn't get very far."

Charlie looked up. "Don't be so sure of that. Have you had any word from that convoy since it pulled out last night?"

"No."

"Just because this fellow doesn't look like a spy or saboteur,"

Charlie continued, "is pretty good proof he was. He could have opened the hood to draw Brown's attention, acted as a decoy while some others got in the real dirty work. It only takes a few seconds to plant a time or incendiary bomb."

Charlie took a pencil from his pocket, leaned over the body and, working carefully with the rubber end, pushed at the stiffened ears. He lifted the hair where it grew close to the forehead and prodded among the roots. "I need an undertaker," he finally said.

"There's only one," answered the surprised Howell. "That's Bickwell. You want me to phone him?"

"Don't phone," Charlie said. "We'll walk over to his place."

Howell gave them the address, and they left the police station.

Wild Horse was a fairly old town, as pioneer settlements go. It sprang into being almost overnight, back in the days of the first Alaska gold rush. Now, work on the Alaskan Highway had brought back the boom days. Wild Horse's main street was mostly mud, and the buildings grouped along either side were unpainted wood. But bright lights gleamed through the windows, and the board paths that served as sidewalks were crowded with people.

Army engineers, contractors and their gangs had brought money to Wild Horse. So had the streams of military convoy trucks that plowed along the unpaved highway day and night. There was even an airport half a mile from the south end of town. The field was dirt, and only small planes could land and take off, but the dirt was fast becoming packed by use.

Charlie and Lew passed an old sourdough who carried a heavy rifle with octagonal barrel in the crook of his elbow.

"See that?" Lew commented. "A big bore Winchester, maybe a fifty caliber. He's getting ready for a spring bear hunt. I told you, as long as we were coming to Alaska, we ought to be fixed so we could shoot two of those big browns, if we had time."

"This isn't a vacation," Charlie replied evenly.

"Sure, I know," Lew said ruefully. "But now, if we do have some time, we won't have a gun."

Lew didn't stop grumbling until they reached the undertaker's office, and the first thing they saw when they got inside was a bearskin hanging on the wall. It must have been 10 feet long and so wide it covered almost all of that side of the room. Lew stared at the hide until a man came in through the rear door.

"I'm Bickwell," he answered Charlie. "I suppose somebody got killed?"

That surprised Lew. Where was the usual undertaker's diffident air of sympathetic understanding? Bickwell seemed more purposeful than polite. He regarded them with hostile eyes that set deep back behind his bulging forehead with heavy pouches beneath.

"We want you to do a little work on a man at the morgue."

"What kind of work?"

"When you get a corpse in with discolored face, don't you paint it to look natural?"

"Sure. Depends on how they died and how well the embalming takes. We watch them for spots and cover them over just before the funeral. But if you think I'm going to fix up a dang spy so he looks pretty, you're mad."

Charlie wasn't surprised that Bickwell knew police business. As the only undertaker in town, he would have a working relationship with the local law.

"I don't want him to look pretty," Charlie said. "Get Police Chief Howell on the phone. He'll give you the OK."

Bickwell unwillingly picked up the phone. "Hello, that you Joe? There's a couple of crazy fellows in here that want me to fix up that dang spy lying in your morgue. I ... what's that? Oh. I see. I didn't know that's the way it is."

The suspicion had faded from his face when he set the phone back. Keen interest had taken its place. "I'll be ready soon as I get some stuff."

He went into a back room, came out with a leather case about the size of a woman's overnight bag. He put on a raincoat and a hat, and they walked back through the rain to police headquarters.

Inside the morgue, Charlie said, "I want this fellow's face all dark, just like those spots that show through."

Bickwell opened his case, took out a sponge and rubbed the corpse's features. He held the sponge up, looked critically at it and gave a low whistle. "Somebody's been painting this fellow already. I guess I see what you want my help for."

"I don't," Howell said. "Of course, I'm only the police chief."

"You'll understand in a minute," Charlie assured him.

"If you want him to look natural," Bickwell said, "all I have to do is get this stuff off."

He worked the sponge deftly, moistening it frequently from one of the jars. Then he straightened up and took two paces back.

"You know your business, all right," Charlie said, studying the dead face, which was now a uniform brown. He bent over and put one hand on each side with his fingertips in the coarse black hair and applied some pressure.

Howell watched with astonishment. Bickwell showed no surprise. Instead, there was half a smile on his lips.

After working several minutes, Charlie said, "Look quick."

They crowded close, looking past his bent shoulders. "I'll be durned," Howell said. "He doesn't look like the same fellow."

"He isn't," Charlie replied grimly.

"I thought, all the time, he was an American," Howell continued. "Now he looks Japanese."

Charlie straightened up, took his hands off the corpse and held them out with a certain repugnance. "He is Japanese. They say dead men don't talk. But this one just told us who he was. Our job should be easier, now that we know what we're up against."

Chapter 2 – Monkey Business

They stood in the morgue that had been added to the police station when the Alaska Highway brought boom times back to the little settlement of Wild Horse. They were looking down at the corpse of a man who had been shot when caught monkeying with one of the trucks carrying World War II supplies north.

"That's pretty slick," Chief of Police Howell told Charlie. "He looked American before. But after you had Bickwell touch up his skin, and after you pulled his face back a certain way with your fingers, he looks Japanese. Must have had something done to his face so people wouldn't spot him as a spy. What put you on to it?"

"The blotches of color on his face were one thing," Charlie replied. "I only suspected the plastic surgery."

"Seems like the plastic surgery would have been enough," Howell said. "Why did he keep his face bleached?"

"The fair skin made his disguise more effective," Charlie explained. "Just another indication we're up against somebody who has a keen mind."

The undertaker Bickwell continued to examine the dead face. "You saw those thin scars where the skin had been cut around the ears?" he asked.

"And those at the edge of the scalp," Charlie added. "And that almost invisible one about the chin. Whoever did this knew his business."

"If there's more of these guys around," Howell complained, "how are we going to know? We can't stop everyone on the street and look at his ears."

Charlie turned quickly. "You understand this is strictly confidential. Not a word must leak out."

"Don't worry about me," Bickwell said. Then he closed his case, put on his hat and walked out.

"He's OK," Howell said, nodding after the departing undertaker. "I don't suppose you want any help from me on this job? You fellows from Washington always want to work alone."

"We'll need a lot of help before we're finished," Charlie assured him. "But for now, keep on with your routine investigation. But keep your men away from the Wild Horse Tavern for at least a day, so we can work that angle alone."

Charlie and Lew went back to the taxi stand to pick up their two suitcases. On the way, they passed a short branch off the main street that looked like an alley but had a painted wooden sign on a post that said "Tenth Street." The second house down had a sign in a window that read "Rooms." It was the only house with such a sign, and they figured it must be where the dead spy had stayed.

"Think it would be too obvious if we rented a room there?" Lew asked.

"No," Charlie answered. "Everyone has to live somewhere. And the town is full of strangers, so nobody is going to pay much attention to us."

"Not yet," Lew said.

Returning with their baggage, they turned up the short street. "Remember, we want single rooms," Charlie said. "There's a chance one of us will draw the one used by the dead man."

"The police searched it," Lew said. "We won't find anything."

"No, I suppose not. But there's a chance the dead man's friends might want to go over the room, too, just to make sure he left nothing behind. It might be nice to meet some of them."

Lew thought not, but he kept that thought to himself.

Number 205 had been built on ground higher than the unpaved street, with the small windows commonly found in northern places spaced sparsely across the two-story front. At one time the place had been painted green, but most of the paint had been stripped away by sun and storm, revealing the more attractive seasoned wood.

They had to climb six steps to reach the narrow porch. Charlie kicked at several of the treads and risers as he climbed, and jerked hard at the handrail. They were sound, and this surprised him. Shaky steps before a boarding house often indicate shabby and rundown insides.

The landlady, Mrs. Fretto, surprised him, too. Most landladies look harassed—the trials of their work, of course—and one would naturally think managing a rooming house in a place like Wild Horse would be more trying than most. But this landlady was comfortably plump and placid. Her dark skin, hair and flashing eyes looked distinctly Italian.

She led them up a rather steep stairway, panting a little at each step, and opened a door in the hall. "This is the best room in the house," she said. "The mattress is new, and the bathroom is only four doors down."

"What we want is two single rooms," Charlie said.

"That's right," Lew added. "He snores like the deuce."

"I only have this room and another across the hall. They're doubles, but you can have them if you pay full price."

"How much?" Charlie asked.

"Ten dollars a week—each."

They handed over the money. She pocketed the bills, went out in the hall and opened the second door. Lew followed with his suitcase. "How about keys?" he asked.

"Don't need them," she replied. "Front door is never locked."

Lew looked around the room. Besides the bed there was one chair, an uncomfortable-looking straight-back thing, and a dresser badly in need of varnish. There was a pair of sheets on the bed and two grayish blankets. He stripped them back to examine the mattress seams. Satisfied when he found no sign of bed bugs, he went across the hall to Charlie's room. Its furniture duplicated his own.

Charlie was lying across the bed. Lew sat down in the chair, winced when his tired muscles met the unyielding seat. He got back up and settled across the other end of the bed, instead.

They were both tired. Neither had slept much on their long trip up from the West Coast, and like most important assignments, this one had come suddenly. After the affair of Danger Isle, they had taken a two-weeks' rest then settled into more or less routine tasks with army intelligence. The work had been necessary, of course, but also dull. They had been glad to receive orders to fly immediately to this outpost on the Alaska Highway. Although the important military road was barely finished, streams of vital war materials were already flowing along its course.

Twice, they were told, a truck loaded with the highly strategic material magnesium had disappeared without a trace. Sabotage was suspected, of course, but there had been no proof. In each case, the last contact with the truck had been when it checked out of the control at Wild Horse. And each time the missing truck had been traveling alone. Before yesterday's events, larger convoys with guards had not been molested, which had convinced their chief that the operation might merely be a test, to try the efficiency of a bigger plot that might later wipe out an entire fleet of vehicles.

Charlie yawned and looked at his watch. It was a quarter past three. They had eaten a late breakfast five hours before. He was hungry, but he was more tired. "Let's get some sleep and then get a real dinner," he suggested.

"Suits me," Lew replied. "I'll go back to my own room and unpack. I wonder who drew the late spy's room?"

"You did," Charlie said.

Back at his room, Lew started to lay out his toilet kit, then hesitated and put it back in the bag. It was expensive, and when he remembered that the front door was never locked and that there didn't seem to be any key for his room, he decided to keep valuables in the bag and keep the bag locked.

He took off his shoes, loosened his belt and lay down. It wasn't quite as hard a bed as he feared it would be, and in a few minutes he went to sleep.

Lew was tired, but he always slept lightly. Sometime later he came out of a dream with a start. In the dream he was trying to dress in a room with many windows. There were no shades or curtains, and people were peeping in to watch him put on his clothes.

For a moment after awakening, Lew lay with his eyes closed, remembering the dream. But the feeling that he was being watched persisted, and he slowly opened one eye. The room was dark, and he wasn't sure, but he thought he saw the door of his room finish closing the inches that separated it from the jamb.

Lew slid out of bed quickly. The springs creaked once from the release of his weight. He sprang across the room and threw the door open. A dim light burned at either end of the empty hall. He stood there watching and listening. His keen ears finally caught the faint click of a door latch pushing home.

Lew went across and opened Charlie's door. His companion was snoring softly. "It's time for us to eat," Lew said softly.

Charlie sat up. "I'm ready."

"Somebody just looked into my room," Lew told Charlie then described what he had heard.

"We may strike pay dirt in this place," he concluded.

"That's the reason we came here," Charlie replied then got

up from the edge of his bed. He picked up a cake of soap from the dresser and a towel hanging from a corner of the mirror. "I'm going down the hall to wash," he said.

Just as Charlie was opening the bathroom door, a girl in a blue dressing gown shot out from the room opposite as if propelled from a gun. She almost collided with him and said, "Oh."

Charlie took his hand from the latch. "I'm in no hurry."

She smiled at him, and he noticed that she was quite attractive. The blue robe wrapped about her slight figure set off her blond hair well. She said, "Thanks," smiled, and darted inside.

Charlie went back to his room and waited until he heard her leave. Then he washed up, and they went out.

They walked through the rain to Wild Horse Tavern, which sat at the other end of town, directly opposite the military control station where trucks were serviced and checked. Four trucks had just entered, and were being gassed and oiled. They stopped to look at the big machines, which were painted olive drab and plastered with mud. The tractors were short and stubby with motors under the cab, and they looked like brutes for power. The closed trailer looked at least 40 feet long, 8 feet wide, and almost as high.

They waded across the muddy street to the tavern. It was dimly lit but warm, and the pleasant smell of cooking food welcomed them. They found a small table against one wall and sat down.

Lew picked up the one-page menu. "Spaghetti and meatballs," he read. "That's me. You want the same?"

A waiter came up and Lew ordered. "Bring us a couple of bottles of soda, too. Unopened."

The waiter looked puzzled.

"All bottles are opened at the bar," he said.

"Ours aren't," Lew told him. "Soda with the caps on, or don't bring any." The man left, looking offended. "Looks like a clip joint to me," Lew said, glancing around at the crowd of tough characters. "I'm not having a Mickey dropped in my soda."

There was a bar across the opposite end of the room. A platform to the right held music stands. A little row of chairs down in front caught and held his eye.

After a long wait, the waiter brought their food and soda. Lew picked up his bottle, saw the cap was OK. He took an opener from his pocket.

The spaghetti was good, though they would have liked more meatballs and sauce. Grated cheese had been sprinkled on top.

Before they finished eating, musicians filed onto the little stage. There were three brass instruments, a violin and drums. A sixth man sat down in front of a baby grand piano.

Then Lew saw the reason for the row of chairs. Six girls in evening gowns came out and sat down on them. The men cheered, and the girls smiled graciously in all directions. They were the hostesses who danced with anybody willing to invest four bits a round for the exercise.

The band burst out in a blare of swing. Charlie watched the girls. "See that girl, second from the left? She's the one who was in such a hurry to wash. She's been watching us since she came in."

"Not bad looking," Lew offered, glancing up over a big twist of spaghetti. The girl stood up and walked over towards them. "Say," he said, "I think she's coming over here. Feel like a dance?"

Chapter 3 – A Cry for Help

The girl Charlie had seen in their rooming house, one of the Wild Horse Tavern's paid hostesses, came straight to their table. "Mind if I sit down?" she asked.

"Of course not," Charlie said. They both stood and Charlie pulled back a chair for her. She sank down with a sigh.

"They keep it so hot in here," she said, "it makes me thirsty."

Lew grinned and beckoned to the waiter who already had edged closer. "A drink for the lady and more soda for us," he said. "And remember, we open our own bottles."

The waiter appeared with the soda and a tall glass partially filled with tea. She took a sip and said, "Thanks for letting me use the bathroom first at the boarding house. They take it out of our pay if we're a minute late."

"At least business ought to be good," Charlie replied, glancing at the check the waiter left. "This swindle sheet says a dollar a drink. You should get at least 20 cents of that."

"I wish. We get a lousy dime."

"You can dump it out and order another drink, if you like," Lew said soothingly. "We don't mind."

She sipped at her glass. The little space out in the center of the room was crowded with dancers. The band actually sounded good.

Charlie studied the girl. She had on plenty of make-up. But a few freckles on her nose showed through. He figured she couldn't be more than 19 years old.

"They told me I'd make 50 dollars a week just in tips," she continued. "And I was sap enough to believe it. I haven't had a tip over 50 cents since I started."

The music paused. Charlie took a bill from his pocket and pushed it over to her. She flushed when she saw that it was a twenty.

"You're going to earn every cent," Charlie said taking her hand. "I haven't danced since I was in high school."

Lew leaned back, watching with lively interest. The girl was a good dancer. And Charlie was light on his feet despite his solid weight of muscle.

Lew wondered if he should cut in, show what he could do. Then another girl approached. She stood by his chair, pressing a thin hip against him. Strong perfume exuded from her clothing, a heady odor that made him uneasy. Lew shifted a little in his chair.

"Mind if I sit down?" she asked.

"Make yourself at home," Lew replied. He couldn't get up; she was too close, so he pulled a chair back with one long leg. She sat, smiling. Her dark hair was piled on top of her head, making her look several inches taller than she really was. Lew guessed she must be at least 10 years older than the girl dancing with Charlie. Still, she was a beauty.

"It's warm in here," she said after a short silence, which Lew did not offer to break. "The heat makes me thirsty."

Lew grinned. "What I like about you girls is your originality."

He couldn't see the waiter, but he held up a hand, and it took three seconds for him to brush Lew's elbow. "Drink for the lady, more soda for me—and I still got my own bottle opener."

Then he looked across the table.

"You're supposed to tell me that you're dissatisfied with your job because there aren't any big tips."

"I'm not dissatisfied," she said coolly, "and I get plenty of tips." Lew was trying to figure out something else to say, when she added, "I suppose your companion's dance partner complained. I could put on an act to get sympathy, but a girl can make plenty of money here, if she plays the angles."

"I'll bet you know them all," Lew thought. But he didn't say it aloud.

"Want to dance?" she asked.

He eyed her thoughtfully. "Not right now."

She frowned.

"I'll dance later," he offered. Then, yielding to a sudden impulse, he added, "I came to look for somebody. A fellow named Pete. Know him?"

"I know half a dozen Petes. What's the last name?"

"I forgot," Lew said. "But he works here as a waiter."

"I don't know everybody who works here. What do you want of him?"

"He owes me money."

"Sure you don't want to dance?"

"I'll hunt you up later."

She stood. "Don't forget."

"I won't," he promised. He stood until she was halfway back to the hostess chairs. Then he wondered if he had made a mistake in not accepting the dance invitation. The band stopped playing and Charlie came back.

"Lew, I want you to dance with Miss LaFrance. She's swell."

"You weren't so bad yourself," she replied. "After the first dozen steps."

Charlie grinned. "How many times did I step on your feet, Miss LaFrance?"

"That's not my real name," she said. "Call me Sadie."

"Okay, Sadie. About the drink?"

"Not now. They don't want us to spend too much time in one place. We have to spread ourselves around."

"Who's that dark girl dancing with the soldier, right in front of the bar now?" Lew asked.

"That's Rita. Why?"

"She came over and asked me to dance with her."

"You should have. Rita's the best." Sadie started off, but had only covered half the distance to her chair before the music began and a short man in a corduroy suit and high-laced boots pulled her to the dance floor.

"Did you learn anything from Sadie?" Lew asked.

"No. She had plenty to say, but only about herself."

"I didn't have any luck, either," Lew said. "I asked that girl Rita if she knew Pete, but she didn't. Which sounded screwy, for she's the kind of babe you'd expect to know everybody."

"You shouldn't have done that," Charlie said quickly. "It was too soon."

"Maybe it was dumb," Lew admitted. "But I promised to dance with her later. Maybe I can fix up that slip."

"Take it easy," Charlie cautioned.

Lew waited until the music stopped and then went to Rita, apparently the most popular girl on the floor, for he saw three other men converging upon her. He shouldered one of them out of his way and said, "I'm ready for that dance."

She stepped inside his arms.

It took only a couple of seconds to discover that Rita was an

84

expert dancer. Lew had a kind of jiggling step other girls found hard to follow. But Rita adapted easily. Not once did his feet scuff against hers, even when he quickened his step a little on purpose. She danced close, but somehow seemed impersonal, even remote. That, he decided, was the touch of a pro.

She glanced up, saw him watching her, and said, "Have you found the man who owes you money?"

"I forgot all about him," Lew replied. "All I can think about is what a great dancer you are."

She shook her head and laughed. "You're doing all right, too."

"Stop kidding," Lew replied. "I know I'm plenty bad. I didn't learn right in the beginning, and I haven't had much practice since."

She eyed him thoughtfully. "I could give you lessons."

"Here?"

"In my room. Any afternoon between 3 o'clock and five." Her perfume was so strong he wondered if that was what was making him dizzy. He leaned back a little.

"I'd like that. Tomorrow?"

"Tomorrow is OK."

"It's a date," Lew said decisively.

The music stopped—it always seemed to be doing that—and Rita was instantly carried off by one of the men he had shouldered aside. Lew went back and sat down.

"I've got a date with Rita tomorrow at three," he told Charlie. "She's going to show me how to dance."

Charlie looked surprised. "You work fast, don't you?"

"Reasonably so," Lew grinned. "You figure she might be one of the gang we're looking for?"

Charlie nodded. "Anyone might be. I suspect them all."

The nearness of the waiter warned them they should either order again or surrender their table. They ordered. A third hostess wandered over and persuaded them to buy her a drink. Charlie danced with the girl, and Lew had a round with Sadie, who was good, but she lacked that special something that distinguished Rita.

The waiter came over and wiped up the wet rings from the tabletop. He was middle-aged with wide shoulders and gray eyebrows that grew straight up and gave him an air of belligerence that fit well with his powerful frame. They decided he would be an ugly customer in a scrap.

"I heard you asking about Pete," he said in a low voice.

Lew started in surprise, but Charlie said evenly, "Did you?"

"Sure. Pete's dead, all right. But I thought you might want to know where he really lived. That room at the boarding house was just a front."

"That might help," Charlie replied evenly, "but it depends on how much you want to tell me."

"I need some dough to move on. How about 50 bucks?"

"For a dead man's address?"

"Well, twenty then."

"I might go that far."

The man nodded then said, "It's hard to find. I'll have to write it out and give it to you tomorrow night. Sorry, gentlemen, but you'll have to order again if you want to hold this table."

Charlie noted the change in the waiter's voice and looked up quickly to see Rita passing behind. "Right, the last wasn't quite as cold as we like."

When they were alone, Lew said quietly, "I don't like the delay. I wish we could get those directions now."

The crowd grew louder as the night advanced. They looked about every few minutes but the waiter did not return. They stayed an hour longer then left.

It was still raining, and there were no street lamps in Wild Horse. Halfway back to their room they passed a vacant lot. A cry that sounded like a woman pierced the night air.

Charlie pulled out his pocket light and swept the beam across the vacant lot, illuminating a group of figures. One figure lay on the wet ground; two others leaned over top, menacingly.

"Let's break that up," Lew said.

Charlie needed no urging. But then, as he passed a pile of crates that littered the edge of the lot, he heard a sound that brought him up sharp. It was the fast, eager breathing of one or more people hiding behind the pile.

"Come back, Lew!" he yelled. "It's a trap!"

Chapter 4 – More Business for the Morgue

Charlie swung his pocket torch in the direction of the face that was rising up from behind the heap of rubbish, hardly 4 feet away. He stepped forward jabbing out his fist at the same time. The face disappeared, and the tingling in his fingers told Charlie he wouldn't have to worry about that one for a while.

But Lew was in a bad spot. A man had come up from somewhere out of the rain and fog and leaped upon his shoulders. Also, the two men who had been leaning over the third figure on the ground had straightened and were running towards them.

Charlie got to Lew just as the fellow on his shoulders lifted up one hand. Charlie seized the wrist and twisted with all his strength. The weapon turned out to be a knife, and the point dipped down and stung into his shoulder. Then Charlie heard bones snapping. The knife slipped down to the ground and, with a savage heave, Charlie jerked the man from Lew's back. Charlie lashed out savagely with one foot. It was dirty fighting to kick a man who was already down, but he had no choice.

Charlie's pull had sent Lew staggering back, and before he could steady himself, the pair was almost on him. Lew ducked and, at the same instant, Charlie's long arms swept up a box of rubbish from the pile and heaved it over his partner's head into the faces of the charging men.

The diversion gave Lew time to straighten up, and he swung at the nearest man, who was clawing at the wet stuff that covered his face. But the ground was wet and he slipped a little. His blow landed but lacked force. The man was only rocked some. He turned, and both the assailants hurried off through the rain. Lew tried to follow, but he slipped again and this time fell. Charlie checked for the person who had been lying on the ground. But there wasn't anybody there.

By the time Lew regained his feet, the fleeing men were out of sight, but he heard light footsteps splashing off through the mist. He started in pursuit. The sound of footsteps died. Still, he ran on until something dark loomed up ahead and, thrusting out his hands, he found it was a high board fence.

He stopped to listen and heard something like the creaking of rusty hinges. He ran along the wall until he reached the end at the rear of the lot. The entire length seemed solid. Yet he knew that somewhere in that length a gate had opened and closed. The night was too dark or the door too well concealed for him to discover it.

When he couldn't find the girl on the ground, Charlie turned to find the man he had struck first. But this one also had disappeared. He did find the knife he had twisted from the other's grasp. It was a very thin blade, about 10 inches long and quite sharp. Then he started off towards Lew.

"Every blamed one of them got away," Lew said in disgust.

"Stop griping," Charlie told him. "You're lucky to be alive. That was a pretty trap. And it almost worked."

"That's why I wanted to grab at least one of them," Lew said. "So we could find out who they were and why they set the trap."

"They're Japanese saboteurs," Charlie replied, "and somehow, they're on to us. Maybe they were watching the police station when we went there."

"That cry for help sounded like a woman," Lew said.

"They knew that would bring us running," Charlie answered, "like a pair of dopes. If I hadn't heard that fellow breathing behind the pile of boxes, we'd both be dead. He was panting like he could hardly hold himself back. He was smelling blood."

And then Charlie remembered that the knife he had twisted from the assailant's hand had nicked his shoulder. He put his hand inside his coat and found the shirt damp with blood. "I got a scratch that needs first aid," he told Lew.

Charlie's wound turned out to be more than a nick. The point of the knife had penetrated almost an inch through the soft place inside his collarbone.

Back at the boarding house, Lew doped it with disinfectant and put a wad of gauze on to stop the bleeding. "You better see a doctor in the morning," he said, and Charlie promised he would if it was sore when he awoke.

Lew went across the hall to his own room. He unbuckled the shoulder holster that fitted so snugly under his arm it could not be noticed as long as he wore a coat, took the automatic pistol out of the leather and shoved it under his pillow. He placed a small flashlight beside the gun, snapped off the room light, and turned in.

It seemed that Rita's intoxicating perfume still lingered in his nostrils. He got up and opened the single window in the room a little, just enough to admit some fresh air without letting in the rain. The big old house was very quiet. Twice he heard the front door open and soft footsteps ascend the stairs.

He didn't know how long it was before he finally went to sleep. All he knew was that sometime afterwards he came wide awake, and somebody was in his room.

Lew didn't want to move because the springs of the bed would protest noisily. So he kept motionless and carefully slid one hand up under the pillow, grasped the gun's butt, and drew it down level with his chest. Then his hand went back for the flashlight.

He had the light in his fingers, but before he could use it, there was a scuffling sound and a body came lunging onto his bed. At the same moment, Lew leaped out on the opposite side, gun in hand, light in the other. He shot a beam towards the bed. What he saw in the circle of light made his mouth gape.

Rita lay half-sprawled over the bed with arms outstretched before her. She was wearing a plaid coat and a little black hat on top of her high hair. She stared into the beam of light with wide eyes. Lew stepped towards the light switch on the wall. He snapped on the ceiling bulb and then turned off his hand-held flashlight.

"I thought we were going to have that dancing lesson this afternoon," he said, keeping the pistol pressed down at his side and out of sight.

Rita got up slowly, pulled the edges of her coat down firmly, and gave her hat a little push, which miraculously put it straight. "What are you doing in my room?" she demanded.

"Your room? Mine, you mean. I'm the one to ask questions."

She looked around. The angry frown left her face. She sighed and rubbed her eyes with a gloved hand. Her hands, he noticed, were very small.

"My gosh," she said, "it is your room. Mine is bad enough, but nobody could mistake it for this kennel."

"If I had known you were going to drop in," Lew retorted, "I might have fixed it up. But you haven't answered my question."

"I guess I can't count straight," she said. "I had a few real drinks tonight. I got to the house all right and up the stairs, but I guess I didn't count doors right. My room is on the same side, next to yours. I'm awfully sorry I fell in and woke you."

She looked down at the floor. Lew's heavy shoes lay there about 3 feet from the bed. "Do you always throw your shoes out in the middle of the room?" she asked.

"It's one of my bad habits. Why didn't you turn the light on? Then you wouldn't have stumbled over my shoes."

"I have habits, too," she replied. "One of them is to never turn on a light at night with the window shade up. It's a good habit for a girl in a place like this."

He walked past the bed towards her. Something on the floor caught his eye. He bent over and picked it up. "You dropped that ornament from your hair when you fell," he said, holding it out. It was heavy and almost 8 inches long, made something like an old-fashioned hairpin, only thicker and topped by a large shield studded with brilliants.

She took it and turned to the door.

Lew opened it, said good night, and closed it when he heard her pause at her own door. He turned around, looked at the single straight-backed chair in his room. It was too tall to set under the door knob. His eye rested on the dresser. It was quite wide with heavy drawers. He pulled one out and tried it under the knob. It fit well enough, and he knew nobody could come in now without making enough noise to awaken him. He put his pistol and light back under the pillow and lay back down.

The room was filled with Rita's perfume, and when he had handed over the long pin, he had caught the odor of liquor on her breath. She had told him the truth about not sticking to the cold tea menu. "Those girls sure have a hard life," he thought.

Charlie came into his room about 7 the next morning. Lew was almost dressed, and he had taken the drawer away from under the doorknob. He told Charlie about Rita's visit.

"That's a sample of your usual hospitality," Charlie said. "Leaving your big shoes out in the middle of the room for visitors to stumble over."

They went in the first restaurant they saw and ordered breakfasts of sausage, buckwheat cakes, coffee, toast, jam and prunes. It was 8 o'clock when they entered the police station. Howell hadn't come down yet, the desk sergeant told them. They sat and waited almost half an hour before Howell arrived. He looked worried, and he wasn't making much of an effort to conceal it.

They went into his office, and Charlie repeated the details of their fight in the empty lot.

"That's all?" Howell asked. "You didn't recognize them?"

"No. It was too dark. But here's the knife I twisted out of one fellow's hand. You can check it for fingerprints, but I think he was wearing gloves."

Howell laid the knife still wrapped in Charlie's handkerchief on his desk. "I'll send some men down there to look over the place. I know that lot. People use it for a shortcut. I can't understand why they opened a gate in the fence, when the back is unfenced. I don't remember any door there, either."

They could see there was something on the chief's mind. Finally, he let them have it. "My boys picked up another dead man early this morning. They found him up one of the alleys that run off the main street."

"You got him in there?" Charlie nodded towards the morgue.

"Yeah. Want to see him?"

Howell led them into the windowless room. There were two bodies on the stone slabs now. Charlie went up and looked at the new one. It was what he expected—the waiter who had promised to tell them where the first dead man had really lived.

Chapter 5 – Lew Buys a Bear Gun

Charlie was not surprised to learn that the dead man found in the alley was the waiter who had offered to sell them information about Pete, the other waiter from the Wild Horse Tavern, a suspected Japanese saboteur who had been shot and killed while monkeying around with a military convoy truck. Now, it appeared that information was out of reach.

"Looks like it isn't lucky to be a waiter at the Wild Horse Tavern," Police Chief Howell observed.

"This man was going to tell us where Pete actually lived," Charlie said. "The room Pete had on Tenth Street was just a front. We agreed to give twenty bucks for the real address, and he said he'd have to write down the way to get there. Then he was called away and said he'd be busy for at least an hour. That was the last time we saw him alive."

"Pete was supposed to have another place?" Howell asked.

"So this one claimed," Charlie replied. "He said it was full of Pete's stuff, and we wanted to get our hands on it. There must be some clue there to his identity, or that of his friends."

"It doesn't look very promising now," Chief Howell said. "But I can put a couple of men on it. I had some photographs taken of Pete's face yesterday, and they can take them around and ask at all the rooming houses if he was ever seen there."

Charlie was still looking down at the corpse. "What killed him? I don't see any wounds."

Howell scratched his chin and then said, "There aren't any. Doc's going to do an autopsy."

"How far from the tavern was he found?" Charlie asked.

"About four long blocks. But I don't think that he was killed there. We found the body at 4:08 a.m. The tavern closes about 3. We rounded up most of the other waiters and a bartender, and they all agreed that this man left somewhere around three or a few minutes later. That seems to prove he was killed outside. Unless maybe the whole bunch is in this thing, and they all lied. Now, I figure he was killed so he couldn't tell you about Pete. You got the same idea?"

Charlie nodded. "It makes sense. It didn't sound like so much then, just the place a dead man had lived, but it has to be big if it justified murder."

"We'll do all we can to run it down," Howell assured them. But they didn't get the impression he had much faith in the words.

Then Charlie asked, "How many doctors in Wild Horse?"

"We got three: Doc Armstrong, the coroner; Doc Phillips; and Doc Faux."

"How long have they been here?"

"Armstrong's been here as long as I can remember. He's been coroner most of the time. Doc Phillips showed up about six months ago. He came in with one of the big construction outfits and liked it so well he decided to stay. I guess the fishing helped him make up his mind. Faux has been in Wild Horse a little longer, about a year."

"Know where Phillips and Faux came from?"

"Phillips came straight from Portland. He's told me about it a dozen times. Faux don't talk so much about where he's been, but I think he was a big shot doctor in the East. Somewhere around New York or Boston. He came here directly from Juneau."

"You wouldn't have a photo of any of them, would you? I suppose not. But will you do this? Write out as complete a description of each man as you can. I want to know their approximate age, height, weight, color of eyes and hair, type of features, and anything else that would help complete an identification."

"Sure, I can do that," Howell agreed. "I'll put down what I can remember and have the sergeant go over it. He's a good man for faces. We can fix it up now if you're in a hurry." Howell apparently welcomed this chance to get into action.

"I am," Charlie replied.

Howell wrote alternately on three sheets for some time. Then he took the work out front. "Jeff will finish them up and bring them back," he said, returning.

They noticed that Howell's eyes were shot with red, that he looked tired. He leaned back in his chair, eyes fixed on the ceiling. Finally, he spoke. "You figure there's a doctor mixed up in this?"

"It's possible," Charlie admitted.

"I guess the plastic surgery you found on Pete started you in that direction. Did you examine the other one's face, to see if his features had been changed, too?"

"No," Charlie admitted. "I didn't think it necessary. I got him lined up as a neutral who stuck his neck out a little too far."

"We got to follow every lead, though," Howell said. "But you're right. I looked him over good. There wasn't any place where his skin had been cut and patched."

"Do Phillips and Faux follow general practice?"

"Phillips does, but Faux likes mental cases, mostly. When Mike Pearson's wife lost her mind, he was down to see her twice a day. Then he persuaded Mike to send her up to his place. He's got a big house just outside town, and it has a few furnished rooms like a sanatorium. He fixed Mrs. Pearson up in less than a week.

"I never heard about him performing any operation, either. He will take on a confirmed drunkard. Had one of our worst at his place for ten days, and when the man came home, he wouldn't touch a drop. He's been sober ever since."

The sergeant came in with the completed descriptions. Charlie looked them over and said, "I want to wire these back to Washington, but I don't want anybody here to know. Can I send these on to the next station and have the operator there wire them in?"

"You could," Howell said, "but I got something better. Jeff used to run the key in a telegraph office. When we got something confidential to send, he goes down to the office, runs the operator out so he can't read the stuff by ear, and sends it himself. I'll have him take these over now. But what about your reply when it comes in? The regular operator will have to receive that."

"Headquarters will mix in enough nonsense that we will understand but no one else will get much sense from the stuff. I can't do that with these descriptions; they have to be exact."

They could see there was still something on Howell's mind. Finally, it came out. "I got more bad news for you. Remember that Pete got shot by a guard riding a convoy of four truckloads of magnesium? That convoy left Wild Horse Sunday night. This is Tuesday. Nobody has heard of it or seen it since. Those four trucks simply disappeared."

Before, it had been only one truck at a time. Now, somebody had taken four at once. And guards were riding these trucks, too.

"How far away is the next military station?" Charlie asked.

"Fifty-five miles. It happened between there and here."

"I've got a detailed map of the highway in my room but I

don't recall if the road touches the coast at any place. Does it?"

"No. It comes about a quarter-mile from the sea, but in between is a ridge so steep a man can hardly climb over, and there's no chance that much magnesium was packed over a box at a time."

"Magnesium is light," Charlie argued. "That's why they use it when they make airplanes."

"Still, that just isn't possible. I've hunted bear along that ridge the last four years, and it was all I could do to lug my rifle up some of those slopes."

"It's being done some way," Charlie insisted. "There isn't any reason to hijack the trucks, unless they can get the cargo off."

"Unless it was sabotage. They could be simply preventing our shipping it across to Russia. That's where it goes, you know."

They thought over that angle for a minute, but Charlie didn't buy it. Howell then said, "I forgot to ask where you're staying. I might want you in a hurry."

"The address is 205 Tenth Street," Charlie told him.

"I should have known. I suppose one of you is sleeping in the room Pete had before he was shot?"

"I am," Lew replied.

Charlie stood up. They had taken enough time already. "We'll come back about noon. I want to know what the coroner finds with his autopsy."

When they reached the street, he told Lew, "I'm going back to the room and study that map. This stuff is going out by sea. There's no other way."

A block farther on they passed a small store with a single dusty window. Neither had noticed the place before, but Lew caught sight of a row of guns behind the glass. "You go on and check the map," he said. "I'll stay a while and study this collection."

The house at 205 Tenth Street was very quiet when Charlie stepped inside. He hadn't seen any of the other roomers, except for the two girls who danced at the tavern. And he hadn't seen the landlady since she had showed them the rooms yesterday.

When he entered his room, he saw the bed was neatly made. The mud that had dropped from his shoes had been swept clean, too. He got out the highway map and spread it over the bed. It was a regular topographical sheet with the highway drawn in by hand. Howell was right about its course. It ran close to the coast beyond

Wild Horse, but the land between was very rough.

Charlie studied the chart for almost an hour. He formulated plan after plan of how the trucks may have been hijacked, but none was sound enough to retain.

Then Lew came in, grinning happily. "My new bear rifle," he announced. "Of course, it's only new to me." He held out a long, heavy gun with a sharp-toed buttstock and an octagonal barrel with the sharp edges worn bright. The wood was scarred, but the metal seemed free of rust.

"It's a .45-82-405, to be exact. Shoots 82 grains of black powder and a 405-grain, 45-caliber lead bullet. And, boy, when she hits something, it goes down to stay."

"I don't doubt that," Charlie agreed. "The only trouble you'll have is in the hitting. At 200 yards, you'll have to aim 2 feet high. And that reminds me, what will you use for bullets? The factories haven't made that stuff for years."

"I'm not dumb enough to buy an orphan rifle," Lew told him and then laid down a package. "There you are, four boxes of 20 each. Genuine factory cartridges. All I lack now is a hunting license before I start after that ten-foot bear rug."

"What did you pay for that cannon?" Charlie asked.

"I got it cheap," Lew said. "Plenty cheap, when you remember how scarce rifles and loads are up here."

"How much?" Charlie insisted.

"Forty-five bucks."

"They sure saw you coming. How's the insides?"

"Pretty good, and it will be perfect after I do some work with rod and oil."

"There's another little job we have to finish first," Charlie reminded. "Solve the disappearance of four trucks with their loads, guards and drivers. Look at this map. See if you can see some angle I've missed."

Lew stood his gun in the corner and bent over the map. Half an hour later, he confessed he was just where he had started. He also confessed he was hungry. They decided to walk back to the police station and find out about the autopsy. Then it would be time to eat.

"Yeah, Doc found out what killed him," Howell said after they arrived. "I guess Doc's a little better than I figured.

"Turns out the man was stabbed through his ear into his brain.

That's why there wasn't any wound or any blood. Doc said it was a very thin, sharp instrument about 6 inches long. It could have been a stiletto, or it could even have been a hat pin."

Something clicked in Lew's brain, and he flashed back to last night, to when he found Rita's hair ornament on the floor. It was at least 6 inches long, and it had a long, thin pin. What a fool he had been. Rita was wearing a hat when he flashed on his light and exposed her collapsed across his bed. A hair ornament would be under a hat, not above it. It couldn't have fallen from her hair when she stumbled over his shoes. It had fallen from her hand.

It was apparent now that she had crept in with the deadly thing clutched in her fingers. She had come to kill him, by thrusting it through his ear into his brain. Only his sixth sense of vigilance and his shoes on the floor before the bed had saved him from death.

Chapter 6 – Lew's Dancing Lesson

Lew was so shaken by what he now realized had been a narrow escape from death the night before, he for a moment forgot his companions. Now he became aware of the fact they watched him with curious eyes.

"What's the matter?" Howell asked.

Lew wasn't sure how to answer. Should he tell Howell he thought the dancer Rita came into his room last night to kill him? Or should he wait until he had proof?

"It's such a horrible way to die," Lew finally answered the police chief. "Stabbing a man through the ear into his brain. It sort of got me for a moment."

"It got him, too," Howell nodded towards the morgue where the corpse lay. "Usually when a man is knocked off around here, there's a reason. He gets into trouble over a woman, or he drinks too much and puts a chip on his shoulder for someone to knock off. We don't have any trouble with those kinds of routine cases. This one ain't routine."

He regarded them soberly then continued, "The only clue we got is the guy wanted to sell you information about a man who was already dead."

"This case is complicated," Charlie agreed. "So far, we've only seen two small links in what must be an intricate chain. Alone, they don't mean much. We've got to uncover more links. When we learn enough, all the little bits will fall together and make a picture we can understand. That's the way these conspiracy cases work. They're like jigsaw puzzles."

Charlie's words seemed to help Howell buck up. "Yeah, I guess you're right," he said. "I'll hunt out this fellow's family or friends. He seems a little better known than the first one. When do you expect an answer to your wire?"

"Tomorrow morning. It's coming in your care. We'll be down about eight."

When they were outside on the street, Charlie said, "All right. Let's have it. What gave you the jitters?"

Lew repeated every detail of his encounter with Rita the night before, and then he added his conclusion, now considerably expanded. "And I got a date with her in her room for dance lessons at three o'clock. That's only two hours. What shall I do?"

"Keep it," Charlie told him.

"And get struck through the ear while we're doing the tango?"

"Don't be a dope. She isn't going to kill you in her room. It's too much trouble to lug the corpse away. And if she tried, would you sit there and get stuck like a hog? What you must do is get your hands on that hair ornament that looks like a stiletto. You've got to find out if she could kill a man with it."

They ate lunch and then sauntered down the main street of Wild Horse until it was time for Lew's dance lesson. Charlie went back to the rooming house with him. "I'll be sitting beside my door with a gun," he said. "Holler when she makes a pass at you."

"This isn't funny," Lew told him.

Rita opened her door with a smile. She looked even better without the makeup and the elaborate hair-do. She had on a straight-cut one-piece dress and black dancing pumps. She was very businesslike. There was a little portable phonograph on the table about as big as a dinner plate. She put on a record, and Lew stepped quickly towards her.

"Wait," she commanded. "You don't reach out for your dance partner like you grab a sandwich at a picnic." Lew flushed and stood back.

"Hold up your arms like this," Rita commanded. "Then she comes forward and inside them."

Gracefully she demonstrated, and they started around the outside of the room. The floor boards were rough but not too bad. Rita didn't seem quite as impersonal as she had at the tavern. She looked up into his face.

"When I tell you how to do things, I'm teaching you what is right for social dancing. Some of those two-legged wolves at the tavern hug so tight I can't breathe."

Lew immediately relaxed his arms.

"The right way," Rita continued, "is to let your partner take the lead. If she wants to be held close, she'll dance inside and let you know. Like this."

She gave a very efficient demonstration.

"She will grip your arm or shoulder tighter," Rita went on. "If you're holding her too close, she will push you back. Like this."

Another skillful example.

"You must be ready to respond, either way."

Then she bumped against a chair.

"You led me straight into it," she admonished. "I put it there on purpose. It is each dancer's responsibility to watch the other when going backward."

Her dresser was in the corner opposite the door. When they passed it, Lew saw the hair ornament lying across an ivory hand mirror. He knew it by its size and by the shield-shaped top studded with shining stones.

The record finished playing, but the needle kept on scratching until Rita went over and shut it off. She turned the spring crank until it was tight again. "We'll try a waltz this time."

"Swell," Lew said. He wandered over to the dresser, picked up the hair ornament, and turned it over in his fingers. "These real diamonds?" he asked.

"If they were, would I be dancing in a place like this? I used to do some stage work. The pin was one of my props. It blazes like fire under a spotlight."

The worry that had kept Lew tense eased. The pin did not have a steel shank, as he had supposed. Instead, the part below the shield that pierced her hair was made of plastic, oval in shape, and duller than a paper knife. The point was blunt.

Quite obviously, this was not the weapon that had stabbed the waiter through the ear.

Lew put the pin down and they danced again. His feet fell eagerly into the rhythm of the waltz. He was definitely enjoying himself. The hour passed quickly. Rita stopped, looked at her tiny wristwatch and said, "You must go now. I need time to rest before work tonight."

He took out his billfold and asked, "What is your fee?"

"Three dollars."

He counted out the money. "How about tomorrow?"

"Sorry. The afternoon is full. Maybe I can spare an hour the day after."

"I'll look you up at the tavern before then, and you can let me know," Lew replied with a smile.

When he went to Charlie's room, he found his companion stretched out comfortably on the bed. "I'll bet you were asleep the whole time," Lew said. "And no, I haven't an earache. The hair ornament is perfectly harmless. You couldn't kill a man with it unless you rammed it down his throat and choked him."

"I haven't been asleep," Charlie replied. "I found out where Doctor Faux lives. Let's walk out that way and see if we can find the place."

"Why pick on Faux? He's one of three doctors in Wild Horse."

"We'll check all of them. I picked Faux first because Howell knows the least about him. The place is supposed to be hard to find," Charlie added as they started down the street.

"It sets on a flat just beyond the edge of town," he continued, walking at a brisk pace. "A high ridge lies between, and the sides are too steep to climb save at one spot. There's a road, but it circles around and is a good three miles farther."

They climbed over two easy hills before they reached a hogback of pure rock, jagged and rough. Scrawny wind-twisted trees lined the top, and the sides were outcrops of stone too steep to be climbed without mountain tackle. The double strands of a telephone wire hung almost vertically down the side from a single short pole at the top.

They found the path after some searching. It was hardly a trail, just flat places in the rock scarcely bigger than the bottom of a boot. But climbing wasn't hard, after you got the hang of it. A stiff wind met them at the crest, and they had to hang onto their hats to keep them. The top of the ridge was about 20 feet wide, and the opposite side plunged precipitously down, just as steep as the side they had climbed.

A two-story wood building sat in the middle of the flat below. It had widely spaced windows and a black composition roof. The unpainted walls had weathered to the customary grayish brown. It was quite a large house for Wild Horse, and might easily contain 10 good rooms.

A second smaller building, maybe a garage or a barn, was partly visible behind the house. A hitching bar sat at one side of the house and deep holes pawed in the ground around it showed that most visitors came to Faux on horseback. Blue smoke spiraled up from one of two chimneys.

"Going down to call?" Lew asked.

"Not now. Later this evening we'll come back. I wanted to find the place and the path in daylight. It's a breath-taker, all right."

"Neck-breaker, too, if you aren't careful," Lew added.

They started back.

"If I owned this setup," Lew said, "I'd get rich. I'd start a reducing sanatorium and wouldn't have to do anything but make my patients climb this ridge half a dozen times a day. The fat would melt off like a kettle of snow on a cook stove."

They went to the Wild Horse Tavern for dinner. Sadie came over and sat with them. They bought her drinks, but they didn't dance. She didn't like that so well, and when Lew called her "Miss LaFrance," she told him off. "You know that isn't my name. I said so last night."

"What is it?" Lew asked. "Smith?"

She surprised them by giggling. "No. My first name is Sadie all right. But the last is Kluke. A girl couldn't get very far carrying a load like that."

Charlie saw she was going to stick to them until one of them danced with her. So, he stood up and led the way to the dance floor. Lew saw Rita, and she waved to him.

She was tied up with a couple of men with chauffeur union badges on their caps.

Howell came in, nodded then sat down a few tables away and ordered dinner.

It hadn't rained all day, but when they paid their meal check and left, they walked out into a fog, and the visibility was about as bad. They had to use flashlights to climb the sharp ridge.

They snapped off the lights when they reached the peak, walked through the fringe of stunted trees and looked down on the valley below. Only one light showed in the big house of Dr. Faux. A shade was pulled down over that glass, but it made a poor job of blocking the glow. That window was in the top floor, facing them.

It was easier going down. The big thing was to avoid loosening pieces of rock, which would bounce noisily down the side of the ridge. They set off only a few, however, and reaching the ground, walked completely around the big building. The light in the upstairs window was the only one. Charlie stopped beneath it.

"We've got to figure out a way to look inside," he said.

Lew had been studying the front of the house. There was a porch across most of it, but the roof stopped about 5 feet short of extending under the window. He knew he could climb the big beams that held the porch roof. The problem would be to then reach the window.

"I can do it," he whispered at last. "If I stand right on the edge as close to the window as I can get and let my body swing out, I can grab the sill with my hands as I fall. That window shade looks old. There should be holes or thin places I can see through. The trouble will be getting back. You'll have to pull me over until I can get balanced again."

"I don't know how important seeing in that room is," Charlie confessed. "But I won't be satisfied until we do it. We should have brought some rope. But we each have a belt, and I'll buckle them together. You fasten one end around your wrist. Then, when you're ready, I can pull you back."

They took off their shoes and climbed the porch post. The roof didn't buckle or creak. Lew poised himself at the edge under the window. From here, it looked even farther away than it had from the ground. He fastened one end of the spliced belts around his left wrist, planted his feet against the roof, and swung out. Charlie set his own feet against Lew's to keep from slipping.

When Lew's outstretched fingers finally touched the windowsill, his body was almost horizontal. Fortunately, the sill was rough and allowed a firm grip.

He stretched his neck and lifted his head. The shade had several splits near the lower edge, and one was close to his eye. He pushed his hands out a little wider to see more readily.

His arms were already beginning to tire from holding the awkward position.

Before Lew got his eye lined up with the split in the shade, a strangled cry came out of the silent house. That startled Lew so badly he almost relaxed his grip on the sill.

But then he dug his fingers harder against the wood and looked through the crack. The light inside was so blindingly bright he saw nothing, at first. Then there was movement just past his direct line of sight. A figure wearing white cut between him and the light. It was a man, slight in stature with steel gray hair. The white garment covered him from neck to feet, and there were shiny gloves on his hands. A white mask was taped over his mouth and nose.

Lew saw it was an operating room, crudely furnished but apparently in working order. About 10 feet away, someone was strapped down to a sheet-covered bench. He or she moved a little when the man in white approached. The latter kept his back to the window, so Lew couldn't see what he did, but that choked groan came again, and it sent shudders up Lew's spine.

He kicked at Charlie, the signal to be pulled back.

There wasn't much strength left in his cramped muscles, and he had to push his weight up past the point of dead center before Charlie could help him. By the time he realized it, he didn't have enough strength to try and was out of other options.

Chapter 7 – They Plan a Raid

Lew was in a tough spot. His feet were jammed against the roof of the porch across the front of Dr. Faux's house while his fingers clung to the windowsill almost 6 feet away. His body was stretched between like the neck of a chicken out to receive the axe. It had been fairly easy to get into that position, but getting back wasn't going to be easy. In fact, his draining strength and the cramps in his arm muscles indicated it might well be impossible.

Lew tried one heaving push with his arms, but it failed to raise him up past the dead center point where Charlie could help by pulling on the belt looped about one wrist. Lew's fingers were numb. In a matter of seconds he would lose his grip.

What he had seen through the window hadn't helped his composure any, either. Neither had the groans of pain that sounded from the room.

The ground was about 14 feet below. He might manage a drop without serious injury, but the landing would be noisy. And it was quite possible he would sprain an ankle. There was only one thing left to do.

Lew whispered to Charlie, "I'm going to let go. Hang on to the belt with all you've got and swing me into the porch post."

His fingers were slipping even then, and he plunged down. He had pulled his feet off from the roof so he wouldn't fall headfirst. He fell the length of his arm and then felt an awful jerk that threatened to dislocate his shoulder. He felt the spliced belts stretch. But they held, as did Charlie's bare feet braced against the rough gravel surface of the composition roofing. Lew swung in against the edge of the roof and the porch post with a bang. It seemed the entire front part of the house shook from the blow.

There was nothing to do but wrap his feet around the post and slide down. Charlie dropped his end of the belt, and Lew went down so fast the weathered wood burned his hands. But he hit the ground running and sprinted to the side of the house where they had set their shoes. Charlie got there at the same time. They didn't wait to pull on their shoes but started running immediately.

Just as they reached the corner of the big house, the front door flew open and feet pounded across the porch floor. The fog had lifted a little, and there wasn't a chance of crossing the yard without being seen. So they ducked around the side of the building and hid inside a small shed attached to the house. A man dashed by, and he carried what looked like a big-gauge shotgun.

They waited several seconds then sprinted for the ridge. No gunshot followed. They found the bottom of the steep path and climbed swiftly. When they reached the top, they paused for a breath and then started down.

They were about halfway down when they heard a grinding noise up above, and then something crashed down the path. They had time only to crouch close against the smooth face of one of the outcrops. The object landed almost on top of their shield, grinding off a shower of stone dust that bit into their faces. It bounced up and again landed with a crash six feet below, grazing Lew's shoulder with a force that left it numb. The big rock continued to bounce down until it rolled to a stop on the level ground below. Lew rubbed his shoulder tenderly.

Charlie grabbed his hand and jerked him along. "We have to get out of here before they pry another one loose," he said.

They went slipping and sliding down with no thought of caution now. Several smaller stones came whizzing down after them, but the aim of their enemy on the summit was poor. They landed at the bottom rolling, got up and started off towards Wild Horse. They passed the big stone that had tumbled down; it was a rough boulder weighing at least 1,000 pounds. "A blockbuster, all right," Lew panted.

After they had run 100 yards, they realized they still carried their shoes in their hands. They pulled on their shoes and ran until they were at the edge of town. There they paused to wipe the dirt from their faces. Lew's shoulder ached, but nothing seemed broken.

"I want to know what you saw through that window," Charlie demanded. "Who made those groans?"

"Somebody strapped down to an operating table," Lew replied. "You remember Howell claimed that Faux didn't operate? He was putting on a good imitation tonight. He had all the trimmings, mask over his face, and enough tools and knives laid out beside the patient to fight a small war."

"Maybe it wasn't Faux," Charlie suggested.

"I don't know about that. I never saw him before. Still, he fit the description Howell gave us to wire into headquarters."

"What was he doing to the patient? Was he working on the face?" Charlie poured out his questions.

"I couldn't see that well. And, remember, I only had a half-inch break in the curtain to peek through."

"Was Faux alone, or did he have an assistant?"

"He was alone except for the patient. Maybe the operation was easy."

"Plastic surgery isn't," Charlie said. "Or I don't think it is. The groans showed Faux didn't use an anesthetic, which is also queer. Why didn't he give the patient a local, at least?"

"I don't know any of the answers," Lew said. "All I know is I ache all over and my feet hurt like the devil."

When they turned off the main street, they bumped into Sadie. Her eyes were red and the rouge was smeared over her face.

"What's wrong?" Charlie asked. "Some of those wolves bothering you?"

"I got fired," she cried. "The manager called me in and said I was through. He wouldn't say why, just that I wasn't satisfactory."

"You can get another job," Charlie said, as they stepped into the boarding house hall. "You can wait tables. None of the restaurants around here seem to have enough help. You won't make as much, but then maybe you will because the tips will be surer."

"That's true," she said, brightening up. "Funny I didn't think about the eating places. Thanks for the tip. Where was that place you ate?"

Charlie told her.

"I'll be there when they open tomorrow morning," Sadie promised and then ran on ahead of them up the stairs.

Charlie and Lew had an appointment, too, for tomorrow morning, and they were in the police station waiting for Chief Howell when he came in. He beckoned for them to follow into his office.

"Anything new on the last murder?" Charlie asked.

"Not a thing. We're stuck right where we were at the beginning. You got anything that will help?"

"We got something, all right." He told Howell about their visit last night to the home of Dr. Faux.

He spoke briefly of their escape from the men who had pursued them, but Howell pounded on that hard. "You got to go a little easier," he warned, "or somebody will kill you. I couldn't do much about it if they did, either. A lot of old-timers take the law into their own hands when it comes to intruders."

"I know," Charlie replied, "but we had to find out what Faux was doing."

"But it doesn't help," Howell said bluntly. "I know I said yesterday that Faux doesn't do surgery that I know about. But an emergency might have turned up last night. On the other hand, if you had actually seen him working over somebody's face, and the person was Japanese, we might be somewhere."

"We still can, if you search his house and find a man there who just had his face operated on," Charlie told him.

Howell shook his head. "I'd have to have a search warrant, and there isn't enough evidence. Besides, it ain't a crime to do facial surgery, if the patient asks for it."

"If faces are changed for illegal purposes," Charlie reminded, "a doctor is held responsible. You know that."

One glance at Howell's features showed he wasn't convinced.

"When Faux heard us, he sent a couple of men out looking with guns," Charlie added.

"Sure. And that's what anybody might do if they heard burglars on their porch roof."

Charlie saw they weren't getting anywhere with Howell. Then Jeff entered with a telegram in hand. Howell looked at the wire then shoved it over to Charlie. The message wasn't code, but the garbling was sufficient to make it meaningless to anyone else. It took him 15 minutes to put it all in coherent order.

The report on Dr. Phillips was short. His actions since leaving an eastern medical school were above suspicion. Dr. Faux's brief was longer. The outstanding facts were he had pioneered in plastic surgery in a city near Boston but had lost his business due to excessive drinking. He had moved west by successive steps: St. Louis, Denver, and finally San Francisco. Then he had shifted northward: Seattle, Winnipeg, and Juneau. The record ended there, but Charlie knew the rest. Wild Horse was the latest stop for Dr. Faux.

"Looks like you might be on the right track," Howell admitted reluctantly. "Nothing conclusive, but it provides some circumstantial facts. You still think I ought to search his place?"

"Yes."

"Aren't you afraid you'll scare the rest of them off that way?"

Charlie admitted a raid might be premature. But it seemed the most logical next step—in fact, the only one holding out any hope of success. He told Howell that.

Howell rubbed his chin slowly. "I got to think it over. You drop in at noon and I'll tell you if it's yes or no."

They hadn't had breakfast yet, and Lew suggested they attend to that now. They went to the restaurant Charlie had recommended to Sadie and found her wearing a white apron and a cap.

"I didn't have any trouble getting the job, and the pay is better than I hoped." She set their water glasses down with a flourish.

They ordered corn flakes, bacon, eggs and coffee. Sadie slid an extra pat of butter on their dishes, and Charlie left a 50-cent tip when they finished.

"If there's nothing else to do," Lew said, "I'll take a few shots with my bear gun. I have to know if the sights are right, and if that old ammunition is any good. It won't be if the grease from the bullets has melted and seeped down into the powder."

Charlie didn't want to go along for the shoot. Lew promised to walk far enough out from town so, when his gun began to boom, the citizens wouldn't think war had come to Wild Horse.

Charlie stayed in his room, studied a large-scale map of Alaska and Canada for some time. Then the room got hot and stuffy with the climbing sun, and he went outside. He walked to the service station for transport trucks. Three huge monsters were receiving gas and oil, the big trailers of extraordinary length.

A driver in a leather jacket and cap stood off several yards from the pump. Charlie walked up to him and casually said, "You can't have very heavy stuff inside that big trailer, or you couldn't pull the load."

The driver grinned. "It's light enough," he replied. "A box don't hardly weigh anything. It's a magnesium alloy of some sort. But it must be valuable, because I got orders to push right along with it. There was four of us started out. We left one fellow behind with ignition trouble. He may catch up with us tonight. He'll lose his bonus if he don't."

Charlie wondered what vital use was being made of this metal.

He wondered, too, why the driver was so free with information. He decided to make a report to headquarters. Somebody should warn these men to be much less talkative with strangers.

Charlie dropped in at the Wild Horse Tavern and ordered a bottle of soda. He failed to see a familiar face. He did note several men staring at him, and when he caught their eyes, they looked in another direction. That may have been perfectly normal. Still, there was an undercurrent of tension in the air. At least it struck Charlie that way.

He went back to the rooming house. Lew came in pretty soon. "She worked fine; only the rear sight was set so high it shot a foot over at 75 yards." He got out a cleaning rod and some oil and swabbed the big bore. Charlie was quiet and thoughtful.

They went back to the police station a few minutes before noon. Howell confronted them with a determined but serious face. "I'm going to do it. I'll get my search warrant right after lunch. I may get broke for this, but you can't say I didn't do all I could. We'll start for Faux's place about sundown. I can only spare two men, so you'll have to come along. It's a big place. We got to watch all sides of it. So meet me here at six tonight, and be sharp."

Chapter 8 – A Light in the Sky

When Charlie and Lew returned to the police station at 6 o'clock, they found Chief Howell in a bad mood, regretting his promise to obtain a warrant and search the house of Dr. Faux for evidence that would tie him in with Japanese saboteurs who had undergone plastic surgery to prevent their faces being recognized.

"I had the hardest time convincing Judge Roberts about that search warrant," he began. "If we don't find something worthwhile, I'm sunk." Charlie knew he was right. Howell would be the one to take the blame if they found nothing. As army intelligence, he and Lew would stay in the background. But if the raid failed, he also knew they couldn't expect any more cooperation from Howell.

They joined two uniformed officers in a light, five-passenger coach then drove through Wild Horse and onto a road that was hardly more than a saddle trail. The road circled out then back around the steep ridge that divided town from the flat where Dr. Faux lived.

Lew sat on the outside, looking ahead at a darkening sky streaked with occasional light spots. He said, "I didn't know there were enough lights in Wild Horse to make that much glow."

Howell grunted. The driver said, "Looks closer than town."

That aroused Howell from his thoughts. He lowered the window glass and thrust his head out.

"That isn't Wild Horse. Gun her, Thompson. She'll do 40 in second gear. I know—I've tried her." They shot to one side of the road, lurched back towards the other, and then leaped ahead as the slipping wheels fastened onto firmer bits of road. The glow in the sky grew brighter. Flames now shot up over the peak of the last ridge intervening. They could hear the crackle of flames devouring seasoned wood. Then they slid around the last curve. Before them stood Faux's house, its entire second story engulfed in flames. Thompson braked the car and they jumped out.

"We won't need that search warrant now," Howell said. "That's Faux's house, and the way she's burning, there won't be anything left but the chimney and foundation in another half-hour."

He seemed more relieved than disappointed. But Charlie had

counted on securing vital information. The second floor, which he particularly wanted to search, was gone. Part of the roof fell in before they were out of the auto.

"See anything strange about that fire?" Charlie said.

"All I see is it's a hot one," the chief replied.

"A house just doesn't burst out all over with flames. But every part of the top story is burning about the same. The only way that could have happened would be for fire to start in every room at the same time."

Howell turned and said, "You think somebody started it?"

"Of course, and that means somebody was tipped off to this search," Charlie replied. "The quickest way to destroy anything they didn't want us to see would be to burn the house."

Just then a man on horseback rode furiously up the muddy trail. He reined the animal with a powerful jerk on the bit. The horse reared a little on its hind legs, and then stood quivering. The man was slight of build with gray hair and ruddy cheeks. He wore an expensive whipcord riding suit with tall, soft leather boots that gleamed from polishing.

"What's happened here, Howell?" he demanded.

"I don't know, Faux. We just got here, and it's too late to do anything. We can't get a bucket brigade from Wild Horse in less than half an hour, and she'll be gone before then. Anybody inside?"

"No. My housekeeper had the day off."

"Any patients in the upstairs?"

"I told you the house was empty." Faux sounded belligerent. "I haven't had a resident patient for weeks."

"I understood you were operating on somebody last night," Howell said.

Charlie was conscious of the sharp look Faux turned on him. Still watching Charlie's face, Faux said, "Who told you that?"

"We hear things," Howell said, and then waited.

Faux made a disagreeable sound probably intended for a laugh. "If you want to call swabbing my housekeeper's throat for tonsillitis an operation. That is all the practicing I did last night."

"Where did she go?" Howell asked.

"To visit her daughter at Salmon Bay," Faux replied quickly. "Why all these questions? Am I suspected of setting my own house on fire?"

112

"Just routine. I got to establish nobody was trapped in there."

What remained of the roof plunged down with a crash that sent clouds of sparks flying high into the air. Faux's horse reared and tried to bolt, but he spurred it hard, raking the steel prongs across the animal's tender flanks. He sat watching the flames with a heavy frown.

"I had ten thousand dollars' worth of equipment upstairs. None of it can be replaced." Faux was talking more to himself than to the group around him.

He turned suddenly to Howell. "Why are you here? Nobody knew my house was burning when I left town."

"We were out at the end of the street and saw the light," Howell evaded. "You must have left town before we did, but I don't remember passing you on the road."

"You didn't. I use shortcuts over the hills to save time."

Charlie saw they wouldn't get anyplace questioning the doctor. Howell apparently had the same thought, for he said, "I'll leave a man here."

"What for?" Faux demanded. "He can't do any good now."

People from Wild Horse who had seen the flames were beginning to climb down the steep ridge, which was part of the shortcut in. Howell called his man aside and said, "Keep your eye on Faux. I want to know who talks most to him tonight. It'll be a job with this crowd milling about, but do the best you can."

Charlie and Lew followed Howell back to the car. Howell climbed in the driver's seat this time. He wheeled around and said, "The more I see of this business, the less I like it. We don't get anywhere fast."

"We will now," Charlie replied.

"Why? Faux's house is gone, and anything it contained that might be evidence against him."

"All we have to do now is watch the doctor. He will leave Wild Horse. He may go tomorrow; he may not go for a week. But soon he must join the rest of his gang. When he goes, we follow."

"It won't be easy," Howell objected. "I think he suspects you tipped me off about that operation upstairs last night. I could tell the way he watched you. You better start locking your door at night."

"They already tried to get us once," Lew reminded.

"The next time they'll try harder," Howell said shortly.

When they reached town, Lew said, "Drop us at the tavern."

They went inside and ordered a soda. Lew kept looking around the room. "Wonder where Rita is?" he finally said. "I want to make a date for another dancing lesson tomorrow."

"You'll be too busy," Charlie replied. "Faux may not leave immediately, but he'll be going soon, and we need to be on his tail."

Lew spoke to the bartender, "Where's Rita?"

"She wasn't feeling good and went home an hour ago."

Lew finished his drink, slid off his stool. "Then we might as well go, too," he told Charlie.

The cheap bulbs Mrs. Fretto kept burning in the upstairs hall of the boarding house were so dim it was easy to see cracks of light under the doors of the rooms that were occupied. The floor was dark, however, beneath Rita's. Lew knocked softly anyway, but got no response. He walked softly down the hall, saw a light under Sadie's door, considered knocking, and then decided he wouldn't. He went back to his room, where Charlie sat waiting.

Charlie had spoken confidently enough to Howell about shadowing Faux, but he knew it would be easy for anyone familiar with the area to drop out of sight. Moreover, Faux suspected them, and a warned man is twice as hard to follow. "We've got to figure out what place they are now using as headquarters," he told Lew.

Lew agreed, but he didn't have any suggestions. They sat in silence. Finally, Lew got up and turned off the light. "I can think better in the dark."

"Also with your eyes shut, I suppose," Charlie replied. "But don't try it. This is no time for sleeping."

Later, after a scream broke the silence in the old house, Charlie accused him of dozing off. Lew denied it, but he had to admit that, although he was nearer to the door, Charlie beat him out—but not before a second scream echoed down the dingy hall.

They ran down the faded strip of carpet and saw the door to Sadie's room partly open. Charlie slammed it all the way open with his arm. The light inside had been turned off, but enough flowed in from the hall to see two figures close to the bed. They whirled around. One rushed him. Charlie stepped nimbly aside and the fellow plunged past, swiping sideways in a half-circle swing. At the same moment, the fellow ran into Lew's fist, which he had thrown from a point close to the floor. The fellow collapsed in the doorway.

"Turn on the light," Charlie ordered as he started for the second man.

This one crouched beside the bed, waiting. He lunged forward, and Charlie saw something gleaming in his hand. Charlie stepped back, grabbed a chair, and sent it sliding forward. It hit the attacker's knees, which checked him for a second.

"The light," Charlie yelled again, and the room blazed up with brightness just as the man rushed past Charlie into the hall. They turned after him, and found to their surprise that the doorway was clear. The first fellow had disappeared, too.

Charlie and Lew momentarily wedged together as both tried to get out through the door at the same time. That gave the man ahead enough time to reach the top of the stairs. They saw him descend in one, wild leap. Charlie jumped too, but the other fellow was out the front door before Charlie landed.

At that moment, Mrs. Fretto burst into the hall, collided with Charlie and flung her arms around him.

"Let me go," he panted.

"What is it? Who screamed?" she demanded shrilly.

"We're going to find out if you get out of the way," Charlie said. He shoved by, flung the street door open and ran out. But the street was clear, and there wasn't any use to try a chase. There were too many dark alleys where a man could hide.

They went back upstairs and found Sadie's room empty. The girl had disappeared. They were sure it was she who had screamed.

Charlie went to the window and pushed the shade up. The lower sash was open. He leaned out, wondered if she had jumped or had been thrown. It was too dark to see the ground, so he started for the door.

Again, he had to wait for Mrs. Fretto to clear the way. "Go ahead, Lew," he said. "See if Sadie is lying on the ground outside."

Lew had his flashlight now, and when he got around the house, he snapped it on. But there was no sign of the girl.

Chapter 9 – High Gear into Danger

Bewildered by the sudden disappearance of the girl Sadie, who until that day had danced at the Wild Horse Tavern, Lew ran back into the rooming house. Charlie had succeeded in quieting the landlady Mrs. Fretto, at least to the extent she was willing to give them a chance to talk.

"There's no trace," Lew said.

"She must have gone out the window," Charlie replied. Then he turned to Mrs. Fretto. "A policeman will be here in a few minutes," he said. "We're going down to the station to report this."

"Sadie wouldn't run from us," Lew said as they crossed the porch. "So it looks like they tossed her out the window to someone waiting below."

They circled around the house for a closer look. A dog in the backyard barked savagely at them. They called Sadie's name, in case she was hiding in the shadows. But there was no reply.

It had started to rain again. As they slopped through the soft mud of Tenth Street, they saw a dark mass that almost blocked off its intersection with the main highway. It was one of the military transport trucks. For a moment, they wondered if the vehicle had any connection with the missing girl. Then they heard somebody groaning inside the cab. Lew stepped up and opened the door. A man was doubled up behind the wheel, arms clamped across his stomach. "What's the matter?" Lew asked.

"I'm sick," the man gasped. "I gotta see a doctor right away."

Charlie walked quickly around the front of the truck and opened the driver's door. "Slide over," he told the driver. Charlie remembered seeing Dr. Phillips' name lettered on the door of a building two blocks beyond the police station. Lew stepped onto the opposite running board, and Charlie slipped the truck into gear.

"It's my appendix," the driver told them between groans. Charlie reached over and lowered the opposite window a little. The cold air, he figured, would do the man good and also give Lew a more secure hold on the door. He hoped Dr. Phillips hadn't gone home for the night.

Charlie pulled in close to the building. Lew jumped off, ran to the door and pounded vigorously with his fist. When it opened, Lew said, "We got a man here with an attack of appendicitis."

Phillips didn't waste any time with questions but ran back with Lew. The three lifted the stricken man out of the truck and carried him inside the office. Phillips put him on a wheeled trailer and felt carefully over his abdomen.

Twice the driver cried out in pain.

"I have to operate at once," Phillips said. "Dr. Armstrong will assist." He already had the phone in his hands.

The driver beckoned to Charlie. "How long will I be laid up?"

"A couple of weeks," Charlie said.

"That truck's got to get on," the driver replied. A spasm of pain contorted his mouth. When it passed, he continued, "I was held up with engine trouble, and the others went on without me. I got to catch up with them tonight."

"You're in no shape to drive," Charlie told him.

"What's the load?" Lew asked.

"Magnesium," the man replied.

Lew looked at Charlie, saw the answering gleam in his eye. He said quickly, "We'll drive it ourselves."

"You can't ..." the driver began.

"Take it easy," Charlie said. "The chief of police will vouch for us."

Phillips handed the phone to Charlie, who dialed Howell. When the chief answered, Charlie spoke quickly into the receiver. "We're going to drive this load through ourselves. That may give us the chance we need to find out what happens to the trucks that disappear. I need you to come over and assure the driver it's OK. Also, you better send a man up to our boarding house. A girl disappeared from her room tonight. Mrs. Fretto will give the story."

The chief got there in less than 2 minutes. Dr. Armstrong arrived a minute later. By then, Phillips had washed his hands, put on gloves, set down a can of ether, and laid out his instruments. Armstrong washed quickly and picked up the ether mask.

Howell flashed his badge before the truck driver. "These men are military intelligence," he said. "Your only problem now is to get well in a hurry."

"All right, if you say so," he replied.

Armstrong set the cone over his face and lifted the ether bottle. Lew, Charlie and the police chief went outside quickly.

"Well, maybe this is the break you have been waiting for," Howell said. "I only hope you have better luck than the other drivers who didn't make it. So long. And good luck."

They climbed in the truck, and Lew said, "Turn her around, I got to go back to the room."

Charlie obeyed, but unwillingly. "Now we'll waste 15 minutes before we can get going," he grumbled.

Lew didn't answer. Fortunately, the street was wide enough to turn without backing. Charlie stopped at the beginning of Tenth Street and started to make the second turn as Lew jumped out. The truck was pointed north again by the time Lew returned.

Charlie's exclamation was half anger, half disgust, when he saw that Lew was carrying the bear rifle. "If I'd known that was what you wanted, I wouldn't have waited," he said. "This isn't a hunting trip. You've got about as much use for that as you have for a slingshot."

"Maybe," Lew answered. He got in and laid the gun in behind the seat. Charlie had the tractor in third gear by the time they reached the edge of town. And as they lumbered along the muddy highway, he experimented with the head lamp buttons, found out how to change from high to low.

Wild Horse was built on a narrow, flat strip of ground, the only place for miles sufficiently level to contain a town of any size. The surrounding country, while not exactly mountainous, was pretty rough, cut into numerous small ravines and steep ridges of rock.

North of Wild Horse, the light beams of the truck showed only rough walls of rock at each side of the highway. The road took a sharp upward turn, and Charlie shifted into a lower gear for more climbing power. They climbed for about a mile, and then the highway plunged down. The truck had air brakes, and Charlie checked to make sure they were working, but he didn't want to ride them any more than he must.

They reached the bottom of the grade. The road ran level for 100 yards and then started to climb again. Charlie was pushing the throttle down to the floor when the headlamps revealed a figure standing beside the road. When they got closer, it lifted an arm and started to jerk an extended thumb.

"What a dope," Lew said. "Doesn't he know the place to thumb rides is at the bottom of a grade, not halfway up? Nobody is going to stop a heavy load here to pick him up."

"We better take him in," Charlie said in a low voice. "This may be the first part of the trap. We can't risk missing any of it, you know." He shifted into the bottom gear.

Lew lowered the glass window and stuck his head out. "Jump aboard," he yelled. "We can't stop on this grade with our load. Make it snappy."

The figure sprang towards him. A hand came up, caught the windowsill, and then fell back as a foot slipped in the soft mud. Lew grasped the hand, caught it and heaved. A head came up level with his, and he heard both feet land on the running board. Two eyes stared into his.

"It's Sadie!" he cried.

"You trying to get me killed?" she demanded. There was enough light in the cab to show her face to be pale but eyes blazing.

Lew could hardly keep from laughing, she looked such a comical mixture of belligerence and helplessness.

"I didn't know it was you," he finally said. "I thought it was just a guy who didn't know better than to flag down a truck on an upgrade. Here, get in." He pushed her light body back so the door could be opened enough for her to slip past.

"Get that soaked coat off or we'll all be wet," he continued. He rolled the garment up and dropped it behind the seat, but off to one side so it didn't touch his bear gun.

Sadie took off her hat and shook it outside the window. "I didn't know you were truck drivers," she said.

Lew lifted her over so she sat between them and then replied, "We aren't."

"Then what are you doing?"

"That's quite a story," Charlie said. "But you won't hear it now. You've got some questions to answer first. And I want answers that are true."

"I never told a lie in my life," she retorted. "Well, I mean about anything so important as what happened tonight."

"That's what we want to know. How'd you get out here on the highway? What happened after you screamed for help?"

The truck seat was not wide. It was a tight fit for three, and

Lew and Charlie both felt the girl tremble.

"I never was so scared in my life," she began slowly. "I was tired when I got home from the restaurant. I threw my coat and hat on the bed and sat down for a minute. Then I picked them up and went to the closet to hang them up. I opened the door and there were two men staring at me. I almost fainted, but I screamed."

"I'll say you did," Lew agreed. "And it's a good thing, too. What happened next?"

"They came out. They didn't run at me, they just moved slowly but in a way that was awful. I screamed again, I guess. And then I heard you running along the hall. One man grabbed at me. I ducked down and he missed. Then you came in. I crawled under the bed. You chased them outside, but I didn't know how it was going to end. So I got up, ran to the window and jumped out. I was so scared. I just started running."

"You should have stuck around," Lew said.

"Why leave town in such a hurry?" Charlie wanted to know. "Where did you expect to go?"

"I don't know. All I could think about was getting away. Anyplace seemed better than Wild Horse."

"Why didn't you go to the police?" Charlie demanded.

"Police?" she cried. "How much did they protect the waiters who got killed?"

They began to realize that Sadie hadn't behaved so strangely, after all. After the shock of being attacked in her own room, nothing but getting out of town as soon as possible made sense to her.

"I think they came there to kill me," she continued. "It showed in their eyes, and the way they closed in so slowly, even after I screamed. That was pretty bad. But something else made me want to get out of Wild Horse just as fast as I could. I didn't realize it at the time it happened. But she almost stabbed me!"

"She? Who?"

"Rita."

Silence filled the cab. Noise from the powerful motor seeped in, but it wasn't enough to drown out the raindrops beating against the windshield.

Chapter 10 – Bullet Through the Windshield

Charlie spoke first. "I want to know how Rita tried to stab you," he said. "Don't omit any detail, however trivial it may seem."

"We have slack time between lunch and dinner at the restaurant," Sadie began, "and we can go home if we like, to freshen up. I came home and went to Rita's room to borrow some lipstick. I opened the door without knocking, and saw she was doing something I thought funny. She was dabbing liquid out of a small bottle onto her face to cover up what looked like a spot of tan."

"Go on."

"When she saw that I saw what she was doing, she just stood holding the bottle in one hand and the little swab of cotton in the other, watching me with a half smile. But there was a frown between her eyes, too, like she was trying to decide something.

"And then I guess I said a dumb thing. I said, 'Were you trying to cover that scar along the side in front of your ear?' I don't know why I said it. I had seen the scar before, but I hadn't mentioned it before. The smile left then. Her eyes flashed, and she picked up that big hair ornament she always wears when she dances in the tavern. Only it looked like a long sharp dagger then, and not very much like an ornament."

"What next?" Charlie urged.

"She changed again, so fast it made me dizzy. She put the pin down. Her eyes softened, and she smiled. 'I didn't mean to scare you, Sadie,' she said. 'I'm sorry. That scar brings back bad memories. A man I loved once tried to kill me. Forgive me, won't you?'"

Sadie shivered again. "I told her sure. But I'll always remember how her eyes were all flecked with little points of red light. I didn't mention the lipstick. I just got out of there as fast as I could. I knocked at your door to tell you about it, but you didn't answer. So I went back to the restaurant.

"Don't tell me I ought to have gone to the police. You know just what they would have told me. That I was imagining things. Isn't that right?"

"I'm afraid so," Charlie replied.

"You came very close to death," Lew said softly. "Fortunately, Rita regained her self-control. It was wiser for her to send the men to kill you later."

Charlie thought it was time to talk about something else. "You told us you wanted to leave Wild Horse and go home. Why did you start off north, then? You should have gone the other way."

"This end of town was nearer, and I wanted to get out as fast as I could. And I was hoping I might meet a load of soldiers who would take me with them. They come back along this road all the time. Most are nice boys, and I felt like I needed protecting."

"We're glad to protect you," Lew said. "But if you stay with us, you'll head into danger, not away from it."

"Why?"

"You remember the first waiter who was killed?" Charlie said. "He belonged to a gang that hijacks the military trucks that travel this highway. We took this truck so we could get hijacked ourselves. Somewhere between here and the next service station 50 miles on, it will probably happen."

The steep grade began to ease, and the truck picked up speed. The transmission still bothered Charlie a little, but he was learning how to shift it. He waited for Sadie to say something, and when she didn't, he said, "You ought to go back. But we can't take you."

"How am I going to get back, then?" she asked.

"You could start back on foot."

"I won't walk," she said firmly.

"Then we'll watch out for a car or truck coming this way and flag it down."

Sadie giggled. That surprised Lew so much he growled, "I don't see anything funny about any of this."

"It isn't funny. I'm just happy."

"Slap happy," Lew corrected. "Did you bump your head when you jumped out of your room window?"

"I landed on my feet, and I'm just not scared anymore. I'm going to stay right in this truck with you. I know you can whip a dozen hijackers."

"Can you shoot a gun?" Lew asked.

"Of course. It's easy. All you do is point, shut your eyes and pull the trigger."

Lew looked past Sadie towards Charlie. "A fellow can't shoot from inside this cab. I'm going up on the trailer roof where I can lay down with my bear rifle and do some real sniping."

"The first bump will roll you off."

"I'll figure out a way to stick," Lew declared. He turned around and began to rummage behind the seat. His fingers encountered a coil of rope. "I've got it. Stop her," he told Charlie.

Lew got out, uncoiled the rope and threw one end up over the trailer. Charlie caught it on the other side and passed it back to him on the underside. Lew worked the loop forward until it was about 6 feet from the front and, pulling the ends tight, tied them.

"I can slip one leg under the rope," he said. "That'll leave my hands free to handle the rifle."

It was easy to see how a rifleman lying up there could cover the highway ahead and to either side. "I guess you got something," Charlie agreed. "Maybe that big gun of yours will be of some use, after all."

Lew took out his pistol and handed it to Sadie. "Use that when the fighting begins. Only don't shut your eyes until you know which way it's pointing."

He reached in the cab, took out his long rifle and gave it to Charlie. Then he climbed to the flat top of the trailer. Charlie handed the rifle up. Lew lay down beside the rope and, after some squirming, discovered that twisting both legs around it afforded the most security. He told Charlie to start driving.

Sadie settled back into the outside corner of the cab. There was plenty of room now, but she missed the reassurance of Lew's shoulder pressing against her own. She shivered a little. The door window was down, and she began to crank it up. Then, remembering the danger ahead and her promise to help fight, she ran the glass down again.

Lew's gun lay on the cushion. She held it forward so more light from the instrument board shone on the breech. "What must I do?" she asked.

Charlie pointed to the safety catch. "Just move that, like this," demonstrating, "and pull the trigger."

Fog drifted across low places in the road, a thick vapor as wet as the rain that had almost ceased. Large drops collected on the windshield, and Charlie knew Lew's clothing would be soaked through, and the wind that hit the exposed trailer roof would chill his muscles and make it hard for him to sight his gun and fire. He decided to stop soon and get Lew down in the cab to thaw out. There was a heater that filled the little space with a blast of hot air when he turned its switch.

Then twin headlamps jumped up from behind a sharp grade and bore into their eyes. Charlie swung nearer the side of the road and stopped. Here, he thought, might be a chance to send Sadie back to Wild Horse. Howell would take care of her until she could start home. He opened the cab door but was only halfway out when the vehicle blasted by. It was a light truck, painted the olive drab of army service and going about twice as fast as he had figured.

Lew called, "If I had a light up here, I could flag them down."

"The next one won't get through," Charlie answered. "I'll pull across the road and block it."

"You seem awfully anxious to get rid of me," Sadie protested.

Charlie laughed. Later, he said, "I've been wondering why your mother let you come to Wild Horse alone."

"My mother died when I was five," she replied. "The two things I remember most about her funeral were the crowds of people and my new dress. Aunt Etta bought the dress. It was pink with blue flowers, and I thought it was the prettiest thing I had ever seen. She made me wash my feet twice before I could put the dress on. After, when I was older and understood, I would lie awake at night and cry because I had thought more of that dress than of my mother's dying."

"I think your aunt was swell to bring something that pretty," Charlie said softly. "How about your father? Does he know you came to Wild Horse to dance in a tavern?"

"He doesn't know where I am. I don't think he cares, either. He went away three years after Mother died. At first, he stayed on the farm and a neighbor girl helped with the work. But her family moved away and she went with them. He couldn't get anybody else. I tried to help, but I was only six years old. Can you imagine a girl like that keeping house?

"Then one morning, when I woke up, he wasn't there. I was almost as scared as I was tonight. The nearest neighbor lived almost four miles away. I walked to their house and told them. Later, I found out that he had run off with a woman from town. I haven't seen him since."

"Poor kid," Charlie said, reaching over to squeeze her hand.

They had been climbing for several minutes. The fog thinned, finally disappeared. Wind whistled past the open cab window. Charlie stopped when he found a level place in the grade, and Lew got down and came inside. His teeth were chattering. They sat there 15 minutes while the heater blasted Lew with warmth. He soaked it in like a sun-baked sponge soaks up water.

"Better make these stops more often," he finally said. "I didn't realize how cold I was until I felt this heat."

They started again after Lew had regained his position on the roof. Charlie kept his speed down to 25 miles an hour. More would increase the force of the wind that hit Lew.

Their headlamps picked up two figures ahead, men plying shovels at the right side of the roadbed. Charlie slowed and, when almost abreast of the pair, stopped. He wanted to ask how far they were from the station ahead. The gas tank showed less than half.

The men straightened, shovels in hand. They were filling in a wide wash, which the rain had gouged from the soft shoulder. It surprised Charlie to find a maintenance crew working at night.

"How far have I come from Wild Horse?" he asked.

"Twelve miles," one of the men replied.

The other stepped off along the edge of the road, picked up a stick and began to scrape the soft mud from his shovel blade. Charlie could just see him in the side glow of the headlights.

"I thought I had driven twenty," he said.

The man laughed. "Ten miles seems like fifty over this road."

Charlie had lost sight of the man cleaning his shovel. He reached towards the gearshift and, suddenly, heard footsteps coming up quickly along his side of the trailer body. Then, before he could depress the clutch, the man he had been talking to dropped his shovel, whipped out a gun from under his coat, and fired a round into the windshield.

Chapter 11 - The Phantom Highway

When the man fired into the truck windshield, Charlie dropped instinctively, although he knew he couldn't duck a bullet. It passed through the windshield of the truck, between his head and Sadie's. The glass wasn't bulletproof, of course, but it didn't shatter, either.

Charlie jerked out his own gun and whirled in the seat, waiting for the man he knew was running along the side of the trailer towards him. Then a noise like the boom of a field gun split the night. Lew had gone into action.

Charlie shot a glance to the right, saw the man who had shot through the windshield fling up his arms and fall backwards. He stuck his pistol around the edge of the cab door and fired twice. He didn't have time to aim, but he knew the man would be coming in close with his head on a level with the seat. A sharp cry followed the second shot.

Charlie flung the door open, but before he could jump out, a salvo of shots filled his ears with a ringing din. Sadie was holding Lew's pistol up level with her eyes, pumping bullets blindly out the window. He reached over, took the gun from her fingers.

"All right," he said. "It's finished."

Charlie jumped out. The second man was sprawled on the ground with his arm and gun under his body. Lew was peering down over the edge of the trailer roof, covering him with his rifle.

Charlie leaned over the man on the ground, turned his flashlight on the face. "More facial surgery," he said. "This fellow seems dead enough. But you better watch the other one, Lew."

Charlie straightened up and took a couple of steps back before Lew said quickly, "Take his gun. I don't care ..." The warning was drowned out by a shot. The man on the ground had suddenly flung up the arm holding the pistol and fired point blank at Charlie.

Particles showered over Charlie, stinging his face. Lew's rifle boomed once more, and this time, when the saboteur settled down with his face in the mud, it was for keeps.

Charlie reached down and picked up the pistol, which had slipped from the dead fingers. The barrel had shattered close to the breach. It looked like the man had jammed the muzzle full of mud when he fell. Charlie's face still stung from the flying pieces of grit and steel, and when he rubbed his jaw, his hand came away bloody. "We better get started," he said and climbed in the cab.

"I knew you could beat them," Sadie cried. "I wasn't afraid."

"I was," Lew said.

"I wonder which man I hit?" she asked seriously.

"Probably both of them," Charlie replied. He slipped back the clutch and the heavy vehicle lurched ahead. Then it stopped. "I can't steer," Charlie said. "Take a look at the front tires."

Lew got out, flashlight in hand. "We had a casualty, all right," he said. "The right one is flat as a flapjack."

"The shot that missed me must have got it," Charlie said, getting tools out from behind the truck seat.

"Sadie," Lew said, "where did you point when you shut your eyes and began pulling that trigger?"

"I pointed it outside," she said. "At the man who shot in through the windshield."

Lew played his light over the truck fender and then left the beam focused on a neat little hole directly over the flat tire.

After they changed the tire, Charlie said thoughtfully, "I never thought we would get through this easy." He looked at the odometer. "If that saboteur didn't lie to me, we've got about 40 miles yet to go. I think you better climb back on the trailer roof."

"I think so, too," Lew replied, and he stepped on the fender and started up.

The truck plowed on through the night. The miles passed without incident. There was no other traffic.

Then they climbed a long, curving grade and saw a row of flares burning ahead. Charlie stopped the truck and called to Lew, who replied, "I'm all set, let's go in."

Charlie eased the truck ahead. He could see figures moving around the smoking iron pots. Charlie laid his pistol down on the seat. He looked at Sadie. She was clutching Lew's gun, this time with eyes wide open.

"Climb behind the seat," he told her, "and this time, let Lew and me do the shooting."

She shook her head "no" and then said, "I won't shoot a tire next time."

They were about 50 yards from the flares when Lew jumped down to the top of the cab. Charlie set the brakes again. Lew slid down on the fender and said, "It's all right. They're American soldiers. I can see their uniforms."

Charlie hesitated. "You ought to stay up there," he objected.

But Lew had already started walking up the grade, swinging the long rifle in one hand. Charlie waited, a little angry with his companion for what appeared to be disregard for caution.

Lew walked right up to the line of flares. They didn't quite fence off the road, just one half. The figures gathered around Lew. Charlie counted six. He saw Lew beckon for him to come on. The truck inched slowly up the grade.

The men were gathered about Lew, pointing to his long rifle and apparently ribbing him about it. Charlie stopped when his front tires were even with the flares. A man with sergeant's stripes on a sleeve came around to the driver's side of the cab. Charlie leaned out, intending to ask about the condition of the road, when the man thrust a machine gun in his face and said, "Get out."

At the same moment, he heard the sound of a blow and shot a fast glance to the right. Someone had struck down Lew from behind. Another jumped on the running board and twisted the pistol from Sadie's fingers. They were trapped, and there wasn't a thing he could do about it. His own gun lay on the seat, but he didn't dare snatch at it.

A figure stepped out of the shadows at the edge of the road. Charlie wasn't surprised when he recognized Rita. He wasn't surprised, either, when he saw she wore a soldier's raincoat and hat. Her gang had captured enough prisoners with the trucks they'd hijacked to supply themselves with uniforms.

Rita spoke sharply. "Get this truck off the road. Number three outpost reports two squad cars coming south." Her eyes swept over Charlie. Nothing in her gaze indicated she knew him.

The phony sergeant barked orders in Japanese. Another man came up and held a gun on Charlie. And then he saw some of the most astounding action he had ever witnessed.

More men came out of the shadows, wearing overalls and jackets, and the entire force shot into action. Attacking the left side of the highway, they rolled aside rocks, plucked trees with 3-inch trunks from the ground and laid them down. A narrow strip of smooth ground leading off from the highway was exposed. A man jumped into the truck cab and pushed Sadie out. He backed the truck up 50 feet, wheeled sharply around, and started up the newly exposed trail. Charlie watched the vehicle lurch and bump along until a turn in the trail hid it from view.

Rita shot a flashlight into Lew's eyes. He was still on his back. He groaned, twisted and sat up. Charlie was wondering if he couldn't rush her and snatch the gun she held in the other hand. Then he heard footsteps behind and gave up that idea.

The Japanese were working fast, putting rocks and trees back in place. They swept the ground to erase the imprints of the truck's big tires. In a few minutes, nobody could tell that a side road existed, or that a loaded truck had been driven off across it.

Lew was on his feet now. Rita motioned for them to follow the workmen. There was a glow to the north, and presently, Charlie could hear those two squad cars grinding up the opposite grade in low gear. Men crowded around him, pushing him and his companions back deeper into the forest. Four detached themselves and ran back to the roadside carrying machine guns.

Two Japanese grabbed Charlie, one covering his mouth with a dirty hand, the other shoved a short gun into his ribs. Charlie gave up any idea he might have entertained about shouting to stop the oncoming cars.

The cars roared past. The machine gunners came back from the roadside. Then they heard their own truck start and, pressed in closely on all sides by Japanese, they followed. The ground was less rocky and contained fewer trees. Men followed, putting these things back into place. "If they've got a place to hide the truck," Charlie thought, "this trail may never be discovered."

He judged they had walked at least half a mile when he saw the truck parked just ahead. The Japanese scurried up to it and went to work. He caught the scent of sea water in the air. The coast apparently was only a few yards off, closer to the highway than the maps had indicated. Lew edged over beside him.

"Sorry," Lew said. "I guess I shot the works."

"Don't waste time being sorry," Charlie replied. He didn't say any more, but he knew Lew would understand.

One of the guards whirled around, hissed something that sounded like "Shut up!" and then struck each of them in the face.

Charlie's hands were free, and he could have grabbed the man and broken his neck in a moment, but he didn't see much hope to escape, not yet. As long as they remained unhurt and untied, there was some sort of a chance.

The Japanese uncovered an opening in the sloping bank. The truck disappeared inside. Charlie saw that the bank had been skillfully covered with rocks and shrubs planted over a supporting frame of thick logs. It was perfectly black inside. After they had stumbled along for 50 yards, Rita turned on a pocket lamp, and Charlie saw they were walking in a narrow tunnel that had been hewed from solid rock. Rotting prop posts lined the sides, and when he stumbled over a section of narrow gauge steel track, Charlie knew they were inside an abandoned mine.

There would be another opening, he figured, at the edge of the sea. That was where the stolen load of magnesium would be loaded onto boats. The banks of mist and fog that always overhung that section of coast would make the sea operation easy to conceal.

The truck stopped, and the driver turned on the lights for a few seconds. Charlie could see other trucks parked before it, at least four or five in single file, because the tunnel was so narrow. Several of the Japanese got out gasoline lanterns and lit them. The driver turned off the truck lights. Then the entire crew, Charlie figured there were at least 20 of them, edged closer to their three prisoners. Charlie felt like he was ringed about by animals eager for a kill.

Charlie could feel Sadie's thin body tremble. Still wearing the service raincoat and hat, Rita pushed through the circle of silent men. She carried a very businesslike pistol in her hand.

Chapter 12 – The Battle in the Mine

Getting captured by Rita and her gang of Japanese spies put Lew, Charlie and Sadie in a tough spot. Of course, Lew and Charlie had been in bad spots before, but it was different with Sadie. Charlie squeezed her arm encouragingly.

Glancing around, he saw that the men who stood behind them were getting out of the path of Rita's gun. That didn't look good. Rita stood five feet away, gun leveled on his chest, a half-smile playing across her elegant features. Charlie realized Rita was enjoying this, trying to break down his courage.

Charlie knew he wouldn't crack; neither would Lew. He wasn't so sure of Sadie. Finally, Rita demanded, "Why did you come here?"

That was what Charlie wanted, to start her talking instead of shooting. He shrugged then said, "I thought you knew we were Military Intelligence."

Rita moved a hand impatiently. "I knew that one hour after you arrived in Wild Horse. But what did you expect to find? Did you come to stop the hijackings, or ..." she stopped abruptly.

Charlie finished the sentence for her. "Or did we come to block something bigger? That's what you want to know, isn't it?"

She didn't reply at first then spit out, "Yes, that is what I need to know."

Charlie thought, "I must keep her talking as long as I can." Then he said aloud, "We knew all along there was something bigger behind this than just hijacking a few truckloads of magnesium. Or were you planning to use the magnesium here, to supplement the real job?"

Charlie noticed that Sadie had stopped trembling. He said, "I'd like to know what your real plan is. It doesn't make any difference what we know, now that you have us."

He hoped her vanity would overcome her training and she would keep talking. He shifted his feet carefully, a few inches back. Sadie and Lew did the same; in fact, he forced them to edge backwards by the pressure of his body.

Rita's vanity apparently won out. "My job is to destroy the Alaska Highway," she declared with pride.

Charlie didn't show his surprise. Instead, he shook his head and said, "I don't think you can swing it. Besides, the highway isn't that important."

Rita's eyes flashed. "It is just like your kind to doubt real resolve, and to not realize the importance of your own highway. We know you plan to invade our country, and the Aleutian Islands are natural stepping stones on the route to Japan, a route we mean to block. We can gain precious time by putting the only highway to the North out of use for several months."

Charlie had moved back another foot, and nobody seemed to notice. "It still looks like too big a job," he said.

"It would, to you," she replied, contempt in her voice. "We will close the highway in less than two hours. Our submarines have brought hundreds of time bombs, and supplemented with tons of your own fiery magnesium, we will bring down every bridge. A bomb will explode atop a dozen banks where rock slides will block key sections of road.

"It will take at least six months to reopen. And that is all the time we need to set up defenses against your invasion route through the Aleutians."

Charlie's back was close to the wall now. He glanced around, saw something lying on the floor. It was a man's body, and it looked familiar. "What happened to Dr. Faux?" Charlie asked.

"He had an accident," Rita said.

"Did he operate on your face?"

"No. That was done in Japan. But when I came to Wild Horse, I needed more men, and Faux was willing to do the work and not ask questions."

"I'm glad he got what was coming to him," Lew growled.

Rita glanced at him, shrugged again. "You are so dumb," she said. "Faux wasn't a traitor. He thought the men he operated on were actually American—that they just wanted their faces changed so they could obtain work and help your war effort. He didn't know we were saboteurs—until tonight."

"I still don't believe you can blow up hundreds of miles of highway in a few hours," Charlie said.

Rita sighed. She was growing tired of his questioning, and

Charlie knew he had to keep her talking. He still hadn't been able to figure out anything to help them escape.

"We have 30 cars stored along the highway, each an exact copy of your army jeep. Our men, wearing American uniforms, will leave on a schedule that will put a bomb at each selected site within two hours."

Charlie didn't believe the timetable, but the rest of the scheme sounded plausible. Devilishly clever, too.

Sadie was squirming against his side. He wondered what she was trying to do. Then he felt something hard and cold poke against his hand. His fingers closed over his own pistol.

Sadie must have picked it up when they were attacked in the truck, and then hidden it under her clothes. It had been lying on the seat between them, he remembered.

He held the gun out of sight, thankful now that there were no Japanese standing behind them.

Charlie studied Rita's gun. It was no more than a .32, maybe a .25, and he believed he could absorb one or two rounds to the body without being disabled. But the man holding the machine gun behind her was different.

He knew Rita was done talking. So he pushed Sadie away, raised the pistol and, shooting from the hip, pumped two shots into the Japanese gunner's face. Then he leaped forward. Rita shot twice before he reached her. He felt one bullet hit his lower chest. He grabbed Rita and felt a bone snap in her wrist as he pried the pistol away. She went limp.

Then Lew hurtled past, barreling full tilt into the line of Japanese saboteurs standing behind Rita. One man leveled a carbine, but before he could fire, Charlie shot him in the head.

Then Charlie swept both of Rita's hands inside his left and, with the same arm, jammed her body up in front of him for a shield. Her eyes glowed with inhuman hatred.

She started to kick at his shins with her hard-soled shoes. He turned slightly and, with a powerful jerk, slammed her stomach against his hipbone. That took the fight out of Rita. She was the leader of this gang, and he figured they wouldn't start shooting as long as her body shielded his.

"Lie on the floor," he commanded Sadie.

Lew had broken through, but most of the Japanese had recovered their balance and were running after him now. Lew headed for the truck. Bullets cracked into the rock wall alongside Lew as he ran. It takes a good marksman to hit a running man, and Lew dived through the open truck door, turned to kick the foremost pursuer in the face, and grabbed his bear rifle.

He didn't have time to turn the gun, so he slammed the steel butt plate into the face of the next pursuer. The impact knocked this man against the next, and both went down.

Charlie seemed to be doing all right, so with sudden decision, Lew put the rifle down and started the truck. He threw the shift in reverse, kicked the throttle flat to the floorboards, and sent the big outfit lurching backward.

The Japanese thought Lew was trying to back out of the tunnel to escape, which was what he wanted them to think.

He grinned when he saw them pouring down the narrow passage in hot pursuit. Some began to shoot, but again their marksmanship was not that good.

Lew hunched down close to the wheel. When the gang was in a tight spot in the tunnel, bunched up pretty well, Lew slammed on the brakes, shifted into second gear and tramped down on the gas. The truck bucked, swayed, and made so much noise he wondered if he had stripped the transmission.

Then the spinning rear wheels bit deeply and the truck leaped forward, back down the tunnel and directly into the Japanese. They didn't have room or time to leap aside, and the front of the tractor hit them hard.

Lew jumped out with his rifle in hand. He shot deliberately, picking off the few panicked Japanese still on their feet. In a matter of moments, it was over.

Sadie got up from the ground. Tears streamed down her cheeks, and she shook like an aspen. "Better get out of here, kid," Lew said, pointing towards the mouth of the tunnel. "Go outside and wait for us there."

He bent over Rita. She was still unconscious. Lew pulled her coat open, found the big jade hair ornament pinned inside. He took it out and showed it to Charlie. "Look, the dull outside is a plastic sheath. Take it off, and there's the thin blade she used to kill that waiter and to try to kill me."

Charlie was beginning to feel faint. "I've got to get to a doctor," he said.

Lew took his arm, and they walked together toward the tunnel exit. Sadie pushed enough of the camouflage aside from the mouth of the tunnel for them to squeeze through.

Lew still held the bear rifle. "I'll stay here and handle anyone who feels like he wants more trouble," he said. "Charlie, you lie down. Sadie, I need you to run back to the highway and stop the first car or truck you see."

Lew looked at his companion. "Doing any better?" he asked. Charlie nodded. But he looked awfully pale.

The sky was growing light, and Lew realized they had been inside the mine much longer than he had supposed. The minutes trickled by.

Then he heard a vehicle climbing up the opposite grade. The brakes squealed and he heard angry shouting. It wasn't long before a group of six men approached. Sadie was doing the best she could to keep abreast of a burly fellow with sergeant stripes on his sleeve. He carried a Garrand, as did the rest of the group.

"The girl says you need help," the sergeant said.

"Isn't it wonderful?" Sadie cried. "I only had to wait a few minutes for them to come along. And when I stepped out in front of them, they had no choice but to stop!"

Lew quickly explained who they were and how things stood. "We've got to get Charlie to a doctor," he urged.

"Take the jeep. My man will drive," the sergeant replied.

Lew and Sadie got in the back seat with Charlie, and the driver wasted no time. Lew was worried about Charlie, of course. But when Charlie gave him a reassuring smile, he started to feel better.

"What are you going to do now?" Sadie asked.

"I'm going to get Charlie to Wild Horse, where Doc Phillips can patch him up."

"I meant after that," she said.

"Oh, I suppose we'll get another job to do. Why?"

"I thought maybe I could tag along. I helped some, didn't I? If I had not picked up that pistol from the truck seat, what would have happened to us?"

"I would rather not think about that," Lew said quietly.

The end

Pacific Outpost

Chapter 1 – Nosedive into Danger

When the light reconnaissance plane dropped down on the big Alaskan army base at eighteen minutes past eight o'clock a.m., there was only one passenger waiting on the sodden ramp. Charlie and Lew didn't get out because the pilot had told them he would make only a brief stop to refuel and unload the three dispatch bags he was carrying for Divisional Headquarters. That suited them fine. They were in a hurry to get back to the States and a bit impatient because the plane on which they had been ordered to return was routed so far west before it would turn south.

The figure that climbed into the cockpit was short and somewhat chunky. The long raincoat and rubber hat were beaded with little drops of water from a soft, persistent rain that had enveloped them ever since they left Wild Horse.

But when the passenger paused just inside the door and took off the hat and coat, they saw with surprise that it was not a man but a woman. A girl, actually, for she didn't appear more than twenty years old. She was wearing a WAC's uniform with the insignia of second lieutenant. Lew thought she didn't look so chunky now, after shedding the bulky coat. In fact, she had a very nice form, and her uniform fit perfectly.

From the way she carried her shoulders you got the idea she knew she had and that it did.

There were two seats in the short cockpit of the plane and they each occupied one. But now they stood up and Lew moved back to share Charlie's and give her more room.

She turned a short glance on him and said "thank you" in a cool voice. She brushed by, sat down and smoothed her uniform out over her knees. It was cut from what looked like very expensive cloth. Then she opened the regulation bag that hung from a shoulder, took out a small pocket book and started to read.

Lew looked around at Charlie, grinned and made a brief gesture of brushing one sleeve off with his hand.

Then he stretched his long legs out as far as they would go, which wasn't far because the seat ahead was only a matter of inches away. His knees bumped into the back of the seat, and the girl jerked forward, looked around with a frown, and then leaned firmly back. Lew retrieved his legs to where they belonged.

Their pilot was back in his seat now, and they started down the rain-drenched runway. It was an emergency strip built of webbed mesh steel laid directly on leveled ground. Little pockets of water had collected in low places, and the fat tires of the plane flipped up splashes that drummed against the bottom of the cabin.

It was rotten flying weather with low, ragged clouds, grayish mist and the ceaseless downpour.

After they had been in the air a few minutes, Lew looked curiously over the WAC's shoulder and saw she was reading a group of selections from Steinbeck. He had just finished the same book a few weeks before, and feeling a sudden esprit de corps, he said, almost without thinking, "That's a good book."

The girl didn't reply. Lew, reading the top of the right page over her shoulder, continued, "It's pretty virile stuff. He doesn't pull any punches."

She leaned forward and said without turning, "Please don't breathe down the back of my neck."

Lew flushed and leaned back so abruptly his knees came up and bored into the back of her seat again.

"Sorry," he said. "I didn't mean to be offensive. I guess I thought since we were flying together we might be friendly."

"I don't care to fraternize with 4-Fs," she retorted.

For a moment Lew wondered if he had got it straight. Then, deciding he had, he straightened up angrily.

"What do you mean by 4-F?" he asked.

She took her time about replying and then, "Just that. You are full-grown and look like you have normal intelligence. But you're not in uniform. What other conclusion can I draw?"

"Listen, you ..." Lew was sputtering when he felt Charlie's elbow dig into his ribs. He glanced and saw his companion was shaking with silent laughter. Lew leaned back with a strong effort and let the angry lines ease from his face.

Then he began to laugh a little himself, and not being as successful as Charlie in keeping it submerged, presently exploded with a noisy outburst.

That wasn't the kind of reaction she had expected. The back of her neck below the carefully arranged curls of blond became pink and she said in an icy tone, "I don't think it very funny."

Lew didn't bother to answer. He was thinking and the more he thought the funnier it seemed to him.

"The little snip believes we're 4-F because we aren't in uniform," he told himself. "I wonder how long she's had hers? It looks pretty new to me. I bet Papa is a politician and wangled a commission for her, because she acts like a spoiled brat and she probably was a problem at home. Why did she have to pick this plane to travel on?"

The weather worsened abruptly, and a flurry of rain hit so hard it made the plane shiver and the left wing dip a bit. Buckets of water sluiced over the little windows. The pilot set the nose up, climbing sharply in an attempt to get out of the storm and into a more calm level. They knew he had been flying blind from the very start, setting his course from bearings received regularly over his radio.

That was no surprise. They knew this kind of flying was more or less the rule here. They had watched him check instruments and gauges at half-minute intervals but hadn't suspected that all wasn't going so well until the pilot pulled off his headphones, turned and beckoned to Charlie.

Charlie went forward. The pilot had been very friendly on the first leg of their trip, and they had learned that 10 of his 35 years had been spent flying over Alaska and the North Dominion. The weather couldn't, by any means, be a surprise. But when Charlie got closer and saw the man's eyes, he realized something unusual had occurred. They were grave with worry.

"The radio's shot," the pilot said. "It fades out and then won't come in again for a couple of minutes. I'm only getting half the stuff they are sending from the base. I want you to take hold of the controls while I check it over. All you have to do is keep them steady. Don't make any change in course or altitude."

Charlie slipped into the pilot's seat. The man got out a long, thin screwdriver and a pair of slender-nose pliers. He took a plate from the back of the receiving set and began to tinker with the parts inside. He said, "I heard your partner trying to talk to the dame who got on back at Headquarters. How's he coming with her?"

Charlie grinned. "He isn't. She's about as friendly as a rattlesnake shedding its skin."

"I don't know what's going to happen to the Army," the pilot replied, shaking his head ruefully. "It used to be a man's outfit. Now there's women underfoot every place I go. They strut around in their uniforms, saluting and snapping out orders just like it was their private war and men didn't count."

"Sounds like you maybe don't like women," Charlie suggested. He was looking straight ahead, and while there wasn't anything to see but clouds and rain, it helped him keep the controls frozen in the position he had received them.

"No, I don't hate women," the pilot replied. "I just understand them. I ought to, I've been married to three."

He put the headphones back over his ears.

"Getting anything?" Charlie asked.

He nodded and wiped his forehead with the back of his hand. He looked a lot relieved.

"I've been keeping pretty well out to sea to miss a storm center that's moving south along the coast. There's a heck of a lot of water under us and when the set went out I got worried. She's coming through fine now, though. Thanks for the help."

Charlie stood up, turned around and bumped into the girl. She had been standing behind him.

"Sorry," he said and squeezed by. She waited until he had reached his own seat and then said to the pilot, "I'm Lieutenant Irene Kelton. Is anything wrong?"

The pilot's eyes swept over her without expression.

"Everything's okay, Lieutenant," he replied.

"I thought if there was any trouble you should give out parachutes. You carry them, don't you?"

"Sure, I got them. And when they're needed I'll get them out. But we don't need them now. Maybe you better go back to your seat, Lieutenant. It's rough riding through these air pockets."

The plane dipped sharply then and threw her off balance. She had to grab the side of the cabin fast to keep from tumbling over. The plane straightened quickly and she began to feel her way back to her seat. When she sat down the back of her neck was very red, and she spent a full minute staring up at the pilot. But he didn't look around, and presently, she started reading again.

Later, Lew saw the pilot eating a sandwich with one hand, which reminded him it was time for lunch. He opened a box he had ordered filled before they left Wild Horse. It held sandwiches of beef, chocolate cake, and a quart thermos bottle of coffee. When he took the cork out and poured a cup, the aroma made the little space inside the plane very cozy and pleasant.

The girl took a chocolate bar from her bag and began to munch it. Lew picked up a sandwich, hesitated, then held it out over her shoulder and said, "Help yourself, Lieutenant. We have more than we can manage."

But she shook her head firmly and said, "No, thank you."

Lew grinned despite the fact that his mouth was full.

When he had swallowed the bite he continued, "There's nothing 4-F about this sandwich. It's 1-A rye bread and grade-A beef. I bet you'd like it."

The WAC didn't answer.

Lew finished the sandwich and picked up another. "This bread isn't salted enough," he commented to no one in particular. "The only kind of rye bread they put plenty of salt in is pumpernickel. I'm going to have a lot of that when we're home. With butter on each slice and layers of onions and Switzer cheese between."

The pilot was beckoning to Charlie again.

"This dang radio is dead again," he growled. "I can't figure it out. Everything tested out okay before we started. Take over again and I'll see if I can get it working."

Charlie felt uneasy now. The bearings were vitally important to a plane flying blind through this kind of soup.

He watched the pilot. The man was trying everything he could to bring life back to the delicate parts. He took small pieces out, examined them and put them back. Finally, he turned a blank face to Charlie. "No go," he mumbled. "She's dead as a doornail."

Charlie got up and gave him his seat.

"What are you going to do?"

"Keep on flying blind. What else can I do? I can't check the sun because there isn't any."

He glanced down at a chart pinned flat over the instrument panel top. "I think I know about where we are. I'll keep flying south for another hundred miles to miss the worst of the storm and then swing in nearer land. If this soup clears up, I can make one of the landing fields along the coast. If it stays thick, we'll just have to bail out when the gas is gone. But there'll be ground under us then."

Charlie turned around to take his seat, but the pilot jerked at his coat. "Don't go yet," he said. His voice was too low for the others to hear. Charlie noticed they were watching intently.

"There's something else I want to tell you." Charlie squatted on his heels, waiting.

The pilot hesitated for almost a minute. "That dead radio isn't all," he said finally. "I have been watching this storm close for the last hour, and it don't act right. I know these rains; I have been flying through them for years. When we left the airstrip the wind hit us about head-on. The way our course is mapped, it should be gradually shifting around until it is hitting us on the right-hand side. But it isn't. Take a look."

Charlie did, and the tension that gripped him started a cold tingle along his spine. The wind and rain were coming hard and steady against the windows on the left side of the cabin. He looked back and met the pilot's eyes. The man shrugged.

"See what I mean? If the storm has changed direction, we're all right. We're following along the coast and pulling obliquely in towards it. But if the wind hasn't changed, and I never saw it change before, then we're dead wrong and heading away from land, out to sea."

"What does the compass say?" Charlie asked quickly.

"It says we're on the right course. But it may be wrong. A compass can go bad just like a radio. For some reason, we have more trouble with them the closer we get to the magnetic pole. You see the jam I'm in, don't you? I don't know whether to trust the compass or the direction of the wind."

"You had bearings from the base within an hour," Charlie said. "What did they tell?"

"I got compass points only. And I followed them. But if the compass is bad ..." he shrugged again.

"I've got a pocket compass," Charlie said.

"No good. Too much metal in the plane. It would have to be specially shielded, and I doubt it is."

Charlie knew it wasn't. He remembered the times he had to

lay his gun on the ground and back away a dozen feet to get an accurate reading from the needle.

"I told you a few minutes back I knew about where we were. What I mean is I know if my compass is right. If it isn't, I haven't any idea of our position or what's ahead. So, I'm going downstairs and have a look. Maybe this miserable rain isn't so thick there."

The plane's nose slanted down.

Watching the altimeter, Charlie saw it creep lower and lower until it registered only 800 feet. The storm was almost as bad as it was higher up. The pilot eased along carefully with a cut throttle. Apparently, he was thinking the same thought as Charlie—the altimeter should be regarded with the same suspicion as the compass.

The plane still nosed down—gently, however—losing only a few feet of altitude every five minutes. The pilot leaned forward in his seat, eyes glued to the glass window.

His fingers were tense on the controls. He was sweating a little, although the air inside the cabin was very cool.

"I'm taking a heck of a chance," he said. "There might be land just ahead with mountains."

The clouds seemed to be less thick here. There were even brief clear spots in between the grayish banks of wind and rain. Then they broke through the lower layer into free air.

The light was dim but they could see the ocean only a few hundred feet below. It looked very bleak, and its unending expanse alarmed them. They were skimming along just under the lowest strata of cloud. Shreds of mist and fog were scattered over the top of the water and on either side.

Charlie looked at the altimeter again. It read 590 feet. He looked back at the ocean. It seemed much closer than that.

Charlie was still glancing down when it happened. He saw a dark gray boat slip out of a fog curl, saw the flash at the craft's prow and felt, simultaneously, their plane rock dangerously.

The shell had struck the left wing, penetrated the thin fabric, and exploded a few feet above. The sound of the report reached him easily over the drone of their engine.

The pilot banked automatically, cursing.

"Can't that fool see we're U.S.?" he yelled.

Charlie saw another flash down on the sea. The boat was well behind them, but the flare burned through the fog like a rocket.

Then a powerful explosion hurled the plane sideways. It rocked like a crazy thing, and for a moment, Charlie thought it would disintegrate in the air.

One side of the pilot's cockpit had been blasted away. The engine was dead, and the pilot had been blown out of his seat. He lay beside it, head doubled under his shoulder. A dark blotch was already spreading out around him. Charlie sprang forward as the plane started to nose over and plunge into the sea.

Chapter 2 – Crash Landing

Charlie knew he had to bring the falling plane out of its dive towards the sea in a hurry or they were doomed. If they hit nose first, the cockpit would fill instantly, and the heavy machine would plummet to the bottom before they could crawl outside.

He jumped over the prostrate pilot and flung himself in the empty seat. The plane twisted sideways, and his face cracked down hard on the edge of the instrument board. But he got both hands on the controls, and he shook his head to clear away the stars dancing in front of his eyes.

Charlie knew in a general way what had to be done.

Earlier in the day he had learned the feel of the plane when he took it over to let the pilot tinker with the failing radio set. He slammed the elevators down in an attempt to bring the nose up and strike a level keel. Something trickled down his forehead and into his right eye. Blood, he figured, from a cut on his head.

The plane still nosed down.

Charlie jammed against the elevators with all his strength. They were down as far as they'd go. What he needed was a quick, hard surge of speed. But he couldn't get it. The engine was dead, what was left of it. It looked from his seat as if a good third of the mechanism was blasted away.

In a moment they would be heading straight down.

Charlie figured there wasn't much of a chance left, so he yelled, "Get ready to jump just before we crash."

He had started to leave the seat when a heavy gust of wind struck the plane, shoved it hard sideways, and then in some way flopped the nose up. That brief impulse forward gave Charlie the advantage he needed. As the plane straightened out more level, he eased back on the elevators.

They were hardly a hundred feet above the waves. He couldn't see the boat that had shot them down, but there were trailing banks of fog dragging along over the top of the sea that could hide it. He had a feeling it wasn't that far away.

The wind had cut their forward momentum down, and the

plane was settling fast.

"I can't keep her up more than another minute," Charlie said. "Lieutenant, examine the pilot. If he is alive we'll try to take him with us. Get the life raft ready, Lew. Get air in it, and stand by to shove it out a moment before we hit."

He swung the plane around a little to head into the wind squarely. That would give them a bit more time. The WAC kneeled gingerly beside the pilot. Her fingers trembled a little but she managed to pull his head out from under his shoulders.

Then she sprang up with a cry. A fragment of shell shrapnel or some metal from the plane's motor had torn one side of his face away. At least the man had died instantly.

As she backed away, Charlie said, "Get your raincoat on."

Lew had the rubber life raft up even with the door. He swung the door open. They were moving so slowly the slipstream pressure was almost zero. He figured he would release the valve that inflated the bag at the same moment he shoved it out.

Charlie had heard that the best way to put a land plane down on water was to aim for a spot about twelve feet over the waves. Then, when you reached that point, you just let the plane drop the rest of the way. The trouble with this plan was the lack of forward speed with the motor out.

They were falling now, already barely inching ahead, and seeing he couldn't do anything more to help, he got up from the pilot's seat and scrambled back to the opened door.

One wing smacked the water, and Lew shoved the raft out in a hurry. It fully inflated as he had hoped. He grasped the WAC around the knees and heaved her out. She landed on her face in the raft.

That didn't surprise Lew, for he had figured she would land that way. What surprised him was she didn't scream.

Charlie was behind him, shoving, so he jumped. He landed close to one side of the raft, almost astride of the big sausage-shaped ring that kept the canvas floor afloat. Then he drew up his legs to make room for Charlie.

Charlie landed on the edge of the raft, thrust his body out and tried to push himself forward with a hard shove of his feet against the plane, when suddenly the plane wasn't there. Consequently, he fell on his face in the sea.

The plane sank like a heavy trolling line weight as he kicked up to the surface, struggling against the suck of the floundered plane. He grasped the line around the edge of the rubber craft. Thankfully, it was rigged to provide handholds.

"Get on the other side to balance me," he sputtered.

Climbing into a rubber raft is more or less a tricky business. It would have been worse, Charlie knew, for a lone man trying to board one, since he would miss the counterweight needed to prevent the craft toppling over on top of him.

Three of them made a tight fit inside the raft.

It was only about 8 feet long and a bit more than 4 wide, and the big sausage-like ring that formed the outside took up most of the total area. One could sit on the bulging ring if he liked, but after trying, Charlie decided it was too risky. A gust of wind or a big wave could rock the boat enough to tip the sitter overboard.

After some squirming around, they found comfortable positions that also trimmed the weight. Charlie took the forward end; Lew and the girl sat in the stern. This made the prow ride high, which they figured was the way it should.

Lew rummaged in the pockets of the raft. He didn't expect, of course, to find such extensive equipment as is carried by the newest type of life raft. Those models even have storm covers and radio signal sets. He did find some "iron" food rations, a canvas bottle of water, a few assorted tools, a compact fishing kit and a jointed paddle. He put the paddle together and started making long, easy strokes. Then he spoke, "Any idea which way?"

Charlie got his pocket compass out, but when he leveled it on the bottom of the raft, he saw that the face had leaked. There were several drops of water inside. Still, the needle moved, although sluggishly, and finally came to rest.

He decided he could still trust its accuracy, although the saltwater would quickly ruin it for good.

"We're west of the continent, of course," he said. "And according to this compass, we must turn and take the opposite direction. That seems about right; I have a sort of instinct that tells me land is behind."

The rain still fell easily, and there was a moderately stiff wind. The air wasn't exactly cold, but it still started Charlie shivering. His clothes were soaked, and he was the only one of the three who hadn't salvaged a raincoat.

He removed his suit coat and squeezed the water from it, pulled the garment back into shape and put it on. His shirt was flannel and didn't feel too uncomfortable wet. Then he inched his hands along the legs of his pants, removing as much water from them as he could. He took off his shoes and wrung out each sock.

Some of the water drained back into the boat, and he got out the bailing pan and scooped it overboard. He glanced at Lieutenant Irene Kelton, Women's Army Corps, U.S.A., and smiled, "What do you think of us so far?" he asked.

"Not much." Her lips tightened. "I don't like being tossed around like a bag of grain. That wasn't at all necessary." She spoke directly to Lew. "I could have climbed into the raft myself."

"Sorry," Lew said. "I didn't mean to be rough. But you can't lose a second when a plane starts to sink. I thought we might be sucked down with it. Tossing you in was the surest way to get you here dry. If it turns cold tonight, as I expect it will, wet clothing could give you pneumonia."

She had been rubbing the tip of her nose. Now she opened the kit bag strapped to a shoulder and took out a combination mirror and powder box. "I thought so," she said grimly and carefully daubed something like cold cream over the skinned place.

"There's going to be some heck raised, too," she continued, sounding oddly calm considering their predicament.

"What about?" Lew asked. He wondered if she meant the way he had heaved her into the raft.

"About one of our boats shooting down a plane like that one just did. It was a torpedo boat, wasn't it?"

"Maybe," Charlie admitted. As he remembered the craft, it had been about 70 feet long. He had seen it briefly during the few seconds it emerged from one bank of fog and disappeared into another. He did know it wasn't large enough to be a destroyer.

"If the gunner had looked, he would have seen the Army insignia on our wings," the lieutenant continued. "But he didn't look. He saw a plane so he started shooting. There's no excuse for that. I'll see that the commander loses his commission."

Charlie didn't say anything, just looked at his watch. It was a high-grade instrument, had cost a considerable sum of cash and was perfectly waterproof. The hands showed 26 minutes after 3:00 p.m.

He figured about 15 minutes had elapsed since the shell had

crashed through their plane and put it down for good.

"Identifying an Allied commander should be easy," he finally said. "All boats keep a log of events like this. All you have to do if you want to locate the commander is find a log that records shooting down a plane at 3:10 p.m. today."

Admiration crept into her eyes.

"You're right. That's clever. But suppose they don't write it down in the log? They may have realized afterwards that they had shot down one of their own planes."

Charlie started to answer, changed his mind and looked at the dial of his compass. It was still active but becoming more sluggish right along.

"A little more to the left," he said, and Lew turned the prow of the bobbing raft slightly. It was hard to manage the wind and waves with only one paddle.

"Something else looks bad," she continued. "Where are they? Why aren't they searching for us?"

"Maybe they're scared of catching some heck like you mentioned," Lew suggested.

"I suppose you think that was funny," she said severely. "But what can I expect from a 4-F?"

That almost made Lew mad again, but he forced a grin.

"I'm not enjoying this any more than you," he replied. "I know how bad we're fixed. But I'm not going to gripe over it. That won't help. Keep cheerful if you can. We're going to need a lot of cheerfulness before we're out of this jam."

Charlie noticed a minute later that Lew would pause between each paddle stroke to listen with his head turned slightly to the left. He watched his companion's face.

"I'm sure, now," Lew finally said. "There's a boat coming towards us."

"I don't hear it," the girl said.

"You wouldn't," Charlie told her. "Lew can usually hear sounds before I and lots of other people can. It's a gift."

"She's coming up behind us," Lew said.

"You're positive?" Charlie asked quickly.

"Absolutely."

Charlie glanced about. A thick wisp of fog hovered over the water at their right.

"Paddle inside that fog, quick!" he ordered.

Lew's long, powerful strokes sent the clumsy craft quivering slowly ahead but in the desired direction.

"What are you doing?" the girl asked sharply.

Charlie glanced thoughtfully at her. Then he said, "We don't want them to run us down, do we?"

"Of course not. But why would we be safer in the fog than out here on open water where they can see us?"

Charlie didn't answer. He was listening, and he caught the deep drumming of multiple motors. The sounds indicated a high rate of speed. The girl was frowning.

"Answer me," she demanded angrily.

"I will in a minute," Charlie replied. "Please don't talk now. Keep silent, and sit perfectly still."

Her body grew more tense and her lips pressed tighter together. She didn't reply, though, and Charlie nodded approvingly.

They were at the edge of the little bank of fog, and Lew thrust the raft inside with a series of powerful strokes.

"This far enough?" he whispered.

Charlie nodded, and the girl's suspicions flared.

"Why are you whispering?" she cried. "What ..."

"Hush!" Charlie ordered sternly.

The sound of the boat engines was very loud. Then the ship smashed out from another drift of fog, and the first thing they saw was a wide wall of white foam curling off either side of the sharp prow. Then its sleek length flashed into view.

"They won't hit us," the girl cried. "But they won't even see us, either. Push out so they can!"

Lew held his paddle poised over the water but didn't dip it down. She opened her mouth, and he knew she was going to cry out to the boat. He dropped the paddle and grabbed her with both hands, one pressed against the back of her neck, the other clamped across her mouth.

She struggled, striking at him with both hands. But Lew lowered his face and shoved it against the front of her jacket for protection against the flailing fists.

Her legs kicked out. Charlie grabbed them and pinned them down against the bottom of the raft.

The gray warship flashed past and disappeared into the opposite fog. When the sound of its motors began to diminish in pitch, they released her.

Her face was red, and her eyes flashed with rage. For a moment she was too angry to talk. Then she stormed furiously.

"Are you mad? You must be if you'd rather drown than have the ship rescue us."

"What made you think they wanted to rescue us?" Charlie asked quietly.

She stared at him amazed. "Do you really think American seamen would leave us drifting on the ocean because they shot us down by mistake?"

"No, I don't," Charlie replied. "But they aren't American seamen. I wasn't sure before, but I am now. That boat was Japanese."

Chapter 3 – You Can't Eat Tin Fish

Lieutenant Irene Kelton, Women's Army Corps, U.S. Army, shook her head when Charlie told her that the patrol boat which had just flashed past their little rubber raft in the fog was Japanese.

"Now I know you're mad," she said. Her anger seemed to abate with the declaration. Lew was glad of that because he had made her angry by clamping his hand across her mouth to keep her from calling to the boat in spite of Charlie's warning to be silent.

"How could a Japanese boat be undetected in this part of the ocean?" she demanded.

"What do you mean by this part of the ocean?" Charlie countered. "Where do you think we are?"

"Where? Don't be silly. We're just a few miles off the Canadian coast. I've been over this route before. The pilots always follow a straight course from Dutch Harbor to Vancouver, and we were in the air long enough to be very close to Victoria."

"I wish you were right," Charlie said. "But there isn't a chance. The Canadian coast is hundreds of miles off, maybe a thousand."

"I don't believe it."

"Whether you do or don't doesn't change the situation. You know our pilot had been flying blind all morning and taking his course from radio signals?"

She nodded and said, "They always do that in bad weather."

"Then his radio went bad," Charlie continued. "You remember that, too? So, he couldn't get any more instructions. But long before that happened, he was already suspecting his compass. It didn't check out with the prevailing direction of the storm.

"The pilot told me he had flown this country for ten years. He knew the prevailing wind and weather by heart. The signals and bearings from headquarters were okay, naturally. But if he had been laying the course with a bad compass, we could be anywhere. In fact, he thought we had actually flown southwest instead of southeast. If so, then we're out somewhere in the Pacific, maybe in line with lower Alaska."

Her eyes showed she didn't like that idea at all.

"Why didn't you tell me these things instead of choking me with your dirty hands?" she demanded.

Lew winced a little and looked down at his hands. They were a bit grimy, especially under the nails. He thought he'd better let Charlie answer.

"I realize now we should have told you," Charlie said. "But you hadn't shown any inclination to be cooperative. There was a good chance you'd disregard our counsel, even resent our advice, since you had decided we were draft dodgers. We couldn't take any chance of you calling out to a Japanese boat, and you know that."

She clearly didn't care much for the way Charlie put things.

"You haven't any proof the boat was Japanese," she argued.

"I have enough. I could tell by her lines. We've studied extensive photography of the craft they use for patrol and torpedo work. Of course, you have only my word for that. But you don't need it for this. The gunner who shot us down saw the plane distinctly. As you pointed out, we were so close he couldn't miss the stars on the underside of each wing. Besides, if we were close to the coast, our own patrol boats wouldn't be so quick on the trigger. They wouldn't expect enemy planes and would have made very sure of our identity before firing."

Charlie took the pistol from its shoulder holster under his coat, dismounted the barrel and started to wipe off the saltwater with Lew's handkerchief, which, fortunately, was almost dry. He knew seawater could ruin a gun in just a few hours, rust it so badly the mechanism would clog and no longer work. He didn't want to risk that. Even if the weapon wasn't needed for defense, it could be used to shoot a fish or bird to eat.

He looked up at the WAC. All of her belligerency was gone. She seemed to have shrunk into a dejected girl of less than average height. The coils of rain-soaked blond hair were straggling down the back of her neck. She tried to push them back up under her cap but didn't have much success.

"I think we should have stopped the boat," she finally said. "I'd rather be a prisoner than drown or starve on the ocean."

"I wouldn't," Charlie replied evenly.

Then he removed one shoe, took out the lace, and started to drag bits of cloth through the pistol's barrel with it.

"Besides, I doubt if they would have bothered taking prisoners. More likely they would have run us down. Whatever the sharp prow left of us would have been chewed up by the propeller."

He moistened some of the cleaning rags with saliva to rinse away the salt. The light, steady rain slackened, and Lew glanced up at the sky. There was a small patch of blue directly overhead.

"I should have been catching water in my raincoat," he said.

"There'll be more rain," Charlie declared. "When it starts again, rinse the coat off first. And then watch it so the sea doesn't splash on it to deposit more salt."

"I'm thirsty," the girl said. She glanced at the canvas bottle of water in the emergency rations.

"So am I," Charlie agreed. "My throat smarts like the devil. I got a mouthful of brine when I fell in. But we mustn't touch that bottle until we get enough rain to replace what we drink. We need that much in reserve. It may have to last a week or longer."

Silence enveloped the little group on the life raft. The girl finally broke it.

"How long do you think it will be before we find land or a ship picks us up?" she asked.

"I haven't any idea," Charlie replied frankly. "We might possibly be in the path of patrol boats or planes working out of Dutch Harbor. If we are, and this fog clears, they'll sight us."

"But we may also reach an island," she persisted. "If we keep on paddling, we'll at least go somewhere. I can paddle. I'll take my turn now."

She held out a hand, and Lew gave her the short oar.

"Take it easy," he cautioned. "Don't flip water into the boat. And don't tire yourself out at the start. We got plenty of time — more of it than anything else."

Fortunately, the sea was calm, almost smooth. The regular swells lifted the little raft up regularly and then let it drop back, but the movement was easy and gradual and almost soothing.

The raft was still clumsy to handle, and one had to continually fight its tendency to go around in a circle. Consequently, their forward progress was slow. But Charlie figured they might be making a couple of miles an hour. He didn't mention that; there wasn't any reason to discourage the girl. She was doing all right with the paddle. Apparently, she had handled boats before.

After a while she said, "That's an army pistol, isn't it?"

Charlie nodded. He was taking the breech plug out, getting ready to dismount it. The only way he could stop the salt's action was to separate the pieces and wipe each as dry as he could.

"If you're enlisted men, you should be wearing army uniforms," she continued.

"That's right," Charlie agreed.

He had found several drops of thick oil down along the side of the magazine. These had accumulated from heavy oiling of the gun, and he was glad they had. He sopped them up with a bit of cloth and rubbed it over the surface he had cleaned.

"Did you desert?" she asked suddenly.

Lew laughed.

"And then thumb a ride in an army plane?" he asked. But he didn't volunteer any information about their status. Her face flushed, and she jerked hard on the paddle.

"Then who are you, and why were you on that plane?" she demanded. "If I've got to live on this raft, or possibly die on this raft with you, I have the right to know."

Charlie agreed with that, and he suddenly regretted his close-mouthed reticence. It really hadn't been fair to the girl.

He wasn't sure they should tell her about their connection with Army Intelligence, but he could reassure her about their reliability. He was mentally casting around for the right phrases when a salvo of heavy gunfire boomed out somewhere in the thick blanket of heavy, wet air surrounding them.

They listened to the echoes of the deep, tremendous sounds rumbling along for what seemed to be minutes. Then there was a single dull boom, followed by the rattle of lighter cannon. The echoes of the big explosion were still glancing back from the horizons when their ears were rent by a different sound. It was so violent it made their heads hurt.

There was a different tone to this report, and they knew it wasn't gunfire. Not even a 14-inch naval rifle could produce so much concussion.

"That was a torpedo or a ship's magazine letting go," Charlie said. "Give me the paddle. There may be a bad wave coming. If we tip over, grab the safety line and hang on."

He indicated the small rope running about the outside edge of the raft, and then he held the paddle poised, ready to dig deep into the sea and steady them if a wave hit.

What seemed like minutes passed. Then they felt the little raft quiver and begin to lift. Up and up it went, and then something struck it on the bottom and shot it even higher. The raft swung sideways from the force of the blow, and Charlie paddled desperately to swing them around in line with the pressure and keep their trim.

The raft kept climbing higher until it appeared to balance on the sharp crest of a gigantic breaker. The prow tipped forward, and Lew flung his weight rearward to offset the action.

For a moment it seemed they must tip forward and go plunging into the sea, but the peak of the wave finally swept forward, and the raft righted and then began to settle.

Charlie balanced for the next wave. It was only about half as violent as the first, and they weathered it nicely. They did ship several inches of water, and Lew began scooping it out.

He glanced at the girl. Her face had turned green with streaks of blue under her eyes and about her mouth. Her lips were set firmly together, and she pressed one hand against her stomach.

Lew knew what that meant. Unless he was mistaken, Second Lieutenant Kelton was going to be very sick in a very short time.

Retching and struggling hard to keep the disconcerting impulse down, she swung suddenly towards the side of the raft with lowered head. Lew grabbed an arm with one hand, hooked the other under her belt. The raft was still bobbing about like a cork float on a trout-fouled line, and there were plenty of chances for her to fall overboard. He knew, too, from his own experience, that when one is very sick he relaxes caution, doesn't care whether he falls into the sea or not. He let her gag over the side for more than a minute.

"Don't try to hold it down," he said. "Let it come."

A wave came up and slapped her in the face. She gasped, choked, wiped her eyes with one hand and sat up. Her face was still white, but the blue marks were gone. The sea was still rough, and Charlie paddled hard to keep the raft ahead of the succeeding swells so they wouldn't be swamped.

"Feel better?" Lew asked and released her arm and belt.

She nodded, pulled her jacket down and settled her cap at its proper slant over one eye. She frowned.

"I never did that before," she said.

"You were never adrift on a life raft in the Pacific when a ship got blown up, either, were you?"

"Look," she said quickly. "There's a fish."

Lew turned sharply, drawing his pistol at the same time. If it was a large fish and if it came close enough he intended to shoot it for food. Then his eyes bulged and he yelled, "Left, Charlie, quick!"

Charlie could always be depended upon in an emergency to keep his head, to act quickly and not ask for explanations.

He swerved the raft, and something long and slim sliced through the water at the precise spot they had been a second before.

It went by with a little churning sound and then disappeared in the rough waves.

Lew took a deep breath.

"That was a fish, alright—a tin one. Am I glad you saw it in time." He patted the girl's knee. She moved enough to escape a second pat of approval. But Lew was so excited he didn't notice and patted the seat of the raft instead.

"Would we give enough resistance to explode one of those things?" he finally asked.

Charlie nodded. "I think so. It doesn't take much of a jolt."

"I'm going to keep my eyes glued on the water from now on," Lew promised. "There might be some more coming our way."

They didn't worry about the torpedo they had avoided so narrowly. It would sink after it had traveled a pre-determined range. But they knew there might be more live ones about.

Such missiles are often fired in salvos, and, apparently, not all had struck the boat they had heard explode. They wondered what sort of craft it had been.

A pair of gray birds wheeled out of the mist, circled over the raft with short, hoarse cries. Then they flashed away from sight. The girl pointed after them and said eagerly.

"That means land is not far," she declared.

Charlie didn't argue. She might even be right. But he knew sea birds are found hundreds of miles from land. Some, apparently live out on the vast ocean wastes. He paddled steadily. Lew offered to take over but he refused. Charlie felt like he needed the exercise. His clothes were still damp, and the air was growing colder.

Although it had stopped raining, visibility was still poor. The sky had clouded over, and the bright blue patch of sky was veiled. They could hardly see more than a hundred yards in any direction.

Charlie looked at his watch. It had survived the saltwater bath and was running fine. It said five o'clock. Night wasn't far off, and he knew it could bring a lot of things that are not good. Cold was only one of them.

"Stop a moment," Lew said.

Charlie listened intently but heard only the rustle of the water as it smacked gently against the blunt end of their raft.

Lew relaxed. "I thought it was a ship, at first. But it isn't. I think I hear breakers over rocks."

The girl straightened up and said excitedly, "I hear it, too. It's land. Hurry, won't you?"

Charlie sped up the paddling a little. He wasn't sure everything was going to be all right, as the WAC apparently believed. Plenty of danger could lie ahead. The first would be the difficulty of running a light raft through breakers.

If they survived that, who knew what other dangers awaited?

Chapter 4 – A Thief in the Night

A few minutes later they caught sight of the land ahead. They couldn't tell much about its size or height because mist enveloped it and hung quite close to the water. What they could see didn't appear very hospitable or friendly, just a strip of bare brown ground, quite rocky and badly cut up with indentations. Charlie steered the rubber life raft towards the deepest of those conveniently near.

The roar came from a belt of white surf that seethed about three hundred feet offshore. Shooting it was going to be a real danger. Charlie eased up on his paddle as they approached. He counted the waves. They were rolling in about four to the minute to hit the submerged barrier with tremendous force and break across it. Beyond was almost quiet water.

Charlie knew the trick of riding safely through bad surf was to time his approach correctly. It looked now like the best plan would be to reach the reef between two of the larger swells. So, he paddled up to within some thirty feet and lay there, backstroking to hold his position. A big breaker lifted then flung them ahead and broke. When Charlie felt the raft plunging down, he paddled fast. They shot onto the barrier, rocking crazily. Twice the bottom of the raft grated on stone and then they floated in the calmer water beyond.

Charlie paddled furiously now to keep ahead of the next big wave. He made it—almost. Its curling crest nicked the stern of their craft, shoved it down until gallons of sea poured over the low gunwale. Lew jumped forward to lighten the stern and began to bail with his hat. Charlie kept plying the paddle and then a third swell pushed them forward and left them on dry land.

The beach they stepped upon was mostly black sand, well-strewn with stones of all sizes. Some were only as large as a man's fist, a few were three and four feet in diameter, and all had been smoothed and grooved by action of the water or some terrific glacial pressure until they were the same color as the sand.

Charlie and Lew grabbed the rubber boat and dragged it inland. The strip of sand beach was narrow. A hundred feet back grass appeared, sparse tufts at first and then these thickened and grew deep as they walked. They dropped the boat in behind two huge boulders well beyond the reach of any sucking tide. Charlie turned the raft over to examine the bottom. It was scratched in places but not damaged enough to leak air.

Lew took the emergency food rations and the bottle of fresh water out and laid them under the raft. Everything was drenched with rain. The big stones glistened in the dim light and the wet grass had soaked their shoes in the first dozen steps. They couldn't see far inland because the beach began to rise and faded out in the low bank of fog.

Charlie started walking away from the sea.

"Where are you going?" the WAC asked him.

"To get some idea of the size of this place. If it has depth then it won't be just a barren ridge of rock."

The grass was very long now and it had dried to fall over into a soft, damp cushion. They sank ankle-deep at each step. Small stunted bushes began to appear. This brush became larger and thicker and finally they walked among short, thin trees that resembled spruce and grew about seven feet high.

The girl stopped beside one of these trees. "Is this wood dry enough to burn?"

Lew broke off some of the dead branches that hung close to the ground. Their centers were dry. "Sure, it'll burn," he said. "After I shave off the wet outside with my knife."

"Will you make a fire right away?" she asked.

Charlie shook his head. "Sorry, but we can't."

"Why?" she demanded.

"The patrol boat that shot our plane down didn't come very far from its base. It couldn't because of its size. This island may be that base. So we have to go slow. A fire might be discovered immediately. We can't risk that. I want to look around first, and if the enemy is here I want to see them before they see us."

He started hiking again. Lew followed but the girl stood there. Charlie paused and waited. She was frowning.

"A Japanese base so close to America?" she said. "That's silly. They wouldn't dare. If we don't have a fire I'll catch pneumonia. I'm shaking with cold and my feet are numb."

Charlie shook his head.

"I'm sorry, but no fire," he repeated.

She drew herself erect.

"Someone," she began firmly, "must take charge here. We won't get anyplace by indecision. Someone must make plans and carry them out. I am a second lieutenant of the WAC. I am going to assume the responsibility of leader here because of that rank. Please gather wood and build a fire. That is an order."

Lew swung about, but Charlie smiled and spoke first.

"I agree someone must take charge, but you are in no position to give orders, and Lew and I both outrank you. I didn't tell you before because our work demands maximum secrecy; everything is on a need to know basis. Since you need to know now, I am telling you we're Army Intelligence."

He paused a moment to let that sink in.

"That is why we wear civilian clothing yet carry army guns under our coats. I am taking charge now by right of my seniority in both experience and rank. I expect to give the orders and I also expect you to obey them and be the good soldier your uniform indicates. The first is no fire, and no noise or sign that might betray our landing to the enemy."

He waited for her reply. It came promptly. She stiffened her shoulders and saluted smartly. "Yes sir. May I know your rank, please, so I can address you correctly?"

"Sure. It is captain. But we use first names only. Here are my credentials. I expect to destroy them as soon as we see any sign of the enemy. Show yours to the lieutenant, Lew."

She examined both carefully, turning them over in her short yet slender fingers. The purplish-red polish had started to chip from the nails. Then she handed the papers back, saluted again, relaxed and smiled. Lew was almost startled at the way her face changed. He had still been judging her from his first impression when she climbed aboard the plane at Dutch Harbor, and that impression had not been a good one.

"I could almost like her if she keeps that up," he thought.

Her next words reaffirmed his change of heart.

"I had to find out who and what you are. Of course I don't want to take the risk of making a fire. I'm cold, but I can wait."

"I'll be," Lew muttered. He had a way of moving his lips to form unspoken words when he did heavy thinking. That habit used to annoy Charlie until he got used to it.

"She put on an act of trying to be boss so we'd give out with our names and our business. But we still need to look out for this pretty lady. She is way too used to getting what she wants, and she knows how to work it."

"You don't mind, my subterfuge, do you?" she asked.

"Not at all," Charlie replied. "We had to get things straightened out sometime and I'm glad we did it now. It wasn't fair to keep you in the dark, but we have our orders, too. You haven't a gun, have you? Then you better walk behind us. If anybody challenges or starts to shoot, drop flat on the ground."

They started walking, still moving away from shore.

Lew decided the short trees were spruce but of a southern kind they had not seen before. The timber grew taller but no more frequent as they progressed. Soon, tree tops were reaching up to disappear into the low-hanging mist. When they had walked about a mile, Charlie turned left.

"An enemy installation will be near water," he explained. "Keeping inland, we should come up on them from behind."

His foot touched something that clinked. He bent and picked up a loop of small iron chain. It was covered thickly with rust and seemed to be fast at either end. A strong jerk lifted a number two steel trap from the matted grass. The jaws were spread and set. Charlie reached under one, pressed on the pan, and the trap snapped shut with a click.

"Some trapper forgot to pick up his trap," Lew said.

"Trappers don't usually forget where they set traps," Charlie said thoughtfully. He wrapped the chain around the springs and shoved the trap in a pocket. This find had eliminated one possibility. The island was large enough to be inhabited. That meant there would be fresh water and game, or at least furbearing animals that would serve for food.

The light was getting bad with the mist dropping lower and gathering intensity. They decided to turn back while there was enough visibility to find the boat they had left cached. Charlie had planned to use it as a shelter from the damp fog and rain.

They hadn't gone very far before Lew stumbled over a second steel trap. It was the same size but had been sprung and the jaws were clamped down about the shriveled leg of a skeleton partly covered with rotten hide.

The reddish-brown hair clinging to the skin identified the skeleton as having belonged to a fox.

Lew pried the jaws apart and released the leg. He jerked the trap loose from the stake and put it in his pocket. Irene watched him with some distaste.

"The man should be punished for that carelessness," she said.

"He wasn't careless," Charlie replied. "Wilderness trappers can't afford to be. They can't afford to lose a fox skin, either. Something happened to this man that made it impossible for him to run these traps."

"Why are you taking them with you?" she asked.

"To catch foxes when our grub is gone," Lew said.

"You mean we'll have to eat foxes?"

"Sure. You can eat anything when you get hungry enough. I've tasted worse than fox, too."

He made a faint smacking sound with his lips.

"Are you hungry now?" Irene demanded.

"He always is," Charlie told her.

"So am I," she said, opening her kit bag. She took out three candy bars. They were big fat ones loaded with peanuts.

"Take one," she invited Lew. Then she added quickly, looking at Charlie, "Unless you think we should save them for later."

"We needn't start to ration our supplies right away," Charlie replied and also took a bar and bit into it. The chocolate-covered caramel tasted good.

They moved nearer the sea, fearing they might pass by their boat without seeing it in the bad light.

"We can have a fire tonight?" Irene asked.

Charlie assured her they could. "We'll prop the raft up on poles and fill in around the back and sides with rocks," he added. They walked a little faster, cheered by the candy bars and the thought of a warm shelter. The two big rocks were just ahead.

They walked around them and stopped. The raft wasn't there. It and the supplies cached beneath it were gone.

"They can't do that to us," Lew muttered.

"Who can't?" she demanded.

"The guys who stole our raft."

Charlie didn't pay any attention. He knew Lew was just talking out loud while he tried to figure this queer business. For it was queer. Why would anybody want to take the raft? It would have been more logical for an enemy to hide behind the stones and ambush them when they returned.

"Stand still," Charlie said. Then he began walking slowly among the rocks, studying the ground. Every few feet he squatted down on his heels. He had learned that old trailing trick years ago. Very slight signs left by feet, which are invisible when one stands to look down on them, can become very plain when you get your eye near the ground and view them sideways.

He finally found what he was searching for.

"Somebody dragged the raft off. See these marks?"

Bending down it was easy, and they followed the trail carefully. About a hundred feet from the sea it turned along the beach in the opposite direction they had taken on their reconnaissance.

Lew took his pistol out, snapped a load in the chamber, put on the safety catch and put the gun in his coat pocket.

"They can't be very far ahead," he said and then took off along the beach at a brisk run. Charlie and Irene followed. The best way to make progress through the rocks was to detour around the really big ones and jump over the rest.

It had started to rain again, lightly but enough to turn their faces wet and chill their hands.

Night was closing in, and it looked as if they might not overtake the man or men who had stolen the raft before total darkness. And then they caught sight of a darker blot against the dark, fog-filled sky.

"There he is—just one man," Lew said quietly. "You stay here. Three pairs of feet make too much noise."

Charlie stopped. Irene paused doubtfully and said, "Do you think he should do that?"

"Lew knows what he is doing," Charlie replied. "The fellow may have a rifle and he would hear three of us coming long before he will know Lew is behind him."

Lew loped at an almost leisurely pace. The thief was moving along slowly, and Lew didn't want to tire himself now that he knew the fellow could not escape. He couldn't see the man, only the raft as it was dragged along over the rough ground.

When he came closer he swerved out to one side and caught a glimpse of the man. He had a short, heavily built figure and considerable strength, for he was pulling the craft with one hand.

The other clutched a short-barreled rifle.

The light was bad, but enough remained to show Lew the gun was a bolt action. He felt better about it, for the fellow would need a second or two to get the weapon into action, and he already had his pistol in his hand. Putting on a burst of speed, he quickly overhauled the other.

When he was just a couple of yards away, he asked in a quiet voice, "Just where do you think you're going with our boat?"

Chapter 5 – I Smell a Fish

The man dragging their rubber raft down the beach didn't act very much surprised when Lew overtook him and spoke. He dropped the boat, turned around and said, "Hello!"

His voice was friendly, his face split with a grin. Lew thought that "split" was exactly the right word, because the man's chin was so heavy and hung so low it put his mouth almost in the middle of a very full, very round face.

"This is your boat? I didn't know. I found it on the beach where I find lots of things the sea brings to me, and I said, 'Joe,' that's me, my name is Joe. I said, 'Joe, you must carry that fine boat home and take good care of it so when the man who owns it comes and says he wants his boat, you can give it to him and say you took good care of it and then maybe he will give you a dollar for going to so much trouble.'"

Joe finished the long sentence in a kind of sing-song lilt like he was reciting a piece committed to memory. Then he grinned again, his round, black eyes darting from Lew's face to the gun in his hand, down to his shoes and then back again to his face, detouring along the way for a sharp, second look at the gun.

Lew changed the pistol into his other hand; he could shoot pretty well with it at close range. Keeping his eyes on Joe's rifle, he reached into his hip pocket, took out his billfold, extracted a dollar bill and held it out. He didn't exactly see how dragging the rubber craft over the rough beach was taking such good care of it, but he figured it was worth a dollar to find the boat intact.

Grinning more than ever, Joe took the money. "Thank you," he said. "I am sorry that your ship was wrecked and you had to float to the island on a raft."

"Don't mention it," Lew replied. "You live here, Joe?"

"Of course. It is a nice island. There are many foxes and their skins are so big and the hair so long the fur buyer pays a fine price for every one I catch."

Lew took the trap they had found a short time ago from his pocket. "This must be yours, then. I found it back in the grass with a fox skeleton in the jaws. You ought to run your traps more carefully. You lost money by missing that pelt."

Joe took the trap. "Thank you," he said again. "It is all the fault of Cham, who married my sister, that I missed this trap and the fox, for when he had to take my sister away two months ago because she was going to have a baby and that made him afraid to leave her here until it happened so he took her to our mother who lives on the big island west of this one, he went in so much hurry he did not have time to show me where every one of the traps he set were, and that is why I missed it."

Listening, Lew began to wonder if Joe would run out of breath, but he didn't. His wind seemed excellent, as it would have to be if he always talked this way without breaking his speech up into normal sentences.

"We found two traps," Lew said. "Charlie has the other." He looked around then and saw his companions were quite close. He motioned to them to hurry. And then he realized that because his back had been towards them and because Joe was facing him, Joe must have seen them all the time. He was going to say something about that but Joe spoke first.

"They must not walk so slowly in the rain. That is right for you to tell them to hurry because this weather is so bad, and if they come faster we can all go to my house where there is a fire, unless it has burned out, which I don't think it has because I put on a very big piece of coal before I left, and you can all get warm and dry your clothes and I will cook a fish."

The mention of food reminded Lew there had been some emergency rations and a canvas water bottle cached underneath the raft. He saw that Joe had put these things neatly back in the pockets built to hold them.

"You burn coal?" Lew asked. "Why ship coal in where there is plenty of wood?"

"We do not ship coal because it is here all the time and all we have to do is dig it, which is not hard work, although Cham says it is, and I think he has always been mad because I found the coal when I came to help him with his traps, and I found it because I knew where to look, and we had always used it in my home, but I do not see why he should be mad because I would rather dig coal than cut down trees."

"Where was your home, Russia?" Lew asked. He thought there was evidence of the Slav in Joe's full, round face and in his short, very thick body.

"Siberia," Joe replied. "But I have lived in Alaska where I learned to talk the United States language and—" he broke off, his beady eyes getting larger and rounder when Irene stepped around beside Charlie and stood looking at him. If Joe was surprised by her appearance he recovered fast and he started off again. "Hello! Hello! I am so glad you are here." He gave Charlie a swift glance and his eyes went back to Irene.

"This is Joe," Lew told them. "Joe, meet Lieutenant Kelton and Charlie. We all came on the raft together."

Joe nodded twice and repeated, "Hello! Hello! I am glad to see you. Let us hurry now and go to my house. It is not really a house because it is made of poles and driftwood we picked up on the shore, but the roof does not leak, although I have thought it would many times because the way Cham made it out of grass when I wanted him to bring some of the black paper that comes in rolls, but he would not pay five dollars for one of the rolls, which is the price the storekeeper asked, so he worked ten days cutting long grass, which would make fine hay to feed a cow if we could bring one to the island, and put on a roof that sheds the rain, because that is the kind of roof Cham was used to in his home."

Joe looked again at Irene and then reluctantly turned, picked up one end of the raft and started off. Lew grabbed up the other end so it wouldn't drag and they followed. Joe turned every dozen steps to look back at them and smile.

After the third look he said, "It is nice to have women in the army. They look so fine in their uniforms."

Irene dropped back a little, and when Charlie paused for her to catch up she whispered, "I don't like the way he keeps looking at me. I get the creeps."

"Forget it," Charlie replied. "He's intrigued by your uniform. I don't think it's so bad myself."

Joe's house was half a mile along the beach where the ground was higher. It was a rambling sort of house with the rear end backed up against a small hill, and it looked like it had started out very small and then grown by abrupt additions, which had undoubtedly supplied more room inside but which had done nothing to help the appearance of the exterior. The roof was low but it had a sharp pitch, and the thatched grass looked very efficient. It was two feet thick with rounded edges and pole anchors.

Joe leaned the raft against the side of the house and opened the door, inviting them with a gesture to enter. They crowded past, and finding themselves in almost darkness, stopped in a tight little group in the center of the room. The windows were small and covered with some opaque material like black sail duck.

Joe struck a match and lighted a kerosene lamp. It was the kind that used a mantle and, after it had warmed up, threw ample light into all corners. The room was quite large, and a partition at the seaward end indicated there was at least one additional adjoining room in the house. The walls were made of different materials—thin poles set on end, rough driftwood boards, and pieces of metal that looked like the sides of oil drums beaten flat.

There was a table and bench made of driftwood. Joe pointed to the latter and said, "Sit down, please. I will cook the fish in just a minute, but first I must wipe the water from my gun, for this is a bad place for guns, and they rust very fast unless they are wiped dry."

He stepped over to the small, flat-top, cast-iron stove and opened the draft. Behind the stove was a box filled with blocks of coal some eight inches square.

Joe pulled the bolt from his Mauser, took cloth and a steel, jointed rod from the table drawer and got to work. The rifle looked like the popular 8mm bore and also looked like it was in excellent shape in spite of Joe's complaint about the weather. It had a sling trap and a sporting aperture rear sight.

Lew remembered he had carried his pistol out in his hand and that it was also wet, so he dismounted the barrel and slide and wiped it with his handkerchief. Charlie made a fast inventory of the room. Its walls were crowded with gear. There was a raincoat and hat, a heavy, wool sailor's pea jacket, several bunches of steel traps hanging from their chains, and clusters of wood stretcher boards. He saw a fishing net, a heavy casting rod, two picks, a shovel, a full-length axe and a pair of oars.

There was a wood bunk against one wall, covered with patched, faded blue blankets. The floor of the room was made of planks worn smooth with use or by the sea and surprisingly clean. Charlie looked down at his muddy shoes regretfully.

Joe glanced up from his work to smile at them, particularly Irene. When he finished, he stood the rifle carefully in a corner, opened a small door almost concealed behind the fish net and went through it.

"He better stop looking at me all the time," Irene said, "or I'm going to do something violent."

Joe came back with a salmon about two feet long. He put a short piece of plank on the floor, laid the fish on it, and took up a long kitchen knife from the box cupboard beside the stove. Charlie always thought he was pretty good at filleting a big fish but he had never done the job any faster. Joe cut behind the fish's head to the backbone, and then, with a continuous cut, sliced the thick meat from the ribs, flipped it over, and cutting back the other way, separated it from the skin.

Lew had finished drying his pistol and offered to help cook. But Joe grinned and said, "You are guests and must not work." That was such a short speech for Joe it surprised Lew into sitting back down. He decided he wouldn't argue the point; it might set Joe off on one of his monologues.

Joe put an iron skillet on the stove and put in grease. He went through the small door again and returned with a pan of flour and a pail of water.

"Got a well in there?" Charlie asked.

"Not a well but a cistern because the ground is too full of rocks to dig a well, and it is also too hard to dig a cistern, so this one is made on top of the ground with a roof over it to keep out the sun and not let the water get warm, and because the water stays cool, it makes a nice place to keep food from being spoiled."

Joe mixed dough, pinched off biscuits, and put them in the drum oven setting in the smoke pipe above the stove. He fried thick slabs of salmon meat and made tea in a two-gallon pail. When they ate he was a very attentive host. As soon as a plate or cup was empty Joe jumped up to refill it. They discovered that the only way not to gorge dangerously was to leave meat and biscuits on their plate and tea in the cup. Despite their keen hunger, they could only handle two pieces of fish. Along with his solicitude for his guests, Joe didn't neglect his own appetite. Lew counted a dozen biscuits and five hunks of meat that disappeared from his plate, and he wouldn't have sworn that he had been able to count them all, either.

The room was very hot and they began getting drowsy. Joe apparently liked the heat, for he jammed coal steadily into the little stove and left the bottom draft partly open. The blocks of fuel were rich in oil or gas and blazed fiercely.

"That was a swell meal, Joe," Charlie said. "Now I want to ask you a question. Where are we?"

Joe's face lost its smile and his eyes grew puzzled. "Why, you are here in my house on the island—"

Charlie interrupted. "I mean, where is this island? I know it's between America and Siberia, but which is closer? Have you got a map to show us?"

Joe's smile returned. "I understand now, but I am sorry, I do not have a map that you can look at which would show you where the island is, but I can answer your question because Siberia is closer and only a little distance away, although I do not know exactly how many hundred miles it is, but I know the big island which is west of here is about three hundred miles, because Cham's boat makes twelve miles an hour and I always remember it is a journey of twenty hours, for when we leave in the middle of the afternoon we get there at noon tomorrow, which I do not like because we must sail all night, and I would rather steer the boat in the daytime, but that is the way we go because the boat belongs to Cham."

"How many hours does it take to go to Siberia in your boat?" Charlie asked, speaking fast because he saw the incredulous look on Irene's face and he didn't want her to interrupt.

"That is something I do not know because I have never gone all the way there in Cham's boat, because I came to this island from the big one, and to that one I came from Alaska, and it was in a ship, and I slept most of the time so I don't remember how long that journey took, but I do not see why you have to ask me about the distance, because you know where your ship was wrecked and how long it took you to float to the island in your raft."

"It wasn't a ship," Irene said. "We were on a plane."

Joe's smile seemed to shrink, or maybe it was their imagination. "That is right and I am not very smart not to know that you came from an airplane, because it would have been a life boat and not a rubber raft if you had been on a wrecked ship, and now I think you are tired and maybe you will want to go to sleep soon, so I will look at the room where my sister sleeps and see if it is clean and a nice place for the Miss Lieutenant to stay."

He took a candle from the cupboard, lighted it and went through the door in the partition wall. Charlie leaned across the table and whispered, "Give me your credentials, Lew. Quick!"

Lew opened his mouth like he might argue on the matter but he gave the notion up when he looked into Charlie's eyes. He took the folder from his pocket and shoved it across the table. Charlie had his own out and with three long strides he reached the hot little stove. He opened the door, dropped the papers inside and then closed the stove carefully to avoid making a noise.

He looked into their questioning eyes. "I'm afraid I waited too long to do that."

"Why?" Irene asked.

"I smell something fishy around here," Charlie told her, "and it isn't the salmon we had for supper!"

Chapter 6 – Death Scores a Miss

"It is a queer business," Lew admitted. "I've been doing some thinking myself. I didn't like that statement Joe made about this island being nearer Siberia than the American coast. Did you?"

"No. Joe might be too dumb to know much about geography, but just the same, we better play our cards close to our vests."

"Was that why you burned your credentials?" Irene said.

Charlie nodded.

"He might go through our clothes while we sleep."

"Why don't we jump Joe when he comes back and put him where he can't do any harm?" Lew suggested.

"You mean kill him?" Irene asked.

"Not quite. But we could immobilize him enough so he wouldn't be dangerous."

"Later maybe," Charlie replied. "But not now. I want to learn more from him, if I can."

Joe came out of the other room. "It is ready whenever you want to go to sleep," he said. "I hope you rest well, although it is not a nice room like the ones you are used to sleeping in."

Irene gave him a forced smile. "You haven't seen many army tents, then."

Joe gathered the dishes from the plank table but refused their offer to help.

"Guests must not work," he insisted, and that was such a short statement for Joe, they yielded without any protest.

"How big is this island?" Charlie asked.

"It is twelve miles the long way and about half as much the short way and that is not very big, and I wanted to find a bigger one where we could trap more foxes, but Cham, who I told you is my sister's husband, liked this place, and because the traps are all his like the boat, we stayed."

"That isn't too much ground for two professional trappers," Charlie agreed. "How many foxes do you catch a year?"

"We did not have the good luck this winter and there were only eighty-three skins when the man who buys them and gives us flour and sugar and smoked meat came in his boat."

Lew did some fast figuring in his head. "Not very big wages for two men," he said.

"It would have been very bad if we had caught nothing but foxes, but besides them there are seals and walrus, and once in a long time we get a sea otter, and those hides bring much money, especially the otter, so we only have to get a few of them, and because we did this winter, we got some money from the fur buyer besides all the supplies he traded to us."

"When will this buyer come again?"

"He only comes two times each year, and since he was here almost two months ago, he will not come back until just before winter begins and that is half a dozen months yet."

Charlie considered this in silence for a minute. Then he asked again, "When will your brother-in-law, Cham, return?"

"That is hard to know because if my sister becomes well quickly, then he will be back very soon, and maybe not more than seven days will pass first, but if she is very bad and does not get strong for a long time Cham will wait until she does, and that may be a month or even two months from now," the man said it all in one unbroken stream of words.

"But," he continued after taking a breath, "I hope it is not going to be that way, for I want my sister to get well fast, and I also want Cham to come back so he can help me dig coal and catch the fish we will eat next winter, because we must catch them when they run, and sometimes they only run once a year, so if we miss them, then we do not have another chance, and the only meat for us will be smoked meat and foxes, and I do not like either very well, especially the way a fox tastes after it is cooked."

"How do you preserve the fish?" Lew asked curiously.

"Some of them we hang up over a fire and smoke until they are hard and dry, and then we hang them from the ceiling of this room near the stove so they don't become damp, but most of the fish we catch are put in barrels with much salt and some water, and that way they stay good for two years, only we have to soak them a long time to get the salt out before we can eat them."

"Will Cham take us to the big island in his boat when he gets back?" Charlie asked.

"I cannot say for sure about that, because Cham is very stubborn and he has strange ideas and does not like to use his boat more than he can help, because it burns a lot of gasoline, but I think if you will pay him for the gasoline and then give him some more money besides, that he will take you, although this is only what I think and not what Cham may really do."

"We'll pay for the fuel and for his time," Charlie declared. "We can raise about a hundred and fifty dollars between us. Think that's enough?"

"It is a lot of money and it would be enough for me if I had a boat, and if Cham does not think it will be a good deal then Cham is a fool, which I have often thought and will now know for sure if he won't take you back to the big island."

Irene stood up.

"I can't stay awake any longer," she declared. "So if you'll excuse me, I'm going to bed."

Joe started to insist that she carry the one gasoline lamp to her room, but she told him the candle he had left burning inside was plenty bright enough. A couple of minutes after she had left them, she opened the door and said, "Charlie, will you help me with this belt buckle, please?"

Charlie went in and saw that the room was much smaller than the other with meager furnishings, just a wooden bed made of driftwood planks, a table with one drawer and a small cheap mirror hanging over it. The bed had the same kind of faded blue blankets and there were no curtains at either of the two windows. There was a row of nails in one wall to hang clothing.

It didn't look to Charlie like a woman had lived there, but the room was clean, and Charlie had to admit to himself he didn't know anything about Joe's sister. She may have been ignorant of or just indifferent to the little luxuries that so many women like to have around the house.

There was a second door at the other end of the room, which opened outside and on to the sea.

Irene pointed to it and whispered, "Neither door has a lock or a bolt. I don't like that."

"Are you afraid?" Charlie asked. He had seen that her belt was already unbuckled, off and lying on the bed.

"Just being cautious. I don't like to be disturbed when I sleep." She opened her kit bag, pulled out a little .25 pistol for Charlie to see and then dropped it back inside.

"I sleep very sound, and anybody could come in through that door without waking me if they moved quietly. If I wake up soon enough to use the gun, I'll be all right. But I'm afraid I won't."

"We can fix that," Charlie said.

He pointed to the heavy bed. "Can you lift one end?"

She demonstrated that she could, and they carried it over and set it down with the tall headpiece pressed solidly against the outside door.

"Now nobody is going to come through that door without waking you," Charlie said.

He took his knife from a pocket, went over to one of the windows to pick up a stick about a foot long that lay on the sill and that, apparently, was used to hold the sash open at the bottom. He whittled the stick into a long wedge.

"After I go out," he told her, "shove this wedge under the bottom of the other door. That will prevent you being surprised from that direction."

Both windows had locking bolts but no screens outside the glass. "You better leave them shut and bolted," Charlie said.

He looked around one more time, nodded and added, "If you suspect trouble, don't wait to yell out. We'll be sleeping only a few yards away."

When Charlie went back into the bigger room he saw Joe held a large bottle in his hand.

"It has been a bad day because you had so much trouble when your plane was wrecked and you drifted on the ocean in the rain, and I said to myself, 'Joe,' I said, 'you should give your guests a drink to help them forget their trouble,' but I thought I should wait until the Miss Lieutenant had gone to bed, because I do not think it is good for women to drink, as my sister never does, and while this is not the best liquor like you are used to, it is the best I have, and if you will pick up the cups on the table I will pour some for you."

"What is it?" Lew asked.

"It is vodka, and I made it myself from some of the potatoes we raised in a little garden behind the house, and I have a small still, which works so slow, yet it makes enough for Cham and I to have a drink when we come home soaked with rain."

While Lew and Charlie weren't drinkers, they didn't want to

alert Cham to their suspicions by turning down such a natural act of simple hospitality.

Charlie nodded, and the liquor he poured out of the 1-gallon glass bottle was absolutely colorless. It was potent, too, for while it went down easily, the reaction that followed when it hit their stomachs was almost violent.

They sipped carefully, and when they had each finished a generous cupful, declined to accept any more. Joe urged them to do so, but when they kept refusing, he poured himself a second draft and tossed it casually down his throat.

They sat before the stove for a short time after that.

Lew's stomach was pleasantly warmed, and he was starting to feel like he ought to go places, at least outside and shout a little. When he saw Joe start to unlace his boots, Lew followed his example and set his own damp footwear back of the stove.

Joe took one blanket from the bed and spread it on the floor saying he would sleep there.

They would have been more comfortable letting him have the bed, but they didn't want to start any more long-winded dissertations. They were very tired and sleepy. Besides, they had won the dispute, if it could be called that, about the second drink and didn't want to stretch their luck.

Joe turned the lamp off.

There were two windows in the room, but Joe made no move to open either. Charlie and Lew would have appreciated a bit of fresh air, but Joe was their host, and they contented themselves by thinking that the little stove would draw out some of the air.

Joe had stoked it well with blocks of coal.

There was no moon outside, and the only light inside the room was the little ring-shaped glow on the floor below the stove's loosely fitted door.

Joe started to breathe heavily a minute after he wrapped the blanket about his thick body. Charlie and Lew went to sleep soon after that, but each had fixed the idea in his mind not to sleep too soundly or too long, and that fixation was probably the reason Charlie awoke later with the memory of a very bad dream in his mind.

In that dream some very large animal was sitting on his chest. The weight was suffocating him, and worse yet, the beast was covering his nostrils with its hot breath while it sucked the breath out from the very bottom of his lungs.

Charlie automatically thrust both hands over his chest when he did awaken. There was nothing sitting on it, of course, save the single layer of blanket.

He tried to sit up. The dream was gone but not the terrible pressure across his lungs. He was gasping for air.

There was a queer smell in the room, too. His eyes seemed to be glued shut or else the lids were just too heavy for his tired strength to lift.

He tried again to sit up, and this time he barely made it, swinging both feet down to the floor. He somehow got his eyes open and looked across the room. Something was different than it had been before he went to sleep.

His dulled mind couldn't grasp it at first; then he saw that the little ring of light under the stove was gone.

The odorous air in the room was choking him.

He flung back the blanket and staggered across the floor. His fingers felt along the hot pipe of the stove until they reached the damper in the joint just above the drum oven. It was turned flat, completely shut. He opened it and flung the feed door wide. He could see a little better now.

Joe's blanket lay on the floor, empty.

Charlie lurched over to the outside door, holding his breath as long as he could, and swung it open. He gulped the fresh air for a moment then ran back to the bed. Lew was breathing with short rasping breaths. Charlie grabbed his shoulders and jerked him upright. The deadly coal gas was draining out of the room fast now, through the door and the opened stove.

He tried to drag Lew out of the bed but didn't have enough strength. Still, he tugged at his companion's arms.

Finally, Lew leaned forward, and when Charlie jerked at the same moment, they both sprawled over on the floor. Lew began to grumble, and then he swore.

Charlie knew, now, that he had been very close to the dangerous stupor that is a part of asphyxiation.

Lew sat up, flinging his fist in a wide arc. Charlie barely dodged the roundhouse punch.

"What's going on?" Lew demanded, his rumbling voice thick and hoarse.

"Get up and come to the door," Charlie ordered. "We just escaped being suffocated with gas from the coal stove."

"Where's Joe?"

"I don't know. But he's gone."

Lew made it to the door, and with the room filling with fresh air, Charlie was starting to feel all right. He pulled on his pants and shoes. Then he picked up his pistol and started out the door.

Then he thought about Irene. The partition between the rooms was pretty tight, but some of the gas could have seeped through.

He rapped on her door but got no responses. Then he pounded and shoved hard against the panel. But the wedge he had whittled and that she had shoved under it held fast. He pounded harder and shouted her name. Then, when he had decided to go outside and break one of the windows in her room, she answered.

"What is it?" Her voice was heavy with sleep.

"Joe turned the stove damper off too much and coal gas leaked out. Any get in there?"

"I don't think so."

"You'd smell it if it did," Charlie said. "How do you feel? Got a headache?"

His own head was splitting.

"No," she replied. "I feel all right. Just sleepy."

"Go back to sleep then. I fixed the stove, and we are airing out our room."

"Where's Joe?"

"Gone."

There was a pause. "Shall I get up?"

"No need. I'd rather you stayed here. I'm going out to look for Joe. But Lew will be staying in the house, too."

Lew still stood in the doorway soaking in fresh night air.

"Joe do it on purpose?" he asked.

"Probably. Though it could have been an accident. He was drinking, and the damper turns very easily in the pipe. It may have even slipped shut. But it looks bad, of course, because Joe is gone.

"I'm going out to look around. If Joe comes back before me, keep an eye on him but just say I went outside, couldn't sleep, the room was too hot or something. Don't mention the coal gas. At least, not tonight. If he's a bad egg, we want to keep him guessing a little longer. He'll be easier to handle that way."

"I can handle him right now," Lew declared.

Charlie shook his head. "Don't start anything."

He went outside and walked down to the edge of the sea. The moon had come out; it hung bright and high in the sky. The shoreline seemed to be solid rock, and Charlie was wondering where Joe and Cham could store the boat. He found out after he had followed the beach a few hundred feet. There was a deep, narrow inlet cutting back into the land to form a perfect small harbor. Charlie could hear the roar of heavy surf beyond its mouth, indicating the entrance was protected by an outside reef, and even a small craft tied up here could weather some heavy storms.

There was a small boat moored on the other side of the inlet. It was an open craft and empty. Charlie walked along the side of the harbor, around its end and back to the coast again. The ground below began to grow higher, and after a bit, he walked along the crest line of a moderately tall cliff.

Up ahead he caught sight of a dark spot. Soon, it began to look suspiciously like a man squatting on his heels or on his knees. Charlie stopped, took off his heavy shoes and backed down away from the top of the cliff. Then, with shoes in one hand and his pistol in the other, he moved in. His sock-covered feet made no noise whatsoever. He had to go within thirty-five feet of the object before he saw that it actually *was* a man and that the man was Joe.

He was rocked back on his heels holding a pair of binoculars to his eyes with both hands. He was moving his head methodically, sweeping a section of night-blanketed horizon with slow, regular swings of the glass.

Chapter 7 – Charlie Opens a Grave

Charlie stood on the cliff for several minutes, watching Joe search the sea with his binoculars. Charlie couldn't see the glasses plainly, but they seemed to be very large in size. He knew that to be of any practical use in such bad light, they would necessarily be of the "night" type of very high grade. It seemed strange that a common trapper would own such expensive equipment.

Charlie backed away, stopped at a safe distance to replace his shoes. When he reached the little natural harbor he went up to the small boat moored there. It was about twenty feet long and built like a New England dory.

Rough steps cut in the rock made an easy path, and Charlie followed them down and stepped into the craft.

He saw a large outboard motor clamped on the stern. The motor was well covered with lashed-on canvas to protect it from the rain. He tried to note the manufacturer's nameplate but couldn't find it without removing the cover, and he didn't want to do that. But the outboard was evidently a very powerful job.

The boat was empty except for a pair of oars tied on the inside of the gunwales. It smelled strongly of fish.

Charlie climbed back up the bank and started toward the house. He was about halfway there when he stopped to listen. It seemed like there was some noise out in the sky over the sea that wasn't made by the surf. He stood there a minute wishing he had Lew's keen sense of hearing.

But the sound didn't increase, and he wondered if he had been mistaken in thinking a plane had passed close to the island.

"What do you think Joe is looking for?" Lew asked him a little later.

"It could be his brother-in-law," Charlie replied. "You know he said Cham liked to travel at night."

"Sure. But it fits in too well. Are you going to ask him when he comes back?"

"It's none of our business. We're just castaways, guests. He took us in, fed us and gave us a place to sleep. Really, we've been treated fine. He even gave us drinks of homemade vodka."

Lew shuddered.

"My stomach still burns from that. And don't forgot that after pouring drinks, Joe also tried to suffocate us with coal gas by shutting off the damper in the stovepipe. I don't think that's mentioned in my book on entertaining guests."

"I haven't forgotten," Charlie assured him.

They closed the door and got back in bed.

Joe came in about an hour later. A faint creaking of the salt-rusted hinges of the door was the only sound. He seemed to have his shoes off because he walked across the plank floor also without making a sound. There was enough light to reveal him as a dim, rather shapeless shadow. Joe went to the stove, opened it, laid several blocks of coal on the fire, turned around and started towards them with his cat-like tread.

Charlie felt Lew's hand go towards the pistol lying under his coat. Charlie already had wrapped his fingers around his own gun. But Joe crept by them and went to the door of Irene's room. He remained there for what seemed a very long time.

They couldn't see if he was trying to shove the door open or if he was just listening with his ear against it. Finally, he came back to his blanket beside the stove. They heard him snore soon after.

When they awoke in the morning the sky had cleared and the sun, although still dim, was definitely in sight.

Joe was gone again, but this time his blanket lay neatly folded on one end of a bench. He returned before they had finished dressing, with his hat in his hands. It was almost filled with eggs.

Joe smiled brightly.

"We will have these duck eggs for our breakfast," he said, "and I am sure you will like them, as they are only one day old, because I went to the nests yesterday morning and took out the egg each duck laid the day before, which is a regular job for me because there are so many sea ducks who use this island for their nesting place, and after I have found a nest I gather the egg from it every day, only I have to leave one egg or the duck will not come back, so I leave an old egg, which I know because I have put a mark on it which is too small for the duck to see and become alarmed, and I think it is a nice thing a duck cannot count or she would wonder why her nest never becomes full and would go away and build a new one."

Joe paused but it was only to catch up on his breathing.

"I hope you slept well and feel rested after your hard day and I hope the nice lieutenant also slept good, and it is time for breakfast, so if you will ask her if she can come out soon I will cook the smoked meat which is much like the ham Americans eat at breakfast and will be fine with the eggs, and you will have the kind of food you are used to eating in the morning."

Irene opened her door and said, "Go ahead with breakfast, Joe. But could I have some water? I don't want to come out until I have washed. I'm a regular sight."

There was a pail on the shelf back of the stove and Lew picked it up. "I'll get the water," he said and started towards the little door leading out into the storeroom and cistern.

Joe's smile had widened when Irene spoke his name, but it sort of went fixed now. He stepped quickly forward and took the pail from Lew's fingers. "My guests must not carry water," he said. "Sit down and I will get some for the Miss Lieutenant."

He almost pushed Lew towards the bench. His hands seemed very strong, and Lew sat down a bit surprised.

Joe beamed at him and then went out to the cistern. Irene met him at her door and took the pail. That reminded Charlie and Lew that they could use a wash, too, and when they mentioned it Joe took a second pail out and filled it for them.

Joe handled the frying pan skillfully. The smoked meat had a little mold on it, but he scraped that off and cut a large number of very thin slices. He browned them on both sides then put a little water in the pan, covered it, and let it cook slowly.

He surprised them by breaking each duck egg carefully into a cup for examination before he put it into a larger bowl with the rest.

"He's probably had some bad luck with eggs that stayed in the nest too long," Lew whispered to his companion.

Irene joined them soon after.

She had done a pretty good job with her hair, combing out the tight little curls to let it flow down over her shoulders. Her cheeks were pink from the cold water and scrubbing, and possibly from the skilled application of a little rouge.

Lew thought that, in spite of her being a little thinner than he might have preferred, she was quite attractive.

"You can have my vote as pinup girl for the castaway club anytime," he smiled at her.

"Don't be silly," she said, but she didn't seem displeased.

Joe frowned a little at this idle talk and looked at them with puzzled eyes. But when Charlie laughed, he joined in and then turned to Irene.

"Hello. You look very nice and I am glad because I know you slept fine in the hard bed that is my sister's, and I was afraid you might not because it has a mattress that is nothing but a bag filled with dead grass which gets hard after a little time, and I think it is time to put new grass in, which I will do when the rain stops."

The duck eggs had a strong flavor, like the eggs of most sea birds. But Joe had fried them in the meat grease until their edges were crisp, and they were seasoned well.

After they had eaten, Joe said, "I think it would be very nice if we went out to fish in the sea today, because I do not have many fish left, and you will have much fun since we will use the net to get small fish for bait, and while there is only one large rod, you can take turns using it while I run the boat."

"How big is your boat?" Lew asked.

Joe thought for a moment and said, "I think it is about as long as this room is wide, and it is funny I have never thought to measure it with a rule and it is something I must do soon."

"Think you could run down to the large island where your brother-in-law is?" Charlie asked casually.

Joe shook his head decisively.

"I could not do that because the sea is very rough and it is a hard journey with Cham's boat, which is two times as long as mine, and besides, there is not enough gasoline left and I have only enough to go out a little distance to fish, which must last until Cham comes back and brings more, and I hope he doesn't forget, which he does sometimes after he has drunk too much vodka."

"I don't think we want to go fishing," Charlie replied. "We had enough of the ocean yesterday, and we would rather take a walk with solid ground under our feet. Why don't you fish while we walk back in the timber and look for fox signs?"

"You are my guests and you will do just the things you like to do, so I will put off fishing and not go today but go tomorrow when you may have changed your mind, and I will be very glad to walk with you and show you the island, for you maybe will want to see the place we mine coal and where the seals lay on the rocks and where I killed an otter."

"Don't bother," Charlie said crisply. "We're not going to take up all of your time because I know you have work that must be done. We'll go alone and be out of your way for a few hours to give you a chance to catch up."

Joe started to protest, but Charlie grabbed Lew with one hand and Irene's arm with the other and hurried them towards the door. As he went through it, Charlie turned and waved a hand cheerfully to Joe and the three walked briskly off.

Irene breathed deep with relief. "This is going to save my sanity," she told them. "That man was driving me mad with his oily smiles and the smirks he keeps turning on me. They're worse than his endless gabble. How long do you think we'll be stranded here?"

"Until his brother-in-law returns," Charlie replied. "Unless Joe will sell us the small boat. It's a dory and very seaworthy. It could make the three hundred miles to the big island all right."

"If there is a big island," Lew added.

"That's right." Charlie's face was thoughtful. "I know Joe's a liar, either a dumb one or a very clever one. In either case, we can't depend on what he tells us about miles and directions."

"My suggestion of last night still stands," Lew said.

"What is that?" Irene asked.

"We immobilize Joe and take the boat. We can pay him for it if we wish."

They had walked straight inland and away from the house towards the line of timber. The fog was lifting fast, and the trees were clearly outlined against the sky.

"We'd have to pay for the boat," Charlie insisted. "We can't steal stuff in our business. Maybe we better make him a generous offer. He has already said Cham might refuse to run us across to the big island when he gets back."

"If there is such a person as Cham," Lew said.

"You are a skeptic, all right," Irene told him. "How do you know I'm really a WAC and not an enemy agent?"

"I don't," Lew said calmly. "You haven't shown us any of your credentials."

She reached for her shoulder bag.

"Papers don't mean much," Lew said shaking his head. "They're easily forged."

That made her mad. "You think I'm a liar?"

"I didn't say that, either. I said you could be, and it would be pretty bad if you were because then we'd have to shoot you, and I'd hate to do it since you are so nice looking."

Then he stopped and declared, "Good Lord! I'm starting to sound like Joe. That loose mouth disease of his must be catching."

They both laughed at that. But a little later when they had reached the timber and had turned to walk parallel with it and the beach, she said, "You don't really think I'm a fake, do you?"

Lew grinned.

"The only thing about you I'm sure of is you're female. Your persistency proves that."

A pit hollowed out of the rocky soil turned out to be Joe's coal mine. It was an open strip mine, of course, where the thin vein of coal pushed up to within a yard of the surface.

The visible coal was crisscrossed with numerous small seams, which would easily separate before the pressure of a bar and break up into the blocks Joe fed into his stove. There was a shovel leaning on the opposite bank of the pit.

"I wouldn't chop wood, either, if I could dig coal this easily," Charlie said.

"Coal's handier, too, when you want to get rid of unwelcome guests," Lew added.

"You didn't tell me about that," Irene said.

Charlie gave her the details without any of the speculation. Then they left the mine and turned out towards the sea.

Charlie wanted to examine the cliff Joe had used in the night to search the ocean with binoculars. But before they reached the cliff, they stumbled on something showing more evidence of digging but which was decidedly not a mine.

It was a small, rounded mound of earth about six feet long. They stopped, regarded it, and then Charlie said gravely, "Bring that shovel from the coal pit, Lew."

They waited in silence until Lew returned.

Charlie expected the digging would be very shallow because of the nature of the ground, and it was. The shovel struck something that wasn't dirt or stone before he had gone three feet down.

He uncovered it carefully, already knowing exactly what he was going to find. The odor that came out of the hole told him he was right.

He exposed the badly decomposed body of a man, short in stature with a heavy crown of long, straight, dark hair.

Irene backed off.

"Don't dig any more," she said sharply. "We know it's a corpse. Fill the grave and leave him alone."

Charlie still plied the shovel. The stench was terrible.

Finally, Lew backed up Irene's protest.

"Haven't we seen enough?"

"No," Charlie said, "we haven't. If I'm right, there's another body under this one."

Charlie pushed the first body over with the blade of the shovel. Below it was another, and the clothing wrapped around this body was pretty well preserved, enough for them to see it had belonged to a woman.

"Joe would probably tell us that these are the bodies of people washed ashore from some other shipwreck," Charlie said slowly. "But I think we've found all that is left of Cham, the real trapper, and his wife.

Chapter 8 – A Hidden Cache

As Charlie shoveled dirt back over the bodies he had discovered in the shallow grave, Irene asked, "If this is Cham, the real fox trapper, and his wife, then who is Joe?"

"Joe is the man who murdered them," he said. "Look."

Charlie prodded gently at the head of the top body with his shovel point, uncovering the thick black hair to expose the dark skin underneath. In the center of the forehead there was a small-caliber bullet hole.

"There'll be one in the other head, too," he added.

"For God's sake, don't look," Irene exclaimed. Her face paled and she turned about with her back to the grave.

"I won't," Charlie assured her. "There isn't any need now."

Then he began shoveling dirt in the hole again.

"What makes you so sure Joe killed them?" Lew asked.

"He's the only one we've seen. So far as we know, the island is uninhabited except for Joe. He has told us as much. And the bullet hole matches his rifle. It's an 8mm Mauser, you know."

"What reason would he have to kill them?" Irene persisted.

"That's what we're going to find out."

"How can you be so sure?" she replied. "There could be so many reasons for this. Joe said he didn't want to stay here but had to because Cham owns the boat. They may have quarreled about that. Or how the money they received for their fox skins should be divided. You know you have no authority here. Joe said he was a native of Siberia."

"Joe said a lot that don't bear up under a little logic," Lew reminded her.

"If this was a quarrel between a couple of trappers," Charlie replied. "I admit we have no authority. But I'm going to be sure it was that and nothing more important."

"Such as?"

"Well, there is a war going on. I have to know what Joe tried to see last night when he sat on the cliff with binoculars."

"He couldn't see anything at night," Irene sounded impatient.

"Oh, yes, he could," Lew cut in. "They make night glasses that are very effective, and it would be easy to pick up light signals with them. We were giving Joe the benefit of the doubt that he might be watching for his brother-in-law's return. But that doesn't hold up if this is Cham in the grave."

Charlie threw the last shovel of dirt over the little mound and patted it flat.

As he straightened something zipped over his head and smacked into the steep bank behind.

In quick succession, two more bullets followed the first, each hitting the dirt and rock background. The sounds of the three shots reached them almost simultaneously.

They dropped flat to the ground. There were a few boulders scattered around, and that made a fair screen of protection. But a dozen small trees about fifty feet to the left looked better to Charlie.

"Get ready to run for the trees," he said. "Keep about six feet apart when you start. Don't bunch up and give him an easy target."

They jumped up and started running. They expected to be fired upon again but there were no more shots. They ran through the little group of trees and dropped down at the far edge.

"Somebody doesn't like us," Lew said, grinning.

"I suppose you think Joe was shooting at us," Irene said.

Lew turned his grin towards her.

"I know it was. But you aren't fooling me anymore. You think it was him, too, only you're trying to start an argument by pretending to think differently so we'll give out what we know."

She smiled but didn't deny his logic.

"Since you're so smart, Lew, how do you know it was Joe?" Charlie asked. "It looked like poor shooting to me, and I don't figure Joe out as a bum marksman."

"Joe couldn't help those misses, because it wasn't his fault. You saw how the three bullets hit the bank at the same level? They were lined up, too, one exactly above each of our heads."

Charlie nodded and grinned himself.

"Okay, let's have it."

"Well," Lew began with a grin, "last night after we awoke and found coal gas in the room, you went out to look for Joe. While you were gone I noticed he had left his rifle inside, which was a very poor decision on his part.

"I picked the gun up and changed the elevation of the rear sight. You remember it was a high-grade sight with click adjustments for each direction? I moved it four clicks, which I figured would not be enough for him to notice but still might save our lives if Joe started shooting at us. And it did, because he did."

"That was smart!" Irene exclaimed.

"Sure," Lew admitted modestly.

"What are we going to do now?" she asked.

"We're in a jam," Charlie replied. "Looks like we must hide out in the woods and dodge Joe when he comes looking for us. And he'll come, all right. He tried to murder us, and he can't stop in the middle of that kind of job. He has to finish us. It won't be much fun, either, matching pistols against a rifle. He'll know something was wrong, and he'll check the sight and fix it."

"We must leave, then," Irene said. "Joe has our rubber raft but we can take his boat and start tonight."

"We can try. But Joe isn't as dumb as he has tried to make us believe. He is going to watch his boat pretty closely, and especially after dark."

"Then what are we going to do?" she insisted.

Joe himself saved Charlie answering that one.

The little harbor where the boat was tied sat less than a half-mile away, and they heard the roar of the powerful outboard motor when it started. Lew got up and ran to the edge of the trees, and Irene and Charlie followed.

He couldn't see the boat because it lay too low in the water, but he could see a man's head moving along behind the top of the bank. The boat apparently had started out to sea.

A moment later, they all saw the craft emerge from the harbor's neck, turn sharply left to avoid the reef of rocks protecting it, and then it turned again into the opening through the barrier and headed straight out to sea.

They watched until it was only a speck on the horizon.

"Come on," Charlie said. "We've got a job to do."

"What job?" Irene asked.

"We're going to take that house apart. And when we do, I'm guessing we'll find things."

"Are you sure the man in the boat was Joe?"

"Sure enough. Anyway, we have to take that chance."

They went back to the house fast. When they reached the door, Charlie said, "You two stay outside until I find out if there's anyone inside. Keep out of line of the doorway, too."

The door was unlocked, as he expected. A swift look through the two rooms showed them to be empty. Lew and Irene came in.

"Irene, I want you to watch the windows and doors so Joe can't surprise us. You'll have to cover all sides of the house and that means moving back and forth constantly."

"Right," she said smartly. She already had the small-bore automatic pistol in her hand.

Charlie opened the door leading into Joe's storeroom.

"Remember how he insisted on bringing water out of here himself? We're going to find what we want in here."

"What are you looking for?" Irene asked. She had opened the outside door and was looking out and around in all directions. Then she closed it and stepped to a window.

Charlie didn't answer, just walked into the storeroom.

It was quite dark because there were no openings in the walls to admit sunlight. Charlie picked up Joe's gasoline lamp and lit it. The room was about twenty feet square with almost a third of the floor space filled by a low, wide tank made of stones and cement. The walls were crooked and uneven and ended in a wide top covered with boards. A short piece of pipe with a faucet stuck out on one side near the bottom.

Charlie climbed up the side of the tank, found the boards loose, pushed several aside and looked in.

It was half full of water. Apparently, the cistern was no more than it appeared to be. He dropped back on the floor.

Lew was searching along the shelves of a cupboard built at the other side of the room. There were eight shelves and most were filled with small bags and boxes. The bags held flour, beans and rice. The boxes contained a good grade of canned vegetables. The labels, they noticed, were American. At the end of one shelf lay three long sides of smoked meat.

Surprisingly enough, everything inside the storeroom was quite dry. One would expect a cistern filled with cool water to sweat and turn the contents of the room damp, but the flour sacks felt flexible and soft. None of them had that stiff glaze which comes from exposure to moisture.

So far, their search had revealed nothing suspicious. There was no space back of the cistern, since it was built directly against the wall. The ceiling was barely two feet over their heads, leaving no room for an attic. They pushed up against it and satisfied themselves it was the genuine roof of the structure.

The food cupboard had a backing of wood but no doors. Charlie started to empty its shelves, heaping the supplies upon the floor. When it was empty they grasped the front edge near one end and pulled. The structure apparently was perfectly solid. But Charlie motioned to the opposite end.

They grabbed that and jerked. The entire cupboard swung out about four feet, pivoting around the secure end. There was room enough behind it for a man to enter.

They walked through the opening and saw a rough stone wall with an opening about four by six feet hewed from the center. The opening was very dark. Charlie went back, picked up the lamp he had set on the floor and carried it through.

"Wow!" Lew exclaimed. "We found it all right."

Irene heard him and ran in. "What did you find?"

They didn't have to answer.

Anyone with eyes could see the answer.

The opening before them ran at least forty feet back, and beyond the doorway it widened abruptly to form a capacious room, which had either been excavated from rock or had been made of huge slabs of stone. The walls were crossed with seams, which could be either man-made seams or faults caused by nature.

Along one side was a tall stack of metal drums marked with queer characters brushed on in black paint. Charlie and Lew couldn't read them but knew the containers were filled with gasoline. A faint odor of the stuff in the close space told them that.

On the other side of the room was a large rack made of very stout timbers and divided into twenty compartments. Eight of these spaces were empty, but the remaining twelve were filled with long, slim, metal cylinders.

"Torpedoes!" Irene exclaimed.

"Correct," Lew concluded. "Naval torpedoes."

"Then Joe is running a supply base for submarines?"

"Not subs," Charlie said. "These are the medium-sized torpedoes used by naval patrol boats. One of them shot our plane down yesterday, you remember. The harbor is big enough for such a boat to anchor while the crew takes on fuel and ammunition, and there's the dolly cart they use to roll out the tin fish. It's a long pull, but the Japanese soldiers don't mind hard work."

"Not a bad layout," Lew acknowledged grudgingly.

"This island isn't as close to Siberia as Joe wanted us to believe. It must be pretty close to the shipping route between Seattle and Dutch Harbor. From here, a patrol boat could raid our shipping and raise the devil with unarmed freighters and tankers."

Charlie walked on past the torpedo rack.

"Here's a grub supply for the crew," he said.

Lew was patting the end, not the fuse nose, of a torpedo.

"I'd like to plant this in the harbor so that patrol boat would bump into it the first time she returns."

Charlie examined the pile of cases.

"It isn't all grub," he said. "Part is ammunition. Shells for machine guns and anti-aircraft cannon."

Irene was frowning.

"Joe didn't look Japanese," she said doubtfully.

Lew laughed. "Looks don't mean much anymore."

He was thinking about their experiences along the Alaska highway, with Japanese soldiers whose faces had been changed by plastic surgery.

"Joe might be Korean," Charlie said. "Or a Siberian as he said. There will be traitors in every country when war comes. I guess we've even got some in our own."

"There's only one thing to do," Charlie said soberly. "We must destroy this stuff. It's the surest way to put that patrol boat out of business. She will be helpless without fuel and ammunition."

"That will be quite a job, won't it?" Irene asked.

"No," Charlie replied. "An easy one. All we have to do is open up a few gasoline drums, fix up a fuse that will fire it a few minutes later, and then get away from here as fast as we can."

"A few minutes isn't enough leeway for me," Lew objected. "There'll be one heck of a blowup when these tin fish let loose. One can sink a ship, and there's an even dozen here. Shall I start unscrewing the plugs?"

Charlie examined a drum. It had a square-headed cap screwed in the end close to the rim. "If we can find a wrench to fit, we won't have to waste any time."

Searching, they found not one wrench but four leaning in a neat row against the end of the tier of drums.

Lew suddenly remembered something.

"Say," he said to Irene, "what are you doing in here? You are supposed to be watching the windows."

"That would not have done any good," a voice said.

Startled, they whirled around.

A figure stepped out from behind the pile of brown ammunition boxes at the rear of the arsenal. It was Joe. But a different Joe than they had seen before. The loose smile was gone from his face. It didn't look flabby now as it had before. The features were hard and firm, and the black eyes shone dangerously in the lamp light.

Joe held his short-barrel Mauser rifle at the level of his belt, the muzzle pointed slightly upwards at Charlie's heart.

Chapter 9 – Trapped!

Charlie was the only one of the three who made no outward sign of surprise when Joe stepped out from behind the pile of ammunition and food boxes and covered them with his rifle.

He was surprised, naturally, but his main feeling was quick, sharp anger at his own carelessness in being so hopelessly trapped. Irene gave a low cry of alarm and backed away from the menacing gun. Lew had been faced the other way, and he whirled around, one hand moving for the pistol in his pocket. But when he saw the Mauser and its position, he stiffened and stood motionless.

Joe looked mostly at Charlie.

"You couldn't keep your nose out of my business," he said in a flat tone. "Or maybe this is your business, too."

"What do you mean?" Charlie asked, sounding puzzled.

"You're American soldiers. I know that. You didn't fool me by not being in uniform. You don't have to pretend any longer."

"I never did," Charlie replied calmly.

Joe frowned as if he was swiftly reviewing the past events.

"You did all the pretending," Charlie added, and the man's frown deepened.

"I saw you burn papers in the stove last night," he finally said.

"Sure," Charlie replied. "They were our stuff and we had a right to burn them if we chose. I suppose you have a peak hole in the partition?"

Joe nodded.

"How the devil did you get in here?" Lew asked.

The cruel hardness in Joe's eyes was unmistakable, but Lew's voice was casual and even.

"Did you think there was but one door?" Joe's terse speech contrasted sharply with his former rambling. "There's another through the rock behind you. Just a crevice covered with grass but very effective."

"No argument there," Lew admitted.

"We saw you start out in the boat and figured you would be gone at least an hour," Charlie said. He stood closer to Joe than either of his companions and he held the gasoline lamp shoulder high in his right hand.

The corners of Joe's mouth twitched a little like he might grin, but he didn't. "I wanted you to think that. It was such a poor trick I hardly expected it would fool you."

Charlie sighed. "I guess we were so anxious to search the house we didn't think straight," he said.

"Why?" Joe shot the word out so forcibly Irene jerked her head back.

"Why?" Charlie echoed. "You mean why we wanted to search the house. Well, there were several reasons." He spoke slowly, pleased with this chance to talk. It had looked at first like Joe would start shooting immediately. Most killing, Charlie knew, is done in the heat of excitement. If you can hold off a killer's impulse to shoot for a few moments right at the start, you have a fair chance of causing a longer delay.

"I suppose it was finding the two bodies in that grave that brought my suspicions to a head. That clinched them, although they had really begun before."

"Tell me," Joe said. It was an order, not a request.

Charlie was perfectly willing

"Sure," he said. "First was your admiration or simulated admiration for Lieutenant Kelton. Mostly, the simple dog-like way you kept looking at her. You overplayed that badly. I don't mean the Lieutenant is hard to look at," Charlie heard her gasp a little then, "for she isn't. But you didn't get the right touch in your acting."

"Perhaps not." Joe's voice sounded a little chagrined. "What else did I do wrong?"

"There was too much contrast between what you tried to make us believe and what you actually were. I mean, you tried to act like a slow-witted almost dumb person, the sort you thought a real trapper would be. But, on the other hand, you were very efficient in everything you did. You didn't make wasted motions. You were a skilled cook, a surprisingly neat housekeeper. The average trapper is often a bad cook and quite careless around the house. The two extremes didn't make sense at all to me."

"Go on. I am very interested."

Searching his face, Charlie saw the man actually was. He did want to know, and badly, just how he had failed to make them believe in his role of a trapper of foxes. Charlie began to wonder why. Could Joe be vain? Or was he seeking information so he could act more convincingly next time? That phrase "next time" didn't sound very good to Charlie.

"About the worst was when you told me about taking our raft home to care for it so the owner would give you a dollar," Lew said. He had to get into the conversation since talking always made him feel easier under danger.

"That dollar stuff was terrible. I swallowed it then because there was just a chance you were so dumb. But your talk began to get better right along. You rambled on in one great long sentence but there were always facts and reasons behind what you said."

Joe looked briefly at him and then turned his eyes back to Charlie. But that didn't fool Lew into believing he could make a swift pass for his pistol without being shot.

He had been thinking over the chances of drawing his gun and letting off one before Joe could swing his short rifle the few inches necessary to cover him. Those chances seemed too poor and too few to risk.

He might have to take them anyway. He had also figured on that. He would get shot, of course. But in the meantime, Charlie could get his own gun out and finish off Joe. Charlie still had the lamp in his right hand. That was bad, Lew figured, since he would have to get rid of it before he could draw.

"Anything else?" Joe prompted.

"Your pretended ignorance of geography," Charlie said after a pause. "It was too big for anybody who had traveled as much as you claimed. I knew, too, that this island wasn't nearer to Siberia than to the American coast. My guess is it lies pretty close to the shipping lane between Seattle and Dutch Harbor."

He waited, hoping Joe would either deny or confirm this statement. But Joe didn't.

So, after another pause, Charlie continued.

"It wasn't any one of these things, you know, it was the combination of them all. Just a case of overacting, as I said before."

Still, Joe didn't break his silence. But, in spite of his bleak eyes and almost blank face, they got the impression he was thinking at a tremendous rate.

Charlie knew he had to keep talking. He didn't dare let the

silences grow too long.

"I've told you quite a lot," he said. "Suppose you give us some information, too."

Joe nodded promptly. "Why not?" he said.

"Did you intend to suffocate us last night with coal gas or did the pipe damper get closed by accident?"

"I closed it. I didn't care much if the gas killed you or if it just put you in a stupor so you wouldn't know I went out. That was another error. I might have known that you would probably wake up when the gas became strong in the room. But it doesn't make any difference now."

None of them liked the way he said that.

Lew started to move a foot to change his balance, then stopped when Joe quickly shifted the rifle. Irene stood beside him and slightly behind Charlie, and he could hear her breathing rapidly. He hadn't noticed that before, and he wondered if she was going to crack. So far, her self-control had been impressive.

"Maybe you'll tell us what you were looking for last night with your binoculars?" Charlie asked.

"Why not?" Joe said again.

"I was watching for signals from the patrol boat. They often flash out a message when they arrive at night."

Something in Joe's tone and in his eyes warned Lew that the end was very near.

"I guess it's now or never," Lew thought. "It's going to be bad getting hit with a high power rifle at such short range, but this is our only chance."

He took a deep breath and was tensing his muscles for a swift move when a piercing scream smashed at his eardrums and froze his hands. The din was truly awful in the low-roofed room.

Joe's eyes darted towards Irene, and he instinctively swung the rifle to cover her.

At the same instant, Charlie hurled the gasoline lamp into Joe's face with a short arm heave. Charlie had a lot of strength in his arms, and he put plenty of power into that heave.

Lew started to get his pistol, changed his mind, and, stooping, swept up the heavy steel wrench used to unscrew the bung caps of the gasoline drums. He jumped forward swinging the tool.

Joe's rifle blasted. The flame scorched his face and deafened his ears. But the bullet somehow missed; at least Lew felt only the shock of the powder blast. He kept swinging, bringing the crude but brutal weapon down before Joe could chamber another cartridge in his rifle.

The room was pretty dark because the gasoline lamp had fortunately gone out instead of exploding when it hit the floor after smashing into Joe's face. Regardless, Lew was still blinded by the flash of the rifle shot, and he had to trust to memory about where the man stood.

The blow landed. It missed Joe's head but hit at the spot where shoulder and neck join. There was a sharp snap, and Joe tumbled backwards then hit the floor hard.

"Get the rifle," Lew said, rubbing his eyes.

Charlie seized the Mauser.

He thought they were marvelously lucky the lamp hadn't broken when it hit Joe; otherwise, the flash from the rifle would have exploded its spilled contents. That flash had burned out before the lamp had splintered on the floor and released its deadly charge of fuel. But now the room was a veritable tinder box, packed with death and disaster in the form of twelve big naval torpedoes, the tons of gasoline, and piles of boxes filled with small arms and cannon ammunition.

Charlie bent over Joe and ran his hands along his clothes, searching for another weapon. There wasn't any. So, after looking carefully around to see that no spark or tiny blaze existed that could kindle the gas fumes rapidly filling the room, he picked up Joe and lugged him out. He didn't dare drag him, for the heavy shoes might scrape against a stone in the floor and cause a spark like flint striking steel.

There was plenty of light in the outside room, and when they got there, he dumped the limp form on the floor.

"I think you broke his neck," Charlie said. "There isn't much chance he will ever bother us again, but I'll make sure."

He took a coil of small rope from the wall and lashed Joe's feet and wrists together. As he worked he spoke to Irene.

"That was great work, back there. The only thing that could have turned the tables. Joe had figured out every other trick we might try, but he had not prepared himself for that piercing scream. I will see to it you get a service medal, or two."

Color came into her white face.

"You weren't so bad yourself. I was afraid you might whirl around to see what made me yell out and forget to throw the lamp. If you had done that, then I would have only ruined any other plan you might have worked out."

"I was going to throw the lamp, anyway. It was the only thing that seemed even remotely liable to succeed. It would give Lew time to drag out his gun."

Lew sat down on a bench. His legs were a little insecure. You can't nonchalantly miss death by such a narrow margin as he had.

Irene looked down at Joe. "He's dead, isn't he?"

"I'm quite sure," Charlie said.

"This is the first time I ever saw a man killed," she said. "And I don't feel upset, either."

"Why should you?" Lew asked. "He wasn't exactly a lovable character. I'm not going to miss him."

"All right," Charlie said. "We've talked plenty, suppose we get to work. I want to leave the island quick. We'll use Joe's boat, but first it must be rigged out for a long trip. Irene, you pick out enough food to last at least two weeks. Take the emergency rations we brought in our raft. Get the rest from those boxes in the back room. Take stuff we won't have to cook."

"Yes sir!" she said smartly. Then she picked up the axe that stood in a corner of the room and went into the other room. The sounds coming from the storeroom indicated she was using the tool to break and pry the lids from wooden food containers.

"We'll roll a couple of drums of gasoline down to the boat," Charlie said. When they got to the craft, they found the outboard motor's tank completely full. So, they put the two drums inside the boat and went back to search for a funnel and smaller pail or can to use in transferring the fuel.

Irene had a pile of supplies on the kitchen floor. She filled the water bottle that had formed a part of their life raft's equipment and two pails. Lids from pots had been jammed down on top of the pails to prevent their contents slopping over.

Lew found a 5-gallon can of lubricating oil to mix with the outboard's fuel and added it to the heap.

Charlie searched the house quickly, hoping to find a map or chart that would help them navigate but had no success. He did find a hundred rounds of ammunition for Joe's Mauser, a cleaning rod and some thin oil.

He noticed Irene had brought out a two-pound package of tea well wrapped in lead foil bearing Japanese letters brushed over the outside wrappings. She said, "I thought we could stand the cold and rain better if we had a hot drink regularly."

"How are you going to heat water for tea?" Charlie asked.

"Haven't you ever gone on a picnic?" she asked. "All I need is a can half full of sand. Then I pour in a quarter cup of gasoline and light it. That will give plenty of heat to make tea. We could even cook eggs over that kind of fire."

"I can hunt for the duck nests Joe robbed each morning," offered Lew.

"We haven't time," Charlie said. He was impatiently walking back and forth studying the pile of goods. "Come, help me carry this stuff down to the boat."

Lew picked up an armful of canned foods and started for the door. When he reached it he stopped, letting the load slip from his arms onto the floor.

"What's the matter?" Charlie asked sharply.

"Plenty. We can't go now. It's too late. That Japanese patrol boat is pulling into the harbor."

Charlie sprang forward. There was a slim chance, he thought, that the boat wasn't Japanese. It might be Canadian or American navy. But it wasn't. When he peered through the doorway he saw the rising sun flag atop the short antenna mast. It was pushed forward stiffly by the offshore wind and very plain to see.

They were trapped!

Chapter 10 – Dead Man Decoy

Charlie jerked Lew back from the door and pushed it almost shut. "Keep away from the window," he warned Irene. "If you have to look out, come here." He was watching through the crack between the edge of the door and its frame.

The Japanese patrol boat had slipped through the gap in the outside reef. They watched her swing parallel to the rock barrier and race along it at a speed that sent white spray plunging off each side of the sharp bow. Charlie thought the craft was about seventy feet long. The hull had nice clean lines but the superstructure placed well forward looked clumsy and a bit top-heavy.

"We mustn't stand here watching it," Irene cried. "We're wasting time. Come on, hurry!"

"Hurry where?" Charlie asked.

"We can go out through the rear door in the rocks."

"Too late," Charlie replied. "They would see us before we ran a hundred yards."

The warship spun about, and with reduced speed, was heading into the little natural harbor where Joe's fishing boat lay moored.

"And they'd pick us off like sitting ducks with those machine guns," Lew added, pointing to the pair of rapid firers mounted near the bow between the two torpedo launching tubes lying along each side of the deck. There were two more guns, longer and heavier, sitting aft. Their breech ends were swathed in canvas covers and the muzzles pointed up. Charlie figured these were anti-aircraft cannon, probably 20mm bore. The machine guns, however, were stripped of covering and a man in a white uniform stood beside them.

"What will we do?" Irene demanded. "We can't stay here."

The ship eased carefully up to the bank. Two men jumped down from the deck with lines in their hands and took quick hitches about the short posts planted in the soil along the edge of the water.

"Yes, we can," Charlie said slowly. "That is the only thing to do now." He saw fear in her eyes and her lips were trembling. That surprised him; Irene didn't display her emotions so plainly.

"You are going to fight cannons with pistols and Joe's rifle?"

Charlie nodded. "And our heads. We have one advantage. They won't dare shoot into the storeroom. They need the stuff in it too badly, and one explosive shell could wreck everything."

"Including us," Lew said. Then he added, "You've got a plan, haven't you?"

"I'm beginning to get one."

Irene's lips ceased to tremble.

"All right," she said. "Just tell me what to do."

"You're okay," Lew reached over and squeezed her hand. "There's one thing you don't have to worry about. They won't make prisoners of us."

"Why not?"

"That stuff back there." Lew jerked his head towards the storeroom where the twelve naval torpedoes and scores of fuel drums were stacked. "I'll blow it up first. And we'll go along with it. Things will happen so quick you'll never feel it, and that's much better than some Japanese prison camp."

Her cheeks paled but she met his eyes steadily.

"I'm with you on that," she replied.

Three short whistle blasts came from the ship. The two sailors on land had finished making the ropes fast and stood beside them at attention. The men on deck were watching the house. Charlie tried to count the crew. He could see only six, counting the two that had landed. He didn't know how many men these boats carried but there wasn't room for more than ten at the most. There would be a commander and two torpedo men. The guns were mounted in pairs but each pair would need two men to both point and load, so he figured on four gunners. Then an engineer and helmsman, and possibly a steward to serve meals.

"Yes," Lew was saying. "I'm going to blow that storeroom sky high if Charlie's plan skids. Then the boat will be helpless. She's probably out of torpedoes and low on fuel now, or she wouldn't be here today. They'll be in a bad spot if we destroy it all."

He seemed almost happy over the thought.

The boat sounded three more sharp whistle blasts.

"They're getting impatient," Charlie said.

"Let's hear that plan of yours," Lew demanded. "There's something to do except just stand here waiting, isn't there?"

"You can clear the floor of the supplies Irene got out," Charlie replied. "Carry them back into the storeroom out of sight."

Lew's eyes narrowed. "We're going to let them come inside?"

"Maybe."

Lew grabbed at the boxes of canned food and the water pails.

"I've just got the beginning of a plan," Charlie continued. He was searching in the little cupboard back of the stove. "But I hope it will work into something good." He turned about and set Joe's vodka bottle on the table.

Again, the ship sounded the three whistle blasts.

"They're worse than impatient now," Lew said. "They're mad or suspicious or both because Joe didn't run down to meet them."

"They know he's home because his boat is tied up," Charlie added. "I don't like those two drums of fuel in it. They look like somebody was getting ready for a long cruise and Joe was probably ordered to stay pretty close." He bent over the body, stripped the ropes from hands and feet. "Help me," he told Lew.

They seized the dead man by the shoulders, dragged him over to the bench and lifted him up on it. The muscles were still flexible and it wasn't too hard to arrange Joe in a fairly natural position, head down on the table and both arms flung out over it. Charlie hung the pieces of rope back on the wall. He picked up a glass, poured it a third full of vodka and placed it with the bottle close to the right arm. Then he stepped back to appraise the picture.

"What do you think?" he asked.

"Looks all right," Lew said. "Just like a guy who sold his own capacity short." He leaned down to straighten one foot. "But I wonder if Joe had the habit of getting tight?"

"What happens now?" Irene asked.

"From now on everything depends on the sailors outside. They'll have to start something soon. Joe apparently is home but he won't answer their signal. So, I think they'll send up a patrol to find out why."

His guess was sound. The two sailors on land turned smartly about to face the boat. Another man handed down two guns. They wheeled again and came marching side by side along the beach to the house.

"Only two. That's a snap," Lew said. "But we can't make any noise when we take them. I'm going to get the wrench."

"Get one for me," Charlie said. He picked up the dead man's

Mauser, loaded it to capacity and handed it to Irene.

"You know how to use this rifle?"

"Of course. I had the small arms training course."

"Go back in the storeroom. Stand close to the door but keep out of sight. I think Lew and I can handle this pair but if we slip up on one, you'll have to shoot him. Don't let any of them get away."

"I won't," she promised. She faced him, cheeks pale, mouth tight, saluted and marched into the storeroom.

"I wish she'd stop that saluting business," Lew grumbled.

"She can't. It's an outlet for her emotions," Charlie whispered. "By keeping everything on a strictly military basis, she holds down her fears."

"I guess I should start saluting then," Lew replied. "I'm scared stiff, myself."

"I'm not so happy with how this business is playing out, either," Charlie said. "But don't let her see it."

The two sailors were pretty close, and their brisk pace had slowed to a cautious shuffle. Charlie and Lew stood by the door at its hinge edge. They didn't like that too well, because they were forced to stand very close together, but it was the only place in the room where they could escape detection through a window.

Fifty yards away the crewmen separated and circled the house in opposite directions. When they met behind the building they paused. A murmur of voices followed. Then there was the sound of feet approaching the door.

Lew gripped the heavy wrench between his knees a moment while he wiped the moisture from his palms. When the sailors finally stopped, they were so close Charlie smelled the rank odor of perspiration on their clothing. The door was still slightly open and Charlie thought he could feel the pressure of a hand against it when one of the men spoke sharply and the pressure apparently ceased. Then, to their intense surprise, the two sailors wheeled about and marched rapidly away.

Lew laid his wrench carefully on the floor. "I don't get it," he said. "Why didn't those monkeys come inside?"

"They probably had orders just to scout the place. Maybe they lack initiative."

They watched the sailors march up to the ship, come to attention and salute. "I think we'll get real action now," Charlie guessed.

They did. A third man jumped down from the deck. He started towards the house at a smart pace with the two sailors falling in behind. The three came straight to the door and halted a few paces away at a sharp command from the leader. A second command and both men stepped ahead and shoved hard on the panel. It swung open, pinning Charlie and Lew against the wall.

There was a third command, the men at the door spread apart and the leader stepped past them inside. He surveyed the room several long, silent seconds. Then he started barking in an angry voice. The two sailors came around and started towards Joe.

Charlie nudged Lew. They squeezed gently out from behind the door, thankful that the floor's driftwood planks were too solid to creak and betray them. The heavy wrenches came down with a swish. The leader and the sailor at his left collapsed under their terrible force. The third man, who was well out in the center of the room, whirled. His eyes bulged when he saw Charlie and Lew. He swung up his short, rapid-firing carbine, thrusting its muzzle at them. They saw the dark fingers tearing at a catch on the bolt's rear. He had made the fatal mistake of not slipping the safety stop as he came through the door.

Lew swung at the gun, hit its breech and sent it clattering to the floor. The man was opening his mouth to yell. Charlie stood too far away for an overhand swing, so he shot the wrench forward in a straight-arm jab that caught the fellow's lower teeth. That plugged his cry, and before he could recover, Lew struck and he tumbled down on top of his gun.

"Not bad," Lew said. He was panting a little.

Charlie examined the Japanese men carefully. They couldn't take the chance of one being just stunned. He lifted each head, felt of the heart. Two undoubtedly were dead. The third, in the uniform of an officer, seemed merely unconscious. There was a faint pulse action so Charlie recovered the pieces of rope and tied him well. He jammed a sailor's cloth hat between the officer's jaws for a gag.

Irene stood in the storeroom doorway. Her eyes flashed with excitement. "You're wonderful," she praised.

Lew grinned. "I knew you'd appreciate us eventually. Even if you did think we were 4-F when we were on the plane."

"I wish you would forget how silly I was then."

"Sure," Lew agreed. "Only we aren't exactly out of this jam

yet. There're plenty of sailors left on the boat—too many." He looked cautiously down at the boat. Two men now stood beside the double machine guns and the twin muzzles had been swung about in direct line with the house.

"How long before they begin to suspect everything isn't okay?" Irene asked.

"We can't wait for that," Charlie said. He was looking down at the commander. The man was bigger than the average Japanese, almost as tall as Lew.

"We've got to keep things moving too fast for them to get suspicious. Help me strip off this fellow's coat and pants."

They had to untie the ropes to do it, but each was replaced when they were done. Several spots of tattooing stuck up above the man's low-necked undershirt. Lew pulled the garment down to examine them, then shoved it back.

"What are you going to do with this stuff?" Lew asked, holding up the uniform.

"You're going to wear it," Charlie told him. "Don't stand there with your mouth open. Put it on!"

Chapter 11 – The Score Is Five

Lew scowled when Charlie told him to get inside the Japanese commander's uniform. "Me wear that stuff? It will make me a spy and they shoot them in war time."

"What did you think they were going to do when they caught us?" Charlie asked. "Fine us a couple of bucks?"

"It would fit Irene better," Lew grumbled. But his fingers were pulling swiftly at the buttons of his shirt. Irene walked back into the storeroom while he made the change. Charlie kept urging him to hurry. The trousers were several inches too short and the jacket strained so tightly across his chest he was afraid a deep breath would split it. But the medals pinned to each side jingled pleasantly when he put on the commander's cap and pistol belt and strutted across the room.

"Go past that window again," Charlie ordered. "And walk like a Japanese officer."

"Please salute when you address a superior officer," Lew snapped at him.

Charlie grinned. "To me, that junk you're wearing ranks lower than a snake's belly."

Lew pulled the front of the jacket smooth.

"What do I do now?"

"Go outside. Halt a couple of feet from the door and motion with your arm for the crew to come up here. Make it good, too. You must convince them. It is our only chance. We can't attack the ship; that would be suicide. We can't wait until night, either. I don't want to be hunted all over the island by those fellows. Our only chance is to lick them on our own ground and by our own way of fighting. That means getting them up here."

"All I do is wave?" Lew objected. "That isn't so hot. I don't think officers make motions. They like to bark too well."

"Of course, if you can speak Japanese and can imitate the commander's voice, go ahead," Charlie replied.

Lew grinned. "You win. I'll just go out and wave. But what happens next?"

"You wheel around and march back into the house. Don't forget to put plenty of snap into it. Don't wait to see what they do. You're the boss. You're giving a command and you expect to be obeyed. This is going to puzzle them pretty badly. The officer is there to do their thinking and tell them what to do. My guess is they'll come. Be sure," he added, "to stoop a little. You're too tall."

"How can a man stoop and walk snappy at the same time?" Lew wanted to know. But he went to the door, squared his shoulders, and with a pretty good imitation of the short, mincing step used by the officer, marched outside. He advanced two steps, stopped to face the harbor, and with an imperious gesture, flung up an arm. Then he wheeled smartly and strode back into the house.

"Not bad," Charlie commended.

"It could have been." Lew jerked off the cap and wiped perspiration from his face. "I started to sweat when I saw that fellow train his binoculars on me. I think I got turned about before he could focus them on my face, but I expected to feel machine gun bullets between my shoulder blades on that last step."

Charlie was looking out past the edge of the half-open door. The three men on the ship's deck had gathered in a tight little group. "There must be more of them down below," Charlie said. "There must be a larger crew and I don't understand why they don't come up." The parley on the deck lasted so long he began to get uneasy.

Lew was worried, too. "Suppose I ought to go out and wave again?" he suggested.

"Absolutely not. That would spoil it. You keep out of sight. They have to decide soon because they can't just ignore an order, even if it came outside the usual way."

Lew walked nervously across the rear end of the room. He picked up the rapid-fire gun he had knocked from one sailor's hand and tried to move the cocking handle. The breech was jammed tight. He picked up the other gun; it worked freely. The magazine sticking out through the left side of the receiver was fully charged. Lew worked a cartridge through the action into his hand.

"Look here," he said. "This is German stuff. The shell is a 7.65 Luger and the gun a Steyr-Solothurn."

Charlie nodded. "It's been reported that the Japanese hadn't developed any short automatic gun of their own. What about the commander's pistol?"

Lew drew it from the holster. "This is Japanese, all right. An 8mm Nambu automatic. Made something like a Luger, too." He looked across the room. "Hadn't we better do some housecleaning before more visitors come?"

They dragged the three men back into the storeroom. Charlie went back to the door and looked out. "This is it, all right," he said. Some of the tension left and he breathed deep in relief. The crew had apparently reached their decision.

Two of them jumped from the deck. The third handed down a pair of guns. Charlie watched, waiting for him to jump down and join the others. But he didn't. He went back to the twin machine guns and swung their muzzles around in a couple of short arcs.

"That guy likes to play with those guns, all right," Lew muttered. The men on the bank started towards the house. One bore the same kind of short, rapid-firing gun Lew held, but the second was armed with a longer, heavier weapon that evidently shot a regular full-power service load.

"That isn't good," Charlie said.

"Why not?" Lew demanded. He laid the gun down, picked up the gasoline drum wrench. "It's what you wanted, isn't it?"

"I wanted all three to come."

"Well, we can handle two easier. They're suckers for my wrench work."

"That fellow with the guns isn't. He won't be a sucker for anything as long as he sticks behind them."

Irene picked up the Mauser and went back in the storeroom. Charlie and Lew squeezed together in back of the door. The two crewmen came on at a brisk trot. They weren't wasting any time in caution now. Charlie began to wonder if they would keep right on and charge through the door at the same speed. It might be somewhat awkward for him if they did. But the sailors stopped abruptly just outside. There was a silence then that seemed to drag out into hours. One of the sailors called. His voice was shrill, almost quavering. He waited a few seconds and repeated the cry. His tone seemed to climb higher.

Charlie looked around the room. A cold tingle crossed the back of his neck. Joe's body was slumped naturally across the table-top and the vodka bottle and partly filled glass were quite convincing. That scene hadn't alarmed the enemy. The incongruity in the picture was the white naval cap belonging to the commander. It lay on the table beside the tall bottle where Lew had flung it just before he took his position behind the door. But there wasn't anything they could do about it now.

Then the sailors showed that they were not the suckers Lew supposed. The man with the heavy automatic rifle dropped on one knee and leveled the gun through the doorway. Almost at the same instant the other slipped nimbly through the opening and jumped to one side out of range of his companion's weapon. He stood close to the door, back pressed against the wall, breathing quickly with his eyes darting around the room.

Charlie knew it would be only a matter of seconds before he discovered them on the other side of the jamb, hardly five feet away. They must work fast. If either man began shooting they were lost. He nudged Lew slightly, holding his breath and hoping his companion would understand what he wanted. With a sweep of his long arms, he dropped the wrench and caught up the short automatic gun lying between their feet.

There was a window two yards away that set fairly high in the wall. Charlie made it in one jump. He jammed the muzzle of his gun through a lower pane and held back on the trigger. It was hard aiming because he had to point the barrel almost parallel with the side of the building.

The man outside swung around facing him when the glass burst. He started shooting. But he couldn't get the muzzle of his heavy weapon high enough at first and his shots went low. One bullet jerked at Charlie's pants leg just above his knee. Then the man fell forward on his weapon and tripped its trigger for a final discharge as his fingers stiffened about it.

Lew did understand Charlie's shove. He pushed the Nambu pistol's muzzle through the crack between the door and jamb and shot the other sailor in the shoulder with his first bullet. The man let off one burst—a short one—before his gun slipped out of his fingers, and the bullets tore through the wood panel so close to Lew's face he jerked away and bumped his head hard against the wall. Lew fired again and still a third time and the crewman slipped down against the wall and doubled up on the floor.

Lew dropped almost simultaneously and pressed his body close to the floorboards. The sailor down on the ship had gone into action. He had tripped the triggers of his twin machine guns, sending a stream of bullets into the building. They gouged long, sharp splinters out of the door, bored jagged holes through the walls and smashed out the remaining panes of glass. Dust seethed in the air. Lew started coughing. He looked over without raising his head—just rolling his eyes—and saw Charlie flattened out before the stove. Lew wondered if Charlie expected its thin, tin body would help any as a shield.

The shooting stopped. Then it started its deadly clatter again. The gunman aimed low now, sweeping the space just above the floor as if he knew they were hiding there. "We got to get out of this," Charlie called. He jumped up and ran towards the storeroom. A line of bullets stitching its way across the space met him. He jumped over the lead stream and darted through the storeroom door. Lew leaped for the tabletop and with a second jump made it a split second behind.

"That monkey knows his guns, all right," Lew panted. His left ear stung. He put a hand up to it and brought away bloody fingers.

Irene cried out, "You're wounded!" She took a clean handkerchief from her kit bag and daubed at the place.

"I thought one of those bullets came awful close," Lew said. "I even felt its heat."

"You have been bleeding all this time and I never noticed," Irene said. "Your shirt is all bloody. Do you feel weak?"

"Awfully weak," Lew replied. He shut his eyes and groaned. "I'm a casualty, Charlie."

"Here, let me look. Get your hand away," Charlie said. "My gosh! It's only a scratch. He won't die, Irene."

"What do you mean a scratch?" Lew howled. "The lower end of my ear is shot away. I can feel the place. My good looks will be spoiled for life."

"You'd have enough ear left if you lost an inch," Charlie told him. "But it does give you a kind of unbalanced look. I'll bet you can wangle a purple heart out of this."

"Don't pay any attention to him, Irene. He's just jealous. Go ahead and fix me up."

She had a few first aid bandages in her kit and stuck one over the wound. Charlie went to the cistern and drew off a pail of water. He was very thirsty. His throat was stiff and dry. The liquid had a tinge of sharpness caused, he thought, by the coal soot washed off the roof with every rain, but the taste wasn't offensive. He looked at his watch. It was fourteen minutes after twelve. The firing from the ship had stopped. The sailor was probably fitting new belts of ammunition to his guns.

Lew took the Mauser. "What are you going to do?" Charlie asked quickly.

"That monkey needn't think he's the only one who can shoot. I'm going to send a few slugs his way."

"Don't." Charlie's voice was sharp. "He mustn't know we have a rifle powerful enough to reach him."

Lew shrugged. "Okay, but how long do you think it will be before he starts shooting into the magazine?"

"I don't know. Maybe not long. But you couldn't kill him. That steel shield over the gun breech protects his entire body."

"His feet stick down below it," Lew argued. "I could give him a hot foot maybe."

He went over to the pail and took a long drink. Then he looked at his watch. "Do you know what time it is?" he demanded. "After twelve. That's what makes me weak. I'm half-starved."

"I'll open some cans," Irene said.

"Wait," Charlie told her. "There isn't time."

He was staring at the floor.

Lew knew the signs. His companion was trying to make a decision, one that was terribly difficult.

He motioned to Irene for silence.

"I know we can't stand here waiting for that guy to make up his mind to shoot into the magazine and blow everything up," Lew addressed Charlie. "You've got a plan; let's have it."

Charlie looked up.

"Our only chance is to kill that gunner. And the only way we can do it is to make him swing his guns around to one side so the shield doesn't cover him from the direction of the house."

Lew regarded him with grave eyes.

"That's straight talk, and it is our only chance. And it means somebody has to be a decoy. Or I should say a target. Somebody has to run outside to get him shooting a different direction."

Charlie nodded.

"All right, then," Lew spoke fast. "I'm it. You're the best shot with the rifle. Here I go." He started towards the outside room.

"No." Charlie grabbed his arm, pulling him back. "We'll toss a coin to see who goes."

His voice was so level it almost sounded monotonous.

"The devil, we will," Lew retorted. "This isn't going to be settled by luck or chance. We're going to use common sense. You know I can't handle a rifle like you can. Besides, I'm a smaller target by twenty pounds."

Chapter 12 – Now I Know How a Rabbit Feels

The room was silent. Charlie slowly put the coin back in his pocket. Irene tried to speak, choked up and then found her voice.

"You're awfully brave to joke when you know you'll be killed," she told Lew, appreciating his jest that he made a smaller target than Charlie by twenty pounds.

"What do you mean, I know I'll be killed?" he demanded. "I don't know that. There's a fifty-fifty chance. That right, Charlie?"

"More," Charlie replied, "if we get some breaks. We've got to make that gunner on the ship swing his machine guns around to one side, so he isn't protected by the steel breech shield. As long as he keeps them trained on the house, he is. But if he sees a man running away from the house he will surely shoot at that man, and if the man is far enough away he'll have to turn his gun mounts, so I can get him with the Mauser. I figure you should be two hundred yards distant before I'll get my chance."

"I'll go out through the entrance at the rear of the storeroom. That will help some."

"When you are outside," Charlie continued, "worm along on your stomach. The ground is covered with dead grass and there are rocks scattered through it. Together they make fair cover. Go slowly and you make a couple hundred yards with ease. But if the gunner doesn't spot you at all, then you'll have to stand up and run so he will. Be sure you're far enough off, though, before you do that."

"I hope you don't have a hang-fire cartridge then," Lew said.

"So do I." Charlie's voice was very earnest.

"I'll take the short machine gun. Maybe I'll have a chance to use it."

"Crawling with a gun is awkward," Charlie warned.

"Not if I shove it inside my pants with the barrel sticking down one leg. I wish I had time to eat something."

"We've lost too much time now," Charlie told him.

Lew changed back into his own dark gray pants. He lashed the gun's magazine to his belt and shoved the gun itself inside the waist and tightened his belt around the stock. Charlie went outside and looked towards the ship. The sailor still stood motionless behind his guns. Both of his feet showed below the shield.

Charlie went back to the storeroom. "We must find the hidden entrance Joe used."

"I've already found it," Irene said. "It's behind a pile of ammunition boxes, just a crack in the rock with a wooden slab door."

Lew pushed the slab around and exposed a short passage which a man could walk through only if he held his head down and kept his back bent. The top sloped sharply downwards towards the far end where a faint glow of light showed.

Lew turned, faced them, waved a hand lightly. "So long. I'll be seeing you." And then he added silently, "I hope."

Charlie lifted a hand in response. The gesture might have seemed casual, even indifferent to a stranger, but Lew knew how much feeling and encouragement it conveyed.

The two were close as brothers. There was a tremendous bond between them, but they seldom, if ever, expressed it.

"Is that all you're going to do?" Irene demanded. "Wave your hand at him when he's going out to die so we can live?"

She pushed her way past Charlie, and declared, "I can do better than that!"

Then he threw her arms around Lew and kissed him soundly.

"Say," Lew said when she released him and stepped back. "Don't you know I've got to keep my cool? You shouldn't shoot my blood pressure up before I even start."

He looked fondly at her.

"You're a swell girl, Irene. I wouldn't hurt your feelings for anything. But I have to be fair to Charlie. His wave meant as much to me as your kiss."

Creeping along behind him, Charlie watched Lew push the long, matted grass away at the tunnel end and crawl through on his stomach. The outlet was hardly bigger than the mouth of a good-sized badger den. Charlie looked through, saw the ground was covered with more dead brow grass and there were even more rocks than he had dared to hope.

Most of the stones were small, about a foot in diameter but there were occasional larger ones plenty big to hide a man.

Lew made good progress. He kept both head and hips down, something the amateur stalker is liable to forget when he tries to move undetected. Actually, Lew was plowing along under the grass as much as through it. He was still hidden from the ship by the small hill against which house and storeroom had been constructed. His real danger would not begin until he had crawled beyond it.

Charlie backed away. He would have liked to watch Lew longer but he didn't dare risk it. The Japanese gunner might spot him any moment now and he had to have the Mauser ready for a fast, straight shot. Irene's pale face stood out sharply in the dim light.

"Listen," Charlie said. "I've got to stay out in the room now. That gunman may decide, however, to blast the house again. If he does, he'll probably get me, so you'll have to take over. We can't let Lew down now. He'll be waiting for us to shoot fast when he starts running for it."

"Yes, Sir!" She saluted. Charlie knew when she did this she was tense with emotion.

"You've got to keep calm," he warned. "One thing more. In case the gunner doesn't swing his guns around so you catch sight of his body, shoot low at his feet. They're always exposed. Aim about six inches in front of them so the bullet will glance up off the deck and hit higher. A shot in the leg may save Lew's life."

"I'll do it," she promised.

Charlie opened the Mauser's breach an inch, saw there was a cartridge in the chamber and went out in the room. He took up his old place beside the door and aimed tentatively several times at the steel gun shield and then at the feet below. He decided the best way to get a steady aim was to grip the edge of the door with one hand and rest the rifle barrel over it.

He glanced at his watch. Only four minutes had elapsed since Lew left them. A man could crawl a hundred feet in four minutes, couldn't he? Charlie didn't know. But it looked like he would have a long wait.

He rubbed the palms of his hands dry on his pants. His eyes narrowed. Had the gun shield down on the ship shifted? He rubbed his eyes carefully; this fixed concentration was tiring them. Now he was sure it had moved. A little short swing to the right. Sweat started out on Charlie's forehead. The guns would have to move right to cover Lew. "But Lew can't be over a hundred yards away now," he muttered.

He almost jumped when the guns exploded sharply. They

fired two short bursts and then settled down into an ominous roar. That meant only one thing. The sailor had spotted Lew, had fired a couple of test volleys to get the approximate range and was now laying down a continuous barrage and moving the deadly hail along to overtake him. "Lew must be running," he thought.

Charlie gripped the edge of the door and laid his gun across it. The body of the gunner was still hidden but Charlie aimed low at the feet. *There's no time to squeeze a trigger slowly*, he thought, and pressed firmly and quickly, praying under his breath that he wouldn't jerk the sights out of line.

The machine guns went dead. Their muzzles wobbled and spun about. Charlie saw the man bent over his feet, clutching at them with both hands. His entire body was exposed now. Charlie sent a fresh cartridge home and fired again.

That finished it. The crewman teetered over headfirst, landing on his shoulder and almost turning a flip-flop before his waving legs settled back to the deck.

Charlie reloaded again and stood watching the figure. He watched, too, the center of the ship where a hatchway led down below and from which might emerge other members of the crew. He watched until he heard Lew's shout outside.

"I'm coming in. Be careful with that gun."

Lew swaggered in with a grin. It wasn't a very big one, though, and Lew's face was colorless and there were lines of strain still etched about his mouth.

Charlie glanced back at the ship. "Did he spot you crawling?"

"Did he ever. The grass got awfully short at one place. He saw me and sent those short bursts so damned close I knew he'd get me with the next. My only chance was to get up and run. If I stayed down I'd be potted like a sitting rabbit. But by running there was a slim chance, although I knew I hadn't got far enough away from the house yet. Did you shoot at his feet?"

Charlie nodded. "The first time. The second time I got him in the chest."

Lew went over to a bench and sat down. He was breathing heavily. "Now I know how a rabbit feels when he's running away from the hunter," he said slowly. After a short pause, he added, "I don't think I want to go rabbit hunting again."

"We have to find out if there are any more seamen on the

ship," Charlie reminded him. "A crew of six doesn't sound right for her size. We have to destroy this dump of gasoline and torpedoes, too. I want to fuel up the boat and get away quick. Chances are more than one patrol craft used the island to refill. So much shooting may bring one in, or at least an enemy plane."

Lew got up. "Okay," he said. He assembled his machine gun. "I'll go down and board her while you cover me with the rifle. I'd be too shaky to protect you." He paused at the door. "Anyway, I like leg work." He started off running.

Down at the ship Lew saw it was going to be rather hard to reach the deck, which was about five feet above the bank of the little harbor. But he shoved his gun in his pants again and started hitching along one of the heavy hawsers that moored the ship fast. He went briskly before his weight pulled enough on the rope to move the ship in closer and let it sag. The hawser took him right up opposite the twin mounted guns. Their muzzles had drifted around so they again covered the house.

Lew walked past them. His job now was to prevent anyone coming up from below to man them and he could do that best with his short rifle. There was only one hatch leading below. He planted himself a dozen feet away and signaled to Charlie. His companion joined him a few minutes later.

"Everything's quiet so far," Lew said. "I think I'll go down and look around."

"Not this time," Charlie told him. "You've done enough rough work. It's my turn."

Like the crew quarters on most Japanese warships, they were cramped in space. But everything was scrupulously clean. Walking carefully, Charlie passed through a small galley hardly wide enough to turn about in and found himself in a space that contained bunks bolted to the floor and wall.

Charlie counted swiftly; there were spaces for ten sleepers. The commander undoubtedly had his own private stateroom. That left five men unaccounted for to date. Something like the rustle of cloth reached his ear. He glanced at the lower right bed. It seemed different from the rest. He leaned over and almost shoved his nose against the muzzle of a pointing pistol. Behind it were unblinking dark eyes, beaded like a snake's. A bloodstained bandage covered most of the man's head. Charlie jerked back and thrust his own gun forward. But before he pressed the trigger he saw that the pistol was weaving in the man's hand and that the beaded eyes stared fixedly ahead and had made no attempt to follow his move. He began to doubt that the man had actually seen him.

He took the pistol out of unresisting fingers. Then he pulled the blanket down, wondering if there could be more weapons concealed underneath, but he pulled the cover back up fast. One of the man's legs was terribly smashed with shell fragments.

"Find anything?" Lew called.

"One sailor, but he's hurt too bad to give trouble." Charlie went on aft, searching the engine room and the little cubicle where the commander lived. It began to dawn on him that any additional members of the crew had been killed in some engagement.

Charlie searched on, glancing behind bulkheads where fuel and food and ammunition were stored. Finally satisfied that the ship was empty save for the wounded crewman, he went up on deck.

"We'll have Irene set out a lunch before we start to work. I can use it, can't you?"

"That," Lew replied, "is an entirely superfluous question."

A big job faced them. The fuel tanks of the ship were very low. It was equipped with a small pump that would suck the gasoline out of the drums and into the tanks, but the barrels had to be rolled down to the edge of the harbor, upended and opened. They carried down stores of food, too, and some extra ammunition for the machine guns. Lew wanted to take on a couple of torpedoes, but Charlie banned that. "We haven't time" was his answer.

"But suppose we run into a Japanese cruiser on the way home?" Lew argued. But he did feel better when he discovered a tin fish neatly loaded in one of the tubes on the forward deck.

There were charts in the commander's cabin. They examined these briefly as they ate. They looked over the engines. Lew decided at once that he could run them. "All you got to do is pour on the gas," he said. He proved his ability by starting them up. They ran very smoothly and with hardly any vibration.

One job now remained—the destruction of the stores of fuel and ammunition back on the island. They decided this would be easy. All they needed to do was set the far end of the house on fire. The flames would reach the magazine some time later, giving them the opportunity to be safely on their way when she blew.

Returning from this work, they met Irene on deck.

"The wounded sailor just died," she said.

"Not now, but later we can bury him at sea," Charlie said.

He was helping Lew drag in the mooring ropes. The fire in the house was burning swiftly, spreading along the seasoned timbers with a greater speed than they had figured.

"Let's go," Charlie said. "Start the engines. I want to get through the outside reef before it gets any darker."

The sky was heavily overcast and a light drizzle started slowly. There was scarcely any sunlight left.

Lew went below and snapped on electric lights in the passage and engine room. They heard the motors pick up speed; then the craft nosed carefully back out of the harbor.

Irene shivered a little. "I don't like this ship," she said. "It is all so very clean but it still smells of the enemy.

"A good sea breeze will fix that," Lew declared. "Especially if it's blowing right off the shore of the good old U.S.A."

Charlie took the helm. The ship cleared the harbor, turned along the side of the offshore reef and turned again to slide through the gap in it. And then, when her nose was pointing east with the open sea ahead, Lew shoved the throttle open wide.

The End